HUNTRESS DEFENDER

HUNTRESS DEFENDER

HUNTRESS CLAN SAGA™ BOOK 6

JAMIE DAVIS

DISRUPTIVE IMAGINATION

Copyright © 2020 Jamie Davis
Cover Art by Jake @ J Caleb Design
http://jcalebdesign.com / jcalebdesign@gmail.com

LMBPN Publishing
PMB 196, 2540 South Maryland Pkwy
Las Vegas, NV 89109

First US Edition, August, 2020
eBook ISBN: 978-1-64971-119-9
Print ISBN: 978-1-64971-120-5

The entire Huntress Clan Saga is dedicated to those people who battle loneliness in this strange pandemic world. Be like Quinn and find your tribe, even if it's a regular Zoom call or FaceTime. Peace.

— Jami Davis

THE HUNTRESS DEFENDER TEAM

Thanks to the JIT Readers

Diane L. Smith
John Ashmore
Larry Omans
Kerry Mortimer
Dorothy Lloyd

If I've missed anyone, please let me know!

Editor
The Skyhunter Editing Team

CHAPTER ONE

Avery Skelton-Smythe moved through the thick brush at the edge of the compound, crouching to avoid detection. She'd been on the road for over a week, tracking down this lead. It had led her from the Pyrenees in Spain to the foothills of the southern Andes. After thousands of miles, she hoped it wasn't another dead end.

Her search for women like her, women raised as Huntresses by Gemma, had led here. All those she'd found were either dead or transformed into demon-kinder. Now, Avery was at the last location on her list. She'd found a reference to this remote outpost while going through Gemma's receipts. They'd been left in a drawer at the castle where Gemma had raised Avery. The collection of financial documents was only a few years old. It mentioned "the little ones" in a written note added to a printed airline voucher.

Avery assumed it was a coded reference to others like her, raised to be killing machines on the model of the Huntress of legend. The thought of the legendary figure brought a smile to her face. Avery had once believed she was the Huntress. Now she knew she had only a portion of the skills it took to do that job. Quinn Faust, on the other hand, was the real deal.

Bringing her hand up to stroke the small silver oval hanging at her throat, Avery smiled. Quinn had sent it to her by special messenger a month ago. She'd had it made for Avery, giving her an amulet of her own.

Quinn had said it possessed most of the protections of the one she wore. She also promised to add the final touches to it once Avery returned to Baltimore.

The amulet grew cold beneath her fingers, drawing Avery's attention back to the job at hand. She raised her head above the cluster of bushes. Movement ahead froze her in place as a shadowy figure emerged from the darkness. The sudden chill of the silver amulet told her it was an enemy, which probably meant another demon-kinder. Avery cursed under her breath. She was tired of facing those enhanced, demon-possessed bodies. The last two she'd run into had fought in tandem. They had almost finished her.

Avery concentrated and summoned her blade to hand. She held the blessed katana down by her side and waited.

The woman walked past Avery's hiding spot.

Avery glanced up the path, one last check to make sure no one followed the woman. Seeing it was clear, she moved out of her hiding place, shrouded in magical silence and shadows.

Slipping up behind the woman as she strode along down the path, Avery gauged the distance to killing range. The magically strengthened demon-kinder carried a hefty battle-axe, and the heavier weapon would make it a difficult fight if Avery didn't make the most of this initial strike. Plus, they were too close to the *estancia* on the map. This was no time for the commotion of a prolonged melee.

Avery needed a few more steps to get into range, so she picked up speed. She raised her blade, preparing to deliver a killing stroke.

The demon-kinder stiffened; she'd detected trouble. Although she was a little too far away, Avery leaned in and took the shot anyway. She swept her long blade around and down, striking the woman's exposed neck from behind.

The blade's sharp tip cut cleanly through cartilage and bone. It wasn't enough to decapitate the guard, but it did sever the spinal cord, dropping the woman to the ground. She lay on her back, struggling to breathe, her mouth moving as if she were trying to say something.

Avery had no time to puzzle out what she was saying. She stepped up and finished the job, removing the head.

To be sure, Avery gave it a deft kick, rolling it into the weeds beside the path. She'd made the mistake of assuming a single blow had done the trick with these demon-possessed things before. That was how she'd found out they had limited regeneration and healing abilities.

It had nearly gotten her killed.

Avery checked the path in both directions. Seeing it was still clear, she stooped and rolled the body behind a nearby bush.

With the guard's body hidden, Avery crossed the path and ran over to stand next to the first of the *estancia*'s outbuildings. From the smell of horse manure, it was likely the ranch's stable. The soft whicker of a horse inside confirmed it.

Gemma had probably kept on a few of the gauchos to keep up the appearance that the *estancia*'s cattle were cared for. She'd done the same at the small castle where Avery had been raised. The sheep and goats they kept had also served as food for those who'd lived there. Given how Gemma liked things to operate, the servants here probably kept to themselves, too. At least, they did if they knew what was good for them.

Avery started around the building but warned once again by the amulet, ducked back just in time to avoid detection. A man in a broad-brimmed hat left the stables.

She followed his progress with her eyes, watching him cross to a long single-story building that was likely a bunkhouse of some sort. A thin plume of smoke rose from the tin stovepipe in the building's center.

She waited until he entered and pulled the door shut behind him. As soon as the door closed, she darted from the corner of the stable for a clump of shrubs planted beside the estancia's main house. A broad porch circled the building, with a low roof over it to keep off the elements. Several wooden chairs had sat on the porch allowing the big house's residents to sit there and survey the land. The porch was empty now, allowing Avery to move past and check the windows on the first floor.

If the women held here were still alive and not converted to demon-kinder, she should find them either in or near the main house. Gemma would want to keep an eye on their progress while she was here.

Of course, that assumed that Gemma hadn't already

killed or possessed these candidates, too. She had no idea how many girls Gemma had taken over this way. All Avery knew was she didn't like being one step behind the other woman and getting there too late every time. It had been months of this cat and mouse game, chasing around the globe.

Avery found herself weary and travel-worn. She was glad this was the final location on her list.

Rising from her crouch by the porch railing, she started toward the nearest set of steps up to the porch. She decided to check the big house first.

Stopping by an open window, Avery froze as a voice came from inside. It had the resonant tone of the possessed ones, like two voices talking at once from the same mouth.

"Did Beckingsly say why she wanted them all dead? Not that I'm complaining. The little runts are a pain to keep track of, underfoot one instant, and hiding from you the next. I'll be happy to be rid of them."

Another demon-kinder voice, this one male, said, "I didn't ask. I don't need a reason to kill little ones. The way a child's fear lights up their auras when they die is delightful."

Little ones?

The term confused Avery. Were they talking about actual children? All of Gemma's potential candidates so far had been around Avery's age. They'd all been babies or toddlers at the time of the Hunter clan purges years before.

Where had Gemma found young children suitable for her purposes so many years after the last of the Hunters were tracked down and killed? It irked her that she didn't have an answer.

Avery gathered herself. None of it mattered. If there were children important to Gemma's plans here on the *estancia*, she'd find them. These were the first survivors she'd found. There was no way she'd let the demon-kinder kill children, not on her watch.

The owners of the voices came closer. Avery slipped over the railing to hide in the bushes lining the porch. The male and female demon-kinder took the nearby steps down into the *estancia*'s courtyard and headed to a small square building opposite the gauchos' bunkhouse. Each carried a machete.

They planned on killing the children now.

Avery rose, stepping with care to avoid any noise. She cleared the shrubs and followed the pair in a crouch, keeping her sword ready. She needed to kill both with as little noise as possible. She had no idea how many more like them were located in the home, or what the ranch-hands in the bunkhouse would do if a fight broke out.

The woman shifted the machete to hold it under her arm while unlocking a heavy iron padlock on the door. She flashed her companion a wicked grin as she retrieved the heavy blade and stepped inside.

Screams rang out.

Cursing, Avery sprinted the last few steps and lunged with her katana, taking the man from behind. Her sword pierced his throat before he could croak a warning. Blackened froth fountained up from his mouth instead of blood as he pitched to the dirt outside the door.

Avery leaped over his twitching form. She'd have to remember to come back and finish him. He might possess the ability to heal himself.

The screaming inside intensified.

Avery charged into the small single room. The female demon-kinder advanced on a cluster of little girls huddled in the corner. There weren't two or three as expected, there were six. None of them could be over the age of ten.

"Hey," Avery said. "Why don't you try out someone your own size?"

The woman spun, her eyebrows raised in surprise.

Avery didn't give her a chance to prepare for an attack. She hacked down, aiming to cut at the arm holding the machete.

With impossible quickness, the woman dodged backward.

Avery's blade missed by a millimeter between it and skin. The move left her stretched out in a lunge and exposed.

The machete snapped out with unnatural speed.

Avery pulled her sword around, parrying the heavier blade. She grunted at the force behind the woman's blow. It twisted her wrist back at an awkward angle that threatened to loosen her grip on the hilt.

She gritted her teeth and held on despite the pain and numbness in her fingers. Shaking her head, Avery snarled in defiance. These hunter-trained women, now turned into demon-kinder, were tough to defeat. That was especially true if you didn't have the jump on them.

Avery danced backward to avoid a swipe at her midsection and regrouped. She was running out of time. Someone was going to hear the commotion or spot the body flopping on the ground outside. Either way, if another of these hell-possessed people showed up, she and these little girls would be dead.

She looked around for some advantage as she parried a pair of incoming blows.

The demon-kinder woman flashed an evil grin. "You're her, aren't you? Beckingsly's first failed experiment to breed a Huntress of her own for the prophecy."

"I prefer to think of myself as her only success. Though these little ones might be added to that number once I kill you."

"Bah, these were her greatest failure yet. It was a foolish plan to breed the hunter-born with demon spawn. Almost all died soon after birth. These six were the only ones to survive. It turned out they ended up being mostly human after all. In the end, they need extermination like all the others."

The woman followed her words with a double slash at Avery's head, seeking to attack while the Huntress was distracted by the conversation.

Avery parried the first attack and ducked under the other. As she did, the tallest of the little girls moved toward them from the huddled group. She had bright orange hair in double-braided pigtails hanging to her shoulders and a determined expression on her face. She caught Avery's eye and then got down on her hands and knees behind the demon-kinder.

Avery smiled. That was a smart girl there.

Taking a risk, Avery feinted to the side as if she'd stumbled.

The other woman lunged at her, hacking down with the machete.

Ducking in rather than pulling away, Avery pushed aside the incoming blade. Then she drove forward with a whirling series of attacks meant more to dazzle than connect.

It worked.

The demon-kinder backpedaled until she reached the crouching girl and shouted in alarm as she tripped, her arms windmilling.

Avery pounced.

She rode the woman to the floor, driving her sword's tip up under her sternum to pierce her heart.

A throaty, gurgling groan came from the woman. She struggled to rise, despite the sword impaling her.

Avery reached out with her free hand and wrenched the machete free from her opponent's weakening fingers. Hacking down, she separated the woman's head with two blows, knocking the head away from the body with the flat of the borrowed blade. It left a trail of black ichor on the floor.

She rose from atop the body and pulled her sword free. Avery glanced at the cowering girls. No, they weren't cowering, at least not now. Instead, curiosity filled the faces staring up at her. The taller ginger haired girl had gotten back to her feet and rejoined her companions in the corner.

Avery nodded. If they could keep themselves from screaming again, it would be good. "I'll be right back. I have to finish the other one. Be quiet and gather your things. We're leaving as soon as I get back."

Avery hefted the machete in one hand and her katana in the other as she went back outside.

"Damn," she muttered. The male demon-kinder's body was missing. She should have finished him off when she had the chance. She scanned the open ground between the outbuildings and the main house. She spotted him, dragging himself up the steps and staggering through the big house's back door.

Avery went back into the little building. "No time left. We have to run now. Everyone hold hands with your neighbor. Red, you take the lead."

The pigtailed girl nodded and grabbed the hand of the smallest of the group. Others reached out until they all stood in a line by the door, hands linked.

"Good. Follow me, and for God's sake, keep up."

Shouts came from the direction of the house as Avery ran for the edge of the compound. It wasn't far to her rented pickup truck. She cursed as she realized they wouldn't all fit in the front with her. The oldest would have to ride in the back and hold on tight. The ride out of here was going to be bumpy as hell, but there wasn't much choice. She was sure pursuit would be close behind. Of course, first they had to make it to the truck.

Avery glanced over her shoulder to check on the girls and was surprised to see them right behind her. She nodded her approval and dug in her pocket for the keys.

"The truck is just down the hill from the *estancia*," she whispered. "It's not far. Keep moving down this path."

She heard more shouting uphill, but none coming this way yet. She could make out the silhouette of the truck's cab against the moonlit sky ahead.

"There—we're almost out of here. Put the three smallest

in the front with me. The others will have to go in the back. Got it?"

The redhead and another of the older ones nodded.

Running up to the truck, Avery pulled open the passenger door. "Inside, quick. Find a seat and hold on."

A little brown-haired girl with a pixie cut climbed into the cab, followed by a pair of what looked like identical blonde twins. She shut the door and pointed to the back.

"The rest in there. Hurry."

Red helped the other two over the side and then pulled herself over to tumble into the pickup bed. Avery raced to the driver's side and started the pickup.

Kicking up gravel behind them as she stomped on the accelerator, Avery steered them down the narrow track as fast as she dared. The paved highway was a few kilometers away. Until then, she did her best to maximize her speed on the rough dirt farm road. Every time she hit a bump, she checked over her shoulder to make sure all three girls still hung on in the back.

"Where are we going?" Pixie Cut asked.

"To see a friend of mine. Don't worry, it's somewhere safe. Quinn will know what to do with the six of you."

Avery closed her mouth and offered a silent prayer that Quinn or the others would have a way to help her get these kids to safety. She wasn't sure what it was, but something about what just happened felt right somehow. It was like she'd put things into motion that couldn't be stopped. Avery hoped Quinn was ready for whatever it was.

CHAPTER TWO

Quinn smiled as she walked down the street toward O'Malley's pub. She'd spent the evening having a productive dinner with leaders of the various shifter communities around the city about better ways to help each other monitor their various pack or den members. The goal was to keep the hidden supernatural world away from curious ordinary humans. The folks living in the shadows didn't need their neighbors learning things like their babysitter was a werewolf.

Some among the human leadership were aware of the supernaturals living in the community, of course. That was why a representative of the mayor's office had been there, too. It also surprised Quinn to meet the governor's chosen representative, a very ancient vampire based in Annapolis who made the trip up to join their dinner in Baltimore's Little Italy neighborhood.

That vampire, who everyone called "Al," turned out to be surprisingly charming. Quinn spent so much time chatting with him, she invited him to visit the clan at O'Malley's anytime.

After the dinner and dessert put out by the restaurant's owner for the special event, Quinn needed to walk off the delicious food. She turned down the offer of a ride home from several attendees and opted to walk back to the pub. Quinn had eaten pasta for dinner and had three cannolis for dessert. Even with her Huntress metabolism, she almost regretted the skinny jeans she'd worn.

Quinn reviewed her mental notes as she walked the final hundred yards to the pub. Clark and Naomi would expect a full report on what was discussed. It had been a big deal for Clark to hand off this to her. This was her first solo meeting, and she wanted to show them how prepared she was to handle it. Things like this came with being the Huntress and the leader of the clan.

She figured the report could wait until breakfast, though. Quinn had left in the early afternoon, and it was now close to midnight. The other clan members had to be asleep by now, except for maybe her vampire mother.

Quinn was wrong.

The bar was hopping, as it always was right up to closing time. The pub's country-western theme was popular among the supernatural patrons. There were still a decent number of people line dancing by the bandstand. To her surprise, all her friends were all still awake, too, even Taylor. The tech witch had risen early that morning. Some magic experiment had her and Miranda working long hours for the last several days.

Quinn wove through the tables to where they all sat.

She didn't miss the way they glowered at her as she crossed the room.

Uh-oh, what now?

"Hi, guys. What's got you all up so late?"

"Who wants to go first?" Naomi asked.

Taylor's hand shot up. "I'll go."

"What's up, T?"

"It's that ogre of yours, Quinn. He's done it again."

Quinn sighed. She'd been afraid it was something like this. It had been two months since she'd returned home with Tadpole in tow and Sylvie on her shoulder, announcing they were both new members of the clan. Since then, there had been adjustment pains for everyone.

"Tadpole's an orc warrior," Quinn reminded her best friend. "He's not an ogre. They're different races entirely, which you know. It would really upset him if he heard you calling him that."

"I honestly don't care, Quinn. He's a menace. He tripped over a stack of kegs in the hallway and fell into my door. Now my workshop has no door, and I have to move all my expensive and sensitive stuff elsewhere in this warren of tunnels until Paddy can fix it."

"I'm sure he didn't mean it. You said he tripped, right?"

"I don't see how he's this super orc warrior when he's such a clumsy oaf all the time. I still haven't replaced the monitor he broke when he poked at it with his big, dumb finger."

Quinn tried to tamp down her anger. Something about the orc's childlike nature brought out the mama bear in her. She bristled at her best friend picking on him.

Taking a deep breath, she said, "You know he didn't

mean to crack the glass on the monitor. He was just pointing at the picture you had on the screen. He just doesn't know his own strength sometimes. I told you I'd get you a new monitor. Just pick out what you want."

Naomi said, "It's not just Taylor's stuff, Quinn. He's creepy. He wanders around the Hunter tunnels all day long, humming weird orc songs to himself. I can't get any rest when he's down there."

"It's not like you need to sleep, Mother," Quinn snapped. She heard the acid in her tone too late.

"You're correct. I, as a vampire, do not technically sleep. I do, however, like to meditate and be alone with my thoughts, darling daughter of mine. I've been close to a deep state of calm on several occasions when he's interrupted me. He just pokes his head into my room and asks, 'Whatcha doin'?' It's infuriating, Quinn."

"He's lonely, that's all. He just wants to belong somewhere, like the rest of us. Surely you all can understand that? He's trying really hard to make friends with you."

Quinn glanced at Clark, hoping he'd lend her some support.

He scowled at her instead.

"Okay, Clark, let's have it. What did Tadpole do to you?"

"Oh, it wasn't your young orc friend this time, Quinn. It's that flying menace you keep up in your room. It got out again and crapped ash and charcoal briquets all over my car and several others parked in the alley."

"Sylvie just likes to chase the pigeons. She can't get out and stretch her wings as much as she'd like."

Taylor snorted a laugh. "More like she likes to *eat* the pigeons, you mean."

Quinn sighed. "I don't know what you want me to do. I had Paddy put thicker bars on my apartment windows. She just melts her way through them. I can't think of anything else to do that'll keep her inside if she wants to leave."

The young dragon, the size of a small house cat with wings, had taken to sitting by her window and watching the various birds fly by. Being a city, that mostly meant pigeons. One day, she'd joined them. After she'd caught and eaten the first one, she'd decided they tasted pretty yummy. Since then, Sylvie used her fiery breath like a plasma torch to cut through every sort of barrier Quinn and the building's owner, Paddy, had been able to come up with.

Naomi said, "You're lucky a young dragon's natural magic shields them from being seen by humans without a spell of their own. We'd have a hard time explaining her to our mundane neighbors."

"Look, Clark, I'm sorry. I'll take your car to the cleaners in the morning, okay?"

"That's not good enough, Quinn," Clark said. "You have to do something about how she's getting out. Otherwise, admit you're in over your head and find somewhere safe to set her free. It's only a matter of time until some unsuspecting mundane human figures out what's going on."

"They won't. Remember, they can't see her."

Miranda said, "They can see the aftermath of her passing, though. And some humans have latent magical talents that could allow them to pierce the protection magic she has."

"Miranda? Not you, too? What did Sylvie do to you?" Quinn's temper boiled over. "You're a ghost. You're not even really here. I'm not sure why you felt the need to say anything at all right now."

"Hey," everyone said at once, coming to Miranda's aid.

Quinn realized she'd gone too far. She held up her hands. "I'm sorry. That was uncalled for, Miranda. I take it back."

The ghost witch nodded. "Quinn, we know it's a lot."

"I'm doing the best I can. I've never raised a wild dragon or fostered an orphaned orc warrior. It will take time to find them a way to fit in. I'm sure they'll both find their place before you know it. I just need a little more time to train them, that's all. Before you know it, they'll both be used to civilized company."

Everyone avoided eye contact when Quinn glanced around for some sign of approval. When she got to her mother, she stopped. Naomi was the only one who'd meet her eyes.

"Quinn, we can give you more time if you really think it will work. Otherwise, come to grips with the possibility that there may not be a way to solve this. Sylvie and Tadpole aren't built to live in a crowded city full of vulnerable people."

"I won't give up on them, Mom. People gave up on me, and life was really hard."

Naomi's brows lowered. "I never gave up on you. I was always nearby, keeping an eye on you."

"It's the same thing," Quinn replied. "I didn't know you were in the shadows protecting me. I still felt abandoned. Tadpole and Sylvie need to know someone cares about them. They need to understand the *clan* cares about them. It's important, not just to them, but to me, too."

Taylor's eyes were filled with doubts, but she gave Quinn a half-smile. "It's just a door. And you're right, I can get a new monitor. We have all that spare VirSync gear in storage. Maybe we just need to make some new rules."

Clark rolled his eyes. "Dragons don't follow rules, Taylor. That's what makes them so dangerous. They aren't pets."

"That's not true," Quinn said. "Chessie follows the rules so well no one knows she's out there, hiding in the Bay. She's lived there for hundreds, maybe thousands of years, with most people never knowing there's a dragon right there."

Taylor nodded. "Chessie is an excellent example. Didn't you promise to check in after Sylvie hatched? Maybe this is a chance to learn more about how to control her."

"I guess I could set up a visit for us to go see Chessie and introduce Sylvie to her."

Clark nodded. "That might be a good idea. See if you can leave her there and let the dragon raise the youngling."

Quinn knew that was wishful thinking on Clark's part. Still, the thought of leaving Sylvie alone with the dragon out there in that cold, dank cave turned Quinn's mood sour. An attachment had formed when she'd helped Sylvie hatch. Would all that go away if the old dragon insisted Sylvie remain there?

"No, that's not going to happen. Look, I'll figure out a way to contain Sylvie better. Maybe I just need to have someone sit with her when I am not here. The rest of the time, she can hang out on my shoulder."

"She's not a toy, Quinn," Miranda said. "Or even a puppy. You can't just hire a dragon-sitter on the internet.

Sylvie is one of the most dangerous creatures ever to walk this earth. She's cute now, but someday, she'll be as big as Chessie, maybe larger. Remember that."

Quinn stared at the table for a few long seconds. "Look, I'm exhausted. I'll start working on all this tomorrow. I promise. For now, though, I need to catch some sleep. Okay?'

"Of course," Naomi said. "We shouldn't have hit you with it all when you got back like that. Go upstairs. We'll all come back fresh in the morning. Maybe some more ideas will come from it."

Quinn gave her mother a nod of thanks for her understanding and left them at their table. She needed rest, and maybe some dragon cuddles. Everything had to look better in the morning.

CHAPTER THREE

The steady vibration of Sylvie's body pressing against her chest kept Quinn in bed for at least an extra half-hour. It wasn't purring, exactly. Sylvie wasn't a cat. As far as Quinn could tell, it was something in a dragon's normal metabolism that did it while resting. A heavy feeding the day before always increased the level of rumbling from the young dragon's tummy the next morning.

Quinn smiled and rubbed the smooth scales of Sylvie's still-bulging stomach. "You ate too many pigeons yesterday, didn't you, silly?"

Sylvie pressed her neck up against Quinn's chin and rubbed her tiny body against the Huntress, snuggling deeper into her chest.

"Sorry, sleepyhead. We both need to get up. You're sticking with me today so I can keep an eye on you."

"Eeeep?"

"Don't play innocent with me. You know what you did.

Come on, I need a shower, and if you get up, I'll let you join me so you can scrub under the hot water, too.

"Eeeep!" The dragon rolled over twice to the edge of the bed, launching into the air and circling over Quinn's bed.

Quinn laughed. "Okay, I'm coming."

She got up and followed the excited dragonling into the bathroom. The little hedonist loved getting scrubbed down under the blast of hot water from the showerhead. In all fairness, Quinn enjoyed it, too. It increased their bonding time.

It was obvious Sylvie was intelligent. However, Quinn was never sure if she understood everything she said. The youngling seemed to understand simple statements or instructions, most of the time.

Quinn kept trying. She worked under the assumption that the little one would someday gain the ability to speak inside her mind as the other dragons she knew did. The problem was, she had no idea when a young dragon got that ability. She'd tried to research it. A young human could understand many words and phrases by one year of age and could speak simple sentences as early as eighteen months. Quinn did not understand how that correlated to a dragon, though.

She knew she needed expert advice and also where that advice would have to come from. If only she wasn't afraid of losing Sylvie to the ancient dragon hidden in the middle of the Chesapeake Bay.

Once in the shower, Sylvie kept hogging the shower-head, making the shower longer than expected. By the time she shut off the water and dried off, Quinn realized how late it was. Breakfast hours were already over down in the pub. She made a quick peanut butter sandwich to take downstairs, along with her morning mug of coffee.

Heading to the door, Quinn called, "Coming, little one?"

Sylvie zipped out of the bedroom hallway, flitting across the apartment to settle gently on Quinn's shoulder. Her long tail snaked around the Huntress' neck to steady her as they set out for the day's fun activities.

Quinn arrived downstairs in the pub to the sounds of arguing from the open kitchen door behind the bar. The few leftover breakfast patrons still seated seemed oblivious to the noise. Or maybe they were doing their best to ignore it, judging from their sideways glances at Quinn. She picked up her pace and headed to the open kitchen door.

"I can't take too many more of these assaults on my kitchen," the cook shouted.

"I told you I'd deal with it, and I will," Paddy replied.

Quinn followed the voices into the kitchen, pulling the door closed behind her to cut down on eavesdropping. "What's the problem? Anything I can do?"

"Oh, great," the short leprechaun cook said. "I suppose your pet dragon is here to finish the job? Maybe she'll set fire to what's left of my freshly baked bread? I spent all morning working on it."

"Sylvie didn't do anything. She's been upstairs with me all night."

Paddy put out a hand to settle the other leprechaun before turning to address the situation himself. "Quinn, dearie, it's not the dragon, not this time."

Quinn hid an inward wince at the accusation and waited for what followed.

"It was that enormous oaf you brought into your clan.

He got hungry early this morning and came into the kitchen while the day's bread was baking. He ate half of it right out of the oven before Cookie showed up to stop him."

"I see."

"I'm always quick to offer my hospitality to all within the supernatural community. You of all people know that, Quinn. But I have to draw the line at creatures that cannot be taught decent manners. I mean, I don't know what possessed you to think you could tame an orc warrior."

"Tadpole is still learning the rules, Paddy. I just need to talk with him. That's all."

"The time for talk is about done, girlie. This has to stop."

Quinn glanced around the kitchen. "Where is he? I'll talk to him right now."

Cookie pointed at the door. "He left as soon as I showed up and started yelling at him. Even with me chasing after him with a cleaver, he still managed to stuff a few extra loaves in his face on the way out."

"I'm sorry, Cookie. I'll go talk with him and come back up to help you make more bread. Okay?"

Cookie shook his head. "I've got it. I already called in a few of the other kitchen staff to come in early and help. Just deal with him. Either he learns how civilized people live and work or get rid of him. I don't care which."

He grumbled something else under his breath as he crossed his arms. Quinn couldn't make out what he said. The cook went back to work on more bread after shooting a glowering glance at her.

Quinn returned his glare with a slight smile. She

followed Paddy back out to the pub. "I'll get this worked out, Paddy. I promise."

"See that you do. I can't lose Cookie. He's the best Irish chef in the entire city."

The pub's owner hopped up and over the bar as Quinn headed to the storeroom door. She had a good idea where Tadpole had gone to hide after he got chased out of the kitchen. She headed for the old Hunter chambers in the tunnels below.

On the way down the stone steps, Quinn ran into her mother.

Naomi must have noticed the grim expression on Quinn's face. "I'll bet you're looking for tall, green, and gruesome, aren't you?"

"He has a name, Mom."

"You're right. I'm sorry. I figured he must be in trouble. I heard him sobbing as he passed through the tunnels leading down to the training maze. I think he's headed for that little den he's set up down there."

"Thanks."

"Anything I can do to help?"

"As a matter of fact, you can. Are you headed to the kitchen for your usual late morning snack?"

"I am," Naomi replied.

"See if you can soothe Cookie's feelings. Tadpole got into the day's fresh bread. I know it was just a misunderstanding, but I need to stop them from happening. I told you all last night that I'd deal with this. That's my primary goal right now."

"I'll see what I can do. What are you planning to say to Tadpole?"

Quinn shrugged. "I'm not sure yet. I'm hoping something will come to me."

"Want some motherly advice?"

"I'm not sure. You said last night you wanted me to get rid of him."

"That's fair. But I also know keeping him here is important to you. Try approaching him in a way that lets him know you care about him, even though he screwed up. It might soften what you have to say."

"I guess I can do that. Where d'you come up with the great motherly advice? It's not like you raised me or anything."

Quinn regretted the quip as soon as she said it. Things had been good between them lately. "I'm sorry. That was uncalled for."

Naomi gave Quinn's shoulder a squeeze with one hand. "It's okay. Even though I wasn't able to raise you as I wanted, I read a lot of books in my spare time. I wanted to know what it was like being a parent, even though I couldn't be there." Naomi smiled and cupped her daughter's cheek. "I'm proud of you and what you've accomplished. If anyone can set Tadpole straight and get him to follow the rules, you can."

"Thanks, and sorry about what I said."

"It's the truth. We also both know it still led to where we are today, which is together. I'm good with that if you are."

"I am." Quinn smiled. "Now, I guess I get to be a mom myself."

"Let me know how it goes," Naomi said over her

shoulder as she left. "I'm sure it'll be worse in your head than it really is."

Quinn watched her mother go. She appreciated how understanding Naomi had been with her. Their relationship was complicated enough without letting Quinn's issues with Tadpole or Sylvie get in the way.

Reaching up to stroke Sylvie's side, Quinn said, "Let's go find your brother, shall we?"

"Eeeep." Sylvie launched from Quinn's shoulder and flapped down the tunnel, leaving Quinn standing alone.

"Hey, wait up!" She sprinted after the dragon as Sylvie led her on the search for the clan's giant orc.

CHAPTER FOUR

Quinn had to open her HUD and boost her speed to keep up with Sylvie as the dragonling flew through the twisting tunnels of the training maze below the Hunters' ceremonial chambers.

Sylvie knew where she was going. She slowed and banked into a small alcove on the left. Quinn heard the orc's sobs as she slowed to a walk, then stopped and listened.

The big orc's crying stopped when Sylvie zipped into the room with an enthusiastic, "Eeeep!"

"Hi, Sylvie. What are you doing here? Did you come down to have some of my bread? There's a little left. That tiny man chased me off before I ate as much as I wanted, but I can always share with you."

"Eeeep, eeep."

"Yeah, I know I'm in trouble. Do you think Quinn will be real mad or just a little mad?"

"Eeeep."

"Yeah, I thought so. I keep messing up, Sylvie. I wish I

was good all the time like you are. Everyone always seems to be angry with me, and I never understand why."

Quinn stepped around the corner into the alcove. It was filled with odds and ends Tadpole had acquired during his time with the clan. A stained and discarded queen-sized mattress covered the floor. A small coffee table with a broken leg had been propped to stand in the corner. Tadpole sat there, perched atop a wooden chair with the back broken off. It creaked under his weight every time he moved. Quinn wondered how long it would last.

"Hey, buddy. Mind if I sit and talk with you for a bit?"

"You're angry with me, Quinn, just like everyone else. I don't know why I keep doing things that make people mad."

"It could be my fault, Tadpole. Maybe I need to do a better job of explaining the rules to you. Tell me, why are you hiding down here by yourself? What do you think happened upstairs?"

"Um, I got hungry and had to go, um, you know."

"Yes, I know. You used the bathroom, right? You didn't pee in the corner again, did you?"

"No, I did just like you said. Clark showed me how grown-up boys like me use toilets. I've been careful ever since."

"That's great. I'm proud of you. So, what happened today?"

"Well..." The big orc paused and scratched his chin. "I went up and peed in the bathroom just like I was supposed to. I was hungry, and something smelled more wonderful than I'd ever smelled before, so I went looking for it. I followed my nose and found a hot box full of this amazing bread waiting for me to eat."

Quinn paused as she searched for the best way to explain it to the orc. "What if that amazing bread was waiting for someone else to eat? What if all of Paddy and Cookie's hungry customers wanted to eat that bread later?"

"You think?" Tadpole asked. He thought some more and frowned. "Maybe that's why the little man shouted at me and chased me out. He banged my knee with a heavy pan. It hurt a lot. Then he grabbed this little knife. I knew I had to leave. You told me I wasn't allowed to hurt anyone here, and I've been real careful."

"I know you have, buddy. Let me see where he banged you with the pan."

Tadpole pointed at his knee. There was a bruise there. She knew it couldn't be too bad since he was nearly invincible to non-magical weapons. Unless it was an enchanted frying pan, it couldn't be too bad.

Quinn studied the bruise a little longer and shook her head. "Looks bad. Should we go find you a healer to look at it?"

"No, it doesn't hurt anymore. It just scared me, mostly."

"I'll bet." Quinn thought about how to proceed. "You know, Tadpole, you've had to learn a lot of rules lately. They're all important so you can live here with us, and there are more you need to know. One of them is never taking anything that isn't given to you, even if it looks like it doesn't belong to anyone else."

"Even if it's just sitting around? That's how I found this cool chair." He grinned and wiggled back and forth. "It groans when I sit on it."

Quinn hid her smile behind her hand. "Yes, even if it's just sitting around. If you want something like that, ask someone in charge. You can ask me or anyone from the clan. Paddy and Juni are good people to ask, too."

"Every time?"

"Yep, every time. That way, if it belongs to someone else, they won't be upset when they can't find it. That's why people get angry with you, because they're sad or worried about something getting lost or broken."

"Does that mean I have to give all this stuff back?"

Quinn scanned the cozy alcove. A one-armed, naked plastic baby doll with singed hair stared back at her from atop a dented aluminum beer keg in the corner beside his chair.

She shook her head. "No, you can keep this stuff unless someone specifically asks for it back. Then you have to give it to them. But as soon as you do, come tell me right away, and I'll get you something even cooler to replace it, okay?"

Tadpole nodded. "An even better thing? Really?"

"Only for the stuff already here. Otherwise, ask before you take anything to eat or to bring down here for decoration. Understand?"

"Yes," Tadpole said. His brow furrowed, and he seemed to be looking at the contents of his little lair in a fresh light.

Quinn hoped her brief talk had gone the way she wanted. She suspected most of Tadpole's problem was that he was bored. There was nothing for him to do to occupy his time with the clan, and the last few months might have gone better if Quinn could have come up with something other than the occasional sparring match with her or

Naomi. They were the only ones he couldn't kill accidentally with one blow. He'd sparred with Clark once and nearly pulled the old Hunter's arm off.

She decided to talk to the others about finding Tadpole a job of some sort to occupy him. That might keep him from wandering around and getting into trouble. She wasn't sure what job suited a veritable killing machine like an orc warrior, other than destruction. If there was one out there, though, she would find it.

Quinn pointed at the door. "Hey, you want to come with Sylvie and me and work on some training? I'm sure Clark can come up with some things for you to do afterward, while they're putting me through my paces."

"I don't like fighting you, Quinn. What if I hurt you?"

"It's not real fighting, buddy. You're helping me be better, so someone else doesn't hurt me. If you don't want to spar, we can find something else for you to do while I work out."

"That's great. What do you think it will be? Maybe it's counting stones, or gathering sticks. No, that's silly. There aren't any sticks down here. It could be—"

Quinn tuned out Tadpole's litany of random and varied job ideas as they left the alcove. The three of them went back up to the main ceremonial chambers. She pulled out her phone and checked for a signal the whole way. She wanted to give Clark a heads up that they were coming. Taylor was supposed to install cellphone repeaters down in the tunnels, but she hadn't put them all the way in the maze yet. Quinn had to wait to send the message when they got back to the ceremonial room.

She finally got off a warning text as they entered the

hallway leading from the chamber to the training room and the old Hunter armory. It reached him barely in time. He was tapping out a reply when Quinn, Sylvie, and Tadpole entered.

Quinn called, "Hey, Clark," to give him warning they were this close.

He looked up from his phone, scowling. His eyes darkened even more when he spotted Tadpole standing hunched over in the hallway behind her.

Quinn flashed a broad grin and adopted a cheerful tone as she said, "I brought Tadpole with me for training this morning. I hope you don't mind."

Tadpole pushed past Quinn into the training room. "Hi, Clark. Quinn said you would come up with something fun to do today. What is it? Can you tell me? I really want to know. Is it a new sword? I love swords, especially when they're really sharp. Dull swords make it very hard to cut things. You can do it, but you have to hit things with them lots of times. I—"

Quinn caught up and stopped him. "Why don't we let Clark surprise you? That way, you won't spoil his plans."

Relief washed across Clark's face. He even turned and mouthed "thank you" at her. "Quinn's right. Just give me a few minutes. I'm sure I can find the perfect thing for you to do today."

Tadpole's eyes brightened, and an enormous grin crossed his face. Quinn smiled, too. She tried to think of a few options for the big orc, as well. Clark's initial idea might run out of steam for Tadpole before they finished whatever training he had in mind for her.

Clark left the training room and headed into the old

armory for a few minutes. Tadpole bounced from foot to foot, trying to contain his anticipation.

The old Hunter returned from the armory with an idea that worked out well for everyone. Clark beckoned to the orc and pointed at the armory opposite the hallway entrance.

"See that door, Tadpole?"

"Uh-huh."

"In there are piles of old weapons. A lot of them are broken and rusted beyond repair."

"What do you want me to do?"

"I want you to go through every weapon in that room and test them to see if they are worth repairing and keeping. If they're not, I want you to put them in a pile by the door. We'll stack all the broken ones we can't fix and carry them out to the alley later."

Tadpole scratched his head. "What're you going to do with them in the alley?"

"I know a weaponsmith outside the city who will come and pick them up to use for scrap." When he saw Tadpole's eyebrows crinkle in question, Clark added, "He'll melt them all down and turn them into tools and things."

"That's horrible. They should get the chance to live again without being melted first."

"Well, Tadpole, I'll tell you what. I need an armory with only usable weapons in it. If you can repair something and show me we can still use it, we'll keep it. Otherwise, it goes to the scrap heap. Deal?"

"Deal, Clark. I'll make sure all the weapons are working. I promise. You won't have to throw any of them away."

"That's not what I meant, exactly," Clark said.

Quinn shook her head. "Clark, let it go. Consider it a win and turn him loose. This is the most excited I've seen him since he first got here and met everyone."

Clark glanced at the towering orc beside him. Tadpole stared at Clark, waiting for permission to start.

Clark sighed. "All right, if you can fix it, we'll keep it. First, you sort through them all for the ones that are in good shape now. No working on repairs until you do that. Go see what you can do."

Tadpole grinned so wide, his usually hidden upper tusks showed beneath the larger ones jutting from his lower lip. He bounded around Clark with surprising grace and disappeared into the old Hunter armory.

"I hope that keeps him busy for more than a few minutes," Clark said.

"Did you see his reaction?" Quinn asked. "That was the perfect thing."

"We'll see. Now, enough time spent trying to distract me from the real work that needs doing. Let's see how far you've come on your acrobatic evasion drills." Clark selected a wooden quarterstaff from the rack on the wall.

Quinn groaned. She hated these because every time she wasn't quick enough, he jabbed her in the ribs with the steel-shod end of that staff.

Clark returned to the mat, spinning the staff in front of him. He counted down from three as Quinn prepared to go through a series of handsprings and somersaults. She focused on the moves that might someday keep her from getting killed.

In the back of her mind, though, she wanted to be somewhere else, with one specific person.

CHAPTER FIVE

Avery returned to the van with two steaming bags of fresh *pastelitos* perched atop the case of bottled water she carried. The giggling from inside brought a tired smile to her lips. The six girls were holding up well so far. Avery hoped hot food would settle them down some. At this late hour, they should all be asleep soon.

She lifted her foot and tapped it against the van's sliding door. "Brea, open up. I've got dinner."

The door's electric lock clicked and the door slid open. Brea's freckled face peered out of the van's darkened interior. The overhead light inside hadn't worked since they traded the pickup truck for it back in Buenos Aires. That was fine with Avery. It made it easier to stay out of sight when they stopped along the road.

"It smells good," Brea said. She grabbed the two paper bags from the top as Avery set the case of water down behind second-row bench seat.

"They're called *pastelitos*. I think they're sort of Honduran empanadas. I got pork, chicken, and bean versions. Eat up. We're getting back on the road as soon as we finish and everyone has had a chance to pee."

"Do we have to use the bathroom at that gas station?" Ola, the dark-skinned seven-year-old, asked. "The last one was disgusting."

"I checked this one while the lady made our food. It's in much better shape. It's a lot better than going by the side of the road. I remember that particular adventure too well."

Kami, the ever-cheerful six-year-old with the pixie cut brown hair, smiled. She held up a roll of toilet paper. "At least we have this now, Avery. We don't have to use icky leaves like the last time."

All the girls said, "Ewwwww," at the memory of their first few days on the road up through Brazil before Avery thought it was safe to stop for provisions. She still feared Gemma's people might find them. The demon-kinder Hunters had almost caught them at the airport's rental car return. Luckily, Avery's amulet warned her away in time to avoid being seen. It also shifted her away from flying and on to plan B, driving north to the United States.

Avery pulled out the burner phone she'd bought at the counter. She'd had to destroy the one she'd been using since arriving in Buenos Aires. She had no idea how Gemma was tracking her or the girls. She couldn't take any chances, so Avery waited an extra few days to be sure they'd shaken pursuit. This was her first opportunity to contact Quinn since she'd rescued the girls. Avery needed her help if she was going to get the girls the rest of the way to Baltimore.

"I'll be right back. I have to make a call. Close the door and lock it. I'll be right over there in the shadows. Brea, see if you can get the others settled for sleep after they finish eating."

Brea nodded. She set her Honduran hot-pocket down, grabbed the door with two hands, and hauled it closed with a grunt. Avery waited to hear the lock click, then walked across the dirt parking lot. It was after dinner time in Baltimore. She dialed the number.

"Okay, mystery caller," Quinn said after picking up. "You've got two seconds to explain yourself, or I hang up."

"Quinn, don't hang up. It's me, Avery."

"My God, Avery, I've been worried sick. Why haven't you called? It's been weeks."

"I had to switch phones. I think Gemma's been tracking my signal and maybe reading my messages somehow."

"How do you know?"

"Because I feel like she's been one step ahead of me since the beginning. Nearly every location I checked from the original list I found came up empty. Everything had been cleaned out."

"You think Gemma knew you were coming?"

"Yes, I picked up the psychic energy of recent pain. Gemma could clean up the physical stuff that might have told me more girls were there, but she couldn't hide the torment of the girls. They have turned some to demon-kinder. I'm pretty sure any who couldn't be possessed were killed."

"How many do you think there were?" Quinn asked.

"It's hard to say," Avery replied. "I've met a few of the demon-kinder on the road. With the Hunter training of the host bodies, they're damned hard to kill. I'm not sure of the total number either way, but I suspect it's somewhere around twenty to thirty girls possessed and maybe as many killed outright."

"Avery, I'm so sorry. I know you were hoping to save them."

"I wasn't completely unsuccessful. The last place on the list was the most remote, so I left it to the end. Before I got there, I dumped my phone and went dark in hopes it would hide my travel plans from Gemma. It must've worked."

"Really? That's great. You found more Huntresses? Ones trained like us?"

"Not exactly," Avery said. "I found six girls, and there's something special about them, but the oldest is just ten."

"Years old?" Quinn paused. "You're bringing them here, aren't you?"

"I'm trying. I couldn't fly with them. I expected one or two women. With six, I couldn't afford forged passports for all of us. Plus, we were almost jumped in Buenos Aires, and again when we got to Rio. I thought it best to keep going by ground for now."

Quinn chuckled on the other end of the phone.

"What's so funny?"

"I'm picturing you driving a carload of schoolgirls through South America by yourself. Are you teaching them road songs to sing?"

"It's not funny, Quinn. We're in actual danger here."

"I know. Sorry. I'd come and help you, but I'm tied up with trouble here, too. What if I send Clark?"

Avery smiled. "That'd be worse than being alone, I think. Look, I'm all right for the drive right now. But I need money for papers, visas, passports, and the rest. I was hoping you could have the Keeper send some more cash to my secure account."

"I'll have Clark call Joshua as soon as I get off the phone. How much?"

Avery cringed and gave her the estimate. "Eighty thousand U.S. dollars. I have a contact in Mexico City who will provide me with what I need, but he won't budge on the price."

"We'll make it work. Joshua will complain, but he'll do what I say. What about getting into Mexico from wherever you are now?"

"We're in Honduras. I have enough left to cover the bribes to get us across the border. If I don't, I'll figure out a way to get there somehow. I'm trying to stay out of sight."

"Be careful. If you run into trouble again, call me. I don't have much of a network beyond Baltimore yet, but I'll mobilize what I can as you get closer."

"Thanks," Avery said. "And Quinn…"

"Yeah?"

"I miss you."

"Me, too. Just get here, then we can carve out some time for the two of us. Promise."

"Sounds like a plan. I'll watch for the deposit to hit. I need to go before the girls get restless and try to leave the van. Bye."

"Bye."

Avery flipped the cover down and slipped it into her pocket. A tingling sensation on the back of her neck and a sudden chill in her amulet sent her into action.

Ducking and spinning in a single smooth motion,

Avery whipped around and threw the compact phone at the target she sensed behind her.

The dark-haired woman creeping up on Avery tried to duck the incoming projectile. Surprise slowed her reaction just enough and the plastic phone slammed into her face, smashing the bridge of her nose.

Black ooze splattered out of her nostrils as both her nose and the plastic phone case shattered from the force of the blow. The woman's eyes rolled up in her head, and she crumpled to the ground.

Avery didn't wait to see what happened. She spotted another woman behind the first, holding a wicked barbed short sword in her hand.

"Brea, start the van now!"

Avery hoped the girl was listening. Summoning her katana, Avery charged the second demon-kinder.

This one's eyes glowed red and her lips moved, though she couldn't make out what she said.

A powerful invisible force punched Avery in the gut, expelling the air from her lungs. Judging by the intense, almost burning cold of her amulet, at least some of the spell's effect had been absorbed. It could have done a lot more than just knock the wind out of her.

Avery recovered and brought up her blade to parry the incoming strike from the barbed sword. She struggled to suck air into her oxygen-starved lungs after the spell attack. Gasping, she twisted and drove an overhead slash at her opponent.

Behind her, the van's engine roared to life, and Avery smiled. Brea *had* been listening. She feinted another lunging attack and then kicked out hard with her booted foot.

She caught the other woman by surprise and connected with her knee, hyper-extending it backward and eliciting a satisfying scream from her. The leg buckled, and she tumbled to the ground.

The first demon-kinder was stirring at this point. Avery decided this was her chance to disengage and get the girls out of here. She ran for the van.

The now-crawling demon-kinder yelled behind her, "We've found you three times now. We'll find you again, girl!"

The van pulled away from the corner of the gravel lot. The sliding door opened as it picked up speed. The eight-year-old blonde twins Jordi and Margie stood in the opening, clutching the door pillars with one hand and reaching out for her with the other.

Avery could make out Brea kneeling on the driver's seat behind the wheel. The girl craned her neck to watch Avery.

Avery shouted, "Go, Brea. More gas, more gas."

The van's rear tires kicked up a spray of gravel and lurched forward. Avery poured every ounce of her remaining strength into a final lunging dive for the open door.

Surprisingly strong hands grabbed her arms and pulled her to safety as the van surged across the parking lot and onto the narrow two-lane road. The door slammed closed behind her.

Avery tried to right herself from her awkward position half-under the bench seat behind the driver. She finally got up onto her knees.

In the driver's seat, Brea held the wheel in a white-knuckled grip, wide-eyed as she steered the speeding vehicle down the dark and deserted road. Avery reached past the girl's waist and flicked the switch to turn on the headlights. As she did, she spotted nine-year-old Suko, the second eldest. She was crouched on the floor in front of the driver's seat and had both hands pressed down on the accelerator while staring up at Brea.

"Hey, you're both doing great. Keep it up for a little longer, and then we'll stop and I'll take over, all right?"

The Asian girl on the floor nodded, a slight smile crossing her face. Brea didn't respond, just kept her fierce gaze on the road ahead.

Kneeling between the front seats, ready to take the wheel if Brea lost control, Avery said, "Brea, I said start the van, not drive it."

Brea stole a quick, angry glance in Avery's direction, then returned her attention to the road. The look of determination in her eyes held more than a little defiance as well.

"It's okay. I shouldn't joke. I'm not mad at you. It all worked out. You're a talented driver for a ten-year-old."

"The one with the broken nose had gotten up and was right behind you. You didn't see her and the glow in her eyes. We had to drive."

"You did the right thing in a tough situation. I'm proud of you. Let me check to make sure no one is behind us, and then we'll pull over so I can take the wheel. Just keep us on the road until then."

Brea nodded.

Avery glanced behind them. She didn't see any headlights, but the demon-kinder were also trained as Hunters. They likely had night-vision abilities like her own.

"We need to get off this highway and find another route across the border. They have to know we're headed north for the United States, so they'll have others watching for us at all the likely crossings."

Avery reached into the pocket in the center console and retrieved the old paper map she'd bought when they'd stopped for gas in the morning. It didn't show all the smaller roads, but it looked like there was another small highway crossing theirs ahead. They'd pull off there and switch drivers.

"Just a few more miles, then we'll turn onto another road. Are you two good?"

Suko nodded.

Brea said, "We can drive as long as you want. I'm letting Suko see through my eyes so she can judge our speed and be ready to brake if we need to stop or slow down."

"Wait, what?" Avery asked. "She can see through your eyes?"

"Miss Gemma did something to us when we were very young. We are all connected mind to mind. What one sees, we all see."

"Well, that explains why you all always finish each other's sentences when you talk to me."

"We usually know what we will say before we say it," Brea said. "But we can't read each other's minds for real. Just send mind-messages to each other."

A lot of the odd things about the girls fell into place for Avery, like when they'd all start laughing at the same time, or one would point out the window at something interesting and the others would just nod without looking up to see it.

"You're sort of like very special sisters, then," Avery said. "Just remember to tell me when there's something important going on. I'm not in your mind with the others."

"We will."

Behind Avery, the other four girls nodded in perfect unison. For some, it might seem creepy. Avery, though, wondered what Gemma had planned for a group with special talents like these. It might explain why she was sending the demon-kinder after them with such zeal. She would have to be even more careful with their travel plans moving forward. She couldn't afford to take them anywhere near major border crossings.

She settled into the passenger seat, letting Brea and Suko drive a bit longer while she pulled out the map and started adjusting their route north to Mexico City. It looked like it would add nearly three days to their trip, but it would bring them into the city from the northeast instead of the south, hopefully avoiding prying eyes working for Gemma. It would have to do.

Avery returned her attention to the road ahead. They were close to the turnoff. She prepared to take over the driving as soon as they were off this road. They'd be driving on dirt roads before long. With thick brush and forest in the way, it was no place for two little girls to be behind the wheel.

CHAPTER SIX

Q uinn pulled out her phone and checked once again for any messages or even a text from Avery. It had been two days since she'd heard from the woman. She was worried about the other Huntress.

Clark had reached out to the Keeper, Joshua Dalton. He took care of the clan records and their limited finances. They'd become a little more financially stable since the addition of the vampire John Handon's substantial fortune. Running a growing clan like theirs wasn't cheap, though. Joshua cautioned Quinn that it was no time to go on a spending spree. He often reminded her the funds weren't bottomless.

After his cautionary speech a week before, Quinn had assumed there'd be pushback from the Keeper about sending Avery the funds.

To her surprise, he didn't even blink. He wired the funds to Avery's international account minutes after the request was made. When Quinn questioned the lack of resistance, Joshua said, "This is an emergency. We're not talking about frivolous expenses here."

Quinn bristled a little at the inference about her other requests for money, but she let it drop. The important thing was to get Avery the money.

That was two days ago. Quinn had expected a text to say Avery had received the money, but to date, there was nothing.

Quinn glanced one last time at the blank screen and slid the phone back into her pocket.

"Eeeep?" Sylvie's long neck extended from her perch on Quinn's shoulder. She stared into Quinn's eyes.

"I'm all right. Just worried, that's all." Quinn scratched the dragon's brow ridges. "Come on, let's see if they're ready for this thing tonight."

She stopped in the hall and rapped on the newly repaired wooden door. The stout new oak door stood open, so she entered Taylor's workshop. Clark and Miranda were there with the tech witch.

"Hey, Quinn, I'll be right with you. I'm just finishing a quick update of the software prototype for the presentation. Once this compiles, I'll be ready to go to the summit."

"I hope this app of yours works," Clark said. "There's never been anything like this in our community. I pulled the relevant leaders together for tonight's summit. It'll be up to you to convince them this program of hers will work."

Quinn said, "The way Taylor explained it, this thing's an emergency phone app for the city's supernaturals. They'll be able to tell us when something bad is going down in real-time."

Clark shook his head. "I have my doubts. This whole 'app for everything' has gotten out of hand."

Miranda laughed as she floated past Taylor. "Your phone is so old it won't even update anymore, so what do you care?"

Clark didn't answer, though he glanced down at the phone cupped in his hand.

Quinn asked, "In the old days, how did Hunters find out when there was trouble?"

"We had patrols out and around the city, and our Hunter mages set wards for particularly dangerous things or powerful magics. It worked pretty well most of the time."

Taylor offered a wry chuckle. "Until it failed to pick up the purges in time to stop them, you mean."

"Ooo, harsh, T," Quinn said.

Taylor looked up, blushing. "I didn't mean to say that out loud. I swear. I'm sorry, Clark."

"You didn't assassinate the Hunters, kid. There's nothing to apologize for."

Quinn checked her phone again out of habit. Still no messages. "Hey, have you heard anything from Joshua? I wondered if he had any way to check and see if Avery had received the money?"

"I know he sent it. He emailed me the receipt for the wire transfer. I'm not sure he can see if she's used it without access to her accounts. I thought you just heard from her."

"That was two days ago. It's been crickets since then."

Taylor closed her laptop. She joined Quinn by the

equipment table. "I'm sure she's all right. We'd hear if there was anything wrong, wouldn't we?"

"Not if she's dead in a Guatemalan jungle."

"That was dark," Taylor replied.

"I'm worried about her. I know she can take care of herself, and I'd be confident in her ability to get away if she was on her own. With six little girls in tow, she'll feel responsible for protecting them. I know how I'd react if it were me."

Taylor smiled. "I wouldn't want to get in the way of either of you if something sent you into mama-bear mode."

Quinn started to respond, but Taylor held up her hand.

"Just saying I'd be more worried for the other guys."

"Maybe." Quinn switched gears and forced herself to think about something else. "All set with the app, T?"

"Everything checks out. I'm sure the others will find a few bugs, but we'll fix them as they crop up."

"Good," Quinn replied. "Is Mom joining us?"

Clark said, "She's going to stay here and babysit Tadpole. I assume you're bringing Sylvie along? She could stay here with Tadpole and Naomi. She volunteered to take this round and watch them for the night."

"I'm good with Sylvie coming along. She'll behave as long as I'm around. As for Tadpole, you have to admit, putting him in charge of sorting the armory was an outstanding idea."

Clark nodded and gave half a grin. "I did not know he had extensive training in the care and repair of weapons like that. I mean, he doesn't come across as all that bright most of the time."

"He only learned what his brothers wanted him to

learn. Mostly that was to kill, but he has skill at fixing things, too. Maybe he's like one of those people who's got a hidden super-skill in one thing."

Miranda said, "It's very possible he's some sort of warrior savant. He understands weapons and their use very well, but never learned to interact with others."

"He tries his best. You all see that, right?"

Clark said, "No one is saying he isn't trying. Until we got him focused on the weapons, though, I was sure we would have to take some drastic steps. Now, it looks like he's found a full-time job for himself. You know, he even figured a way to recharge the waning magic in the oldest weapons from the collection?"

"I didn't," Quinn answered. "He can't cast spells. How is he doing it?"

Clark shook his head. "I'm not sure. He said it's something to do with the magic being dull, not diminished."

Miranda brought her hand to her chin. "That's an interesting way to look at that. I suppose it might be possible to hone a spell back into its correct shape in much the way you bring an edge back into alignment."

Clark smiled. "I don't really care how he does it if he gets results. Ever since he settled into working the armory, he's a whole new orc. The first few swords he worked on look like they're brand new."

"I'm glad. I'll still take Sylvie to the summit. She needs practice being out and about in public with other supernaturals. She generally keeps herself cloaked, anyway. Most people won't even see her, even among the most powerful supernaturals. I'll check on Tadpole when we get back and thank Mom for watching him."

Taylor started for the door. "Let's go, then. It's time to release *TeleHuntress*, the app to bring the clan running to the rescue."

Quinn laughed. "You're really going for *TeleHuntress*?"

"Sure. It's catchy, plus the app's set up so they can do a face-chat with one of us before we send out an all-hands alert. That should weed out those who just need a little advice."

Clark grunted. "I'll believe it works when I see it."

"Come on, grumpy pants," Quinn said. "Let's get going, or we'll be late. I had a good visit with them the last time I was there and hinted at what I'd be coming back with. I think the reception from the community's leadership will be positive."

Miranda waved as they left. "I'll wander down and hang with Naomi until you get back. Have fun. Knock 'em dead, Taylor."

Clark, Quinn, and Taylor loaded into the old sedan and headed across town. Their meet-up was to be held at a private social club for local werewolves called The Harvest Moon. The parking lot was full of cars by the time they arrived, and they had to park all the way at the back.

As the trio walked up to the front doors, Quinn remarked, "It looks like the entire community turned out. There are a lot of people here."

Taylor shook her head. "It's awfully quiet for a place with this many werewolves and other shifters inside."

"Maybe there's a lull in the action," Quinn suggested. "Or the band's taking a break."

"Taylor's right," Clark said. He nodded at Taylor. "You're the shifter here. What do you sense?"

Taylor stopped just outside the front doors and stared into space for a few seconds. She frowned. "You're right. I don't sense any other shifters nearby."

"Let's go inside, but be ready for anything."

Quinn stepped even with Clark and drew her Bowie. Sylvie's claws dug into the padded shoulder of her leather jacket as she leaned forward, ready to spring.

"Easy, girl," Quinn said, stroking the dragon's long neck with her free hand. She reached for the door, pulling it open. The coppery taint of fresh blood hung like a fog in the air as she entered the club. It was like she could taste it.

Behind Clark and Quinn, Taylor let out a low growl. Sylvie hissed as her tongue flicked out again and again to taste the air.

Quinn pressed forward until she almost tripped over the first body.

Catching herself on the vintage jukebox by the door, Quinn stared down. A grizzled middle-aged man in biker leathers lay against the neon lights of the jukebox's base.

At least half of him did.

They had cut him in two at the waist. The lower half was a few feet away, closer to the bar. The guy had bled out on the floor while he dragged himself toward the door.

Bodies and pieces of bodies lay scattered everywhere.

Taylor's snarling growl increased in volume. The shift had started as soon as she scented the blood.

"T, you all right? Maybe you should stay outside."

The voice that responded was only half that of her friend. There was a snarl beneath it now. "I'm in control, but I want to kill someone, Quinn. The smell of death is overwhelming."

"Be careful. If you need to go out for some air, you do it." Quinn glanced over her shoulder to make sure her friend heard her.

Taylor's facial features had shifted and elongated to accommodate her wolf's fangs. Short blonde hair covered her face and arms, and one-inch talons had sprouted where her fingernails used to be.

Clark stood behind Taylor, his short sword drawn. "Where was our meeting supposed to be held?"

Quinn nodded to the back of the main clubroom. "I was told there's a smaller conference room at the back where the social club's board meets. The summit's supposed to be in there."

Clark pointed at a door in the far corner at the end of the bar. "Let's look in there first. Taylor, you check for survivors."

The tech witch-werewolf nodded. She stepped past the guy on the floor and started searching among the dozens of bodies scattered around the room and behind the bar.

Quinn and Clark worked their way through the carnage, focused on the door in the far corner. It was ajar a few inches.

When she reached it, Quinn tried to push it open, but something blocked it from the other side. She checked the floor and spotted the hand gripping the bottom. It belonged to a body on the other side.

Sylvie launched before Quinn could stop her and flew through the narrow crack.

Putting her shoulder to the door, Quinn shoved the body back enough so she and Clark could squeeze through.

When she got into the room, Quinn just stood there and surveyed the carnage. It was hard to be sure everyone she'd expected was in here, but she recognized a few of the faces among the bodies. "Goddess, Clark, they're all dead."

"Looks like it," Clark said. He knelt beside the closest corpses. "A heavy sword, maybe an axe, did this. Maybe both. It's hard to be certain. Look at the cuts. They're all clean and deep, done in single strokes."

"You're thinking magical blades like we carry?"

"To kill them all like this, there'd have to be silver infused into the blade somehow. The Hunters aren't the only ones who have that technology, but we were the best at it."

"Avery mentioned Gemma had created demon-kinder from at least some of her Huntress trainees. If she's brought them to town, the entire city's in danger."

"I'm more worried about how they knew to come here tonight. This all happened recently, only a few hours ago."

"Eeeep."

Quinn searched for Sylvie, spotting her at last on the floor next to a gray-haired woman. The dragon nuzzled the woman's cheek, eliciting a low groan. Quinn raced over, trying to place the woman's face in her memory. She thought she represented a coven of witches to the south. They'd met only once, at the previous meet up, so Quinn wasn't sure.

The woman had a broad gash just below her ribs. The puddle of blood on the floor around her torso had already congealed. Quinn wasn't sure how the old woman was even still alive.

Bending down and struggling to remember her name, Quinn said, "Lie still. We'll get some help."

The eyes fluttered open, and the lips curved with the hint of a smile. "Foolish girl, don't lie to me. I know I'm dead. My old body is just stubborn and hasn't decided to go yet."

"Who did this?"

"It was one like you."

"A girl my age?"

"Not exactly, but she was another Huntress. At least that's how she announced herself. She was something more, too. The girl wasn't alone, judging from the shouts and screams outside in the bar. Before she attacked, she said, 'We are the Huntresses of the Change. Prepare for a new world order.'"

Clark knelt beside the woman, taking her hand. "Ainsley, it's Clark. What did her voice sound like?"

The woman stared up at him, smiling. "Clark Hunter, I haven't seen you in many years."

"Too long," he replied. "The voice, what did it sound like?"

"It sounded odd, almost like it was two voices speaking at once. I figured it was a Hunter trick of some sort designed to magnify your voice."

Clark shook his head. "She was one of the demon-kinder, a possessed girl. They're pretending to be Hunters to confuse people."

"I believed her," Ainsley said. "She can certainly kill us like a Hunter could, at least before you became civilized."

Quinn ignored the accusation. "Did she say anything

else? Please, anything you can tell us will help me track them down. I will make them pay for this."

"I'm sorry, child. I've told you all I know." The old woman's back arched as she groaned again. A fresh flow of blood spilled from the gash in her stomach.

"Ma'am," Quinn said, struggling again with the name. "Uh, Ainsley, don't give up. There has to be something else. Think." Quinn gripped the woman's shoulders and stared into the wide-open eyes.

"She's gone, Quinn."

Quinn held the woman's vacant gaze for a few seconds longer, refusing to believe she'd died before telling them more. Letting out a lengthy sigh, Quinn reached up and used her fingertips to slide the eyelids closed.

Standing, she shook her head. "This isn't good. I wonder if Avery's escape with the girls pushed up Gemma's timetable? It can't be a coincidence that demon-kinder Huntresses attacked Avery down south and came here to Baltimore at the same time."

"I don't think so, either," Clark said. "It means there's something here they either need or have to stop to put their plan into place."

"Why didn't they wait for us to come before they sprang the attack? They must've known we were coming tonight. It can't be a coincidence."

"It isn't. Knowing Gemma, this is a challenge. She wants us to run around and chase them while we try to figure out what she really wants. It's her twisted idea of a joke."

"So we can expect more attacks like this one? We have to warn people." Quinn stopped. "What if they know we're here and O'Malley's is unguarded? That could be their next stop."

Clark pulled out his phone and tapped in a number. "That's neutral ground. They'd be fools to attack. The protections there are formidable. Maybe, though, that's all out the window now. I'll warn Paddy, just in case. Check on Taylor. I'll be right out."

Quinn nodded and waved for Sylvie to join her. Together, the two headed back out to the bar. When she returned to the main room, Taylor was nowhere in sight. Quinn panicked, worried something had happened to her best friend.

Running to the door, Quinn called, "T, where are you?"

"Over here."

The voice came from behind the bar.

Sylvie launched from her shoulder as Quinn shifted direction. The dragon beat her to the bar and leaned over to peer at the far side.

Quinn joined Sylvie and stretched to look and see.

Taylor crouched on the floor, staring at something beneath the bar. "You can come out. It'll be all right. We're here now, and we can protect you."

"No, you can't. Four of them killed every shifter in this bar. You two can't stand up to them."

"My friend is the Huntress. There's nothing she can't do."

"The Huntress is here? For real?" A small head covered in curly hair poked out from under a shelf full of glasses and beer mugs. It was a boy of maybe ten or eleven.

Quinn waved. "I'm here. For real. Come on out and sit

there beside my friend Taylor." She pointed at the glasses. "Get him some water, T."

Taylor nodded and grabbed the handle of a mug, then filled it with some ice water from a pitcher atop the sink.

"I'm Quinn. What's your name?"

"Zane."

"Hi, Zane. Aren't you kind of young to come in here?"

"My dad's the bartender. I come in to help him sometimes." The boy started to stand so he could see over the bar.

Quinn reached out to nudge him back down. He didn't need to see all the carnage. "Why don't you stay seated for now? There's nothing worth seeing out here."

"I wanted to look for my dad. Can you see him? Is he okay?"

"I don't know, Zane. I promise we'll check everyone and help the ones we can. Do you remember the women who did this? Can you remember anything they said?"

"After all the screaming stopped, I heard them talking. Their voices were weird. One of them said something about this stopping the Huntress from helping save the little ones. I guess they meant you."

Quinn's eyes met Taylor's. The shifter crouched and handed Zane the mug of ice water.

"Here, sip this." She stood back up and said, "This is all about Avery. They're trying to keep us away so they can stop her coming here. What is it she's done that's got Gemma's panties in such a bunch?"

"Whatever it is, Avery holds the key with those girls. I wish she'd reach out to me. I can't go down to Mexico and try to track her down blind. I'd never find her if she didn't want to be found."

Clark came out of the back room. "Everything is fine at O'Malley's, for now. Paddy said he'd use leprechaun magic to put more wards around the place. I'm not sure it'll be enough after what's happened here, but it's better than nothing."

"This is tied to Avery and those girls, Clark. They're trying to keep me from helping them. The problem is, I don't know where they are, even if I wanted to help."

"Maybe they don't know that," Taylor said. "Maybe they think you'll run off and lead them to her. You said you wouldn't be able to find her if she went into stealth mode."

"So, what do I do? Nothing?"

Clark nodded. "We deal with this mess and harden our defenses. When Avery reaches out again, we'll fill her in and ask her what she wants us to do."

"But—"

"Clark's right, Quinn. For now, we prepare as best as we can. Gemma's shown at least part of her hand in a gamble that will not pay off, at least not yet. She's waiting for you to make the next move. Wait for Avery's next call. Until then, there's nothing else to do. We have to deal with the problems we already have."

Clark pulled out his phone again. "I'll call for help to come and clean this up. I also have to alert our contact in the city police department. We don't want any nosy patrol officers poking around in here."

Quinn nodded. "The bartender's son survived. He hid behind the bar during the fight. We need to find someone else from his family. They need to come pick him up."

Clark smiled at the boy on the other side of the bar. "Taylor, you take care of that. He looks old enough to tell you who to call. I'll deal with the police. Quinn, call your mother and fill her in. Then we'll wait for the cleanup team to arrive. After that, we can go home."

Quinn nodded and pulled out her phone. She stared at it for a long time, trying to will Avery to call or text to let her know she was all right. When nothing appeared after a few seconds, she tapped out a long text to her mother. She slid the phone back into her pocket and started helping Clark check the bodies again so they'd be ready for whoever this cleanup team was.

It would be a long night. All Quinn wanted to do was go home. She couldn't, though. She had to be here and be seen by those who responded. The people she'd stepped up to protect here in Baltimore needed to see her being involved and on top of what happened here. She looked down at her stained shirt and jeans, smeared with the blood of those she'd checked.

She cursed as she moved to the next body. Sometimes it sucked being the Huntress.

CHAPTER SEVEN

An hour after the cleanup team arrived, Clark said, "I have to stay a bit longer, Quinn, but you and Taylor can head home if you want. I can have Paddy send someone out to pick you both up."

"You sure?" Quinn asked. She tried to hide her exhaustion, emotional and physical. The day's training and the short night's rest the evening before had caught up with her.

"Yeah. I've got to help the cleaners finish up and give a report to the police department's supernatural liaison so they can document things on their end in a way that keeps all this under the radar." He nodded at Taylor, seated in the corner with the bartender's son. "She's overwhelmed with all the carnage. She's done well keeping the boy occupied, but I think she's on the verge of full-on shift to wolf. Take her home. His family is on the way to get him and should be here soon. If I learn anything else about the attacks, I'll fill you in over breakfast."

"Can you make it lunch?" Quinn checked the time. "It's

2:30. I'd like to sleep in, and I have to do a few things in the morning with Tadpole."

"That works. It'll give me time to sleep, too. I'll call Paddy, and he can send someone from his late kitchen staff to pick you up. Go down to the corner so they don't have to pull into the lot. The cleaners have it blocked with their panel van."

Quinn went to give Taylor the good news. She and Sylvie were playing a game with Zane where he balled up bits of paper cocktail napkin and tossed them in the air for the dragon. Sylvie's head tracked them as they came close, then she torched each one in a quick burst of magical flame.

It had kept the boy occupied well enough, though Quinn was surprised it hadn't set off the smoke detectors mounted on the club's ceiling. She switched her attention to her best friend.

Clark was right; Taylor didn't look well. Every time someone moved inside the club's bar, her eyes jerked in their direction and her talons emerged. That had to be taking a toll on her ability to remain in control.

Quinn approached slowly and forced herself to relax as she said, "T, come on. Let's go outside. Clark's sending us home."

"What about Zane? We can't leave him alone in here. It's mostly cleaned up, but—"

"I can handle it, Taylor," Zane interrupted.

"I didn't say you couldn't. You're doing better than I am."

"It's all right, T. His family should be here soon. It's time for both of us to go home."

Taylor nodded, a brief jerky motion. "We taking Clark's car?"

"No, Paddy's sending someone. They'll meet us outside."

Taylor stood, "Bye, Zane. Is it okay if I call and check on how you're doing in a few days?"

"I'd like that, Taylor. Thank you."

Taylor smiled and nodded at another shifter who showed up as they were talking. "Leslie will sit with you until your family shows up. Take care."

Zane waved goodbye.

Sylvie flew up to land on Quinn's shoulder, balancing there as they headed outside.

The cool night air struck Quinn with a blast of freshness. She hadn't realized how foul it was inside the club with the odor of death. She wondered how a person's nose became used to something like that. It must've been even worse for Taylor, with her heightened senses.

Quinn glanced at her friend. The change of location seemed to have an immediate positive effect. "Good to get some fresh air, isn't it?"

"I should have come out here a long time ago. I'm not as used to this kind of carnage as you are. I work my magic behind a desk with monitors and keyboards and stuff. This is way above my comfort zone."

"I know. I wouldn't have brought you if I had thought this was a possibility. You'll feel a lot better after a shower and some rest."

They started down the street toward the corner at the end of the street. Quinn glanced back up the street. A large panel van belonging to the cleanup crew blocked their view of the club from here.

Quinn's phone chirped with a text. It was Clark.

One of the new cooks is on the way. Be there to get you soon.

As Quinn put the phone back in her pocket, a silver SUV pulled to the curb and the woman behind the wheel asked, "Need a ride?" She had an accent Quinn couldn't place.

Taylor smiled. "That was fast."

"Yeah, maybe Paddy called someone who lives nearby." Quinn turned to the woman. "Thanks so much. You got here fast."

The driver nodded and smiled. "I was in the neighborhood."

Quinn pulled open the front passenger door and smiled at Taylor. "You can ride shotgun. You deserve it."

The tech witch climbed in with a nod of thanks. Quinn got in the back seat. The little dragon moved from Quinn's shoulder to her lap.

"You two going back home?" the woman asked as she pulled away from the curb.

"Yes, it's been a long night," Quinn replied. "I don't remember seeing you around O'Malley's. Clark said you're new?"

"Uh, yeah, I, uh, just started. I haven't been in the States very long."

Taylor asked, "Where are you from?"

"Macedonia. It's one of the Baltic states. Most people haven't heard of it."

Quinn had to admit she had no idea where it was on a map. Maybe Taylor did. She changed the subject. "I'm Quinn, and this is Taylor. Sorry, I don't remember your name."

"Safka. It is okay. I never told you my name."

Quinn smiled. "What's your specialty, Safka?"

Safka glanced back at Quinn with her eyebrows raised. "What do you mean?"

"Clark said you were one of the new cooks. What do you cook at Paddy's? Maybe Taylor and I can try it next time. I didn't see anything new on the menu recently."

"Uh, yes, I am a cook. I am best at preparing lamb."

Taylor frowned. "There's no lamb on the pub's menu."

"Not yet, but maybe soon."

Quinn glanced out the window as they drove along. Safka wasn't taking the route she would have used to get back to the eastern side of town.

"Hey, Safka," Quinn said. "I know you're new to the city, but there's a faster way to get to the pub."

"I use the way I know best."

Quinn shrugged. She was tired and just wanted to get home and go to bed. She let her eyes close for a minute to rest them.

The SUV jerked to a halt, and Taylor screamed, "Quinn!"

Quinn's eyelids popped up as someone yanked open the car door as she leaned on it.

Hands reached for her and slammed her to the sidewalk beside the vehicle. A deep-throated growl came from Taylor in the front seat.

Quinn rolled over just in time to avoid a sword stabbing at her back. Sparks flew when the tip skittered across the concrete.

She drew her Bowie as she rolled, trying to get back to her feet so she could defend herself. All she could do, though, was keep rolling across the sidewalk as the sword came down at her again and again.

Quinn rolled against something hard, a fire hydrant. It stopped her and gave the woman chasing her the chance to catch up. The Bowie came around in time to catch the heavy blade descending toward her head.

"*EEEEEEEEEP!*"

Sylvie's tiny battle cry split the night. The dragon swooped in and delivered a blast of fire to the face of the woman standing over Quinn.

The attack likely saved Quinn's life since the woman dodged back. She beat at the wisps of smoke rising from the scorched ends of her bright red hair.

Quinn grabbed the top of the hydrant and pulled herself up. Sylvie circled around and shot another jet of flame at the woman. This time the flame was much smaller and lacked the distance to reach the target. The woman dodged with ease, ducking under the weak attack.

Damn, Sylvie's earlier antics back at the social club to keep Zane occupied had used up her fire breath reserves. Quinn charged in. "Get clear, Sylvie. I've got this."

She caught the redhead by surprise as she tried to recover from ducking the dragon's attack. The heavy sword came up at an awkward angle.

Quinn ducked beneath the sword, twisting to jab the blade into Red's thigh.

The woman screamed as the blade cut into her leg.

Quinn kicked out, catching the woman in the hip. It launched her backward to tumble to the ground about five feet away.

Using the momentary break to get her bearings, Quinn spotted Taylor in full werewolf mode, locked in combat with Safka. The woman's eyes glowed red as she and Taylor wrestled for control of a hooked silver knife.

There was no time to come to Taylor's aid, though. The other attacker bounced back to her feet. She charged in at Quinn, sword raised. "Time to get rid of you once and for all." This time the woman's voice had the otherness typical of most demon kinder. They only gained the control to normalize it with time and practice. Safka's demon self had been around long enough to do that.

Quinn beckoned with her free hand. "Come and get some. I'm in the mood for killing."

The woman rushed in, weaving her longer blade in a series of attacks. Quinn raised her Bowie, parrying the blade as it came in at her.

She missed Red's forward snap-kick and it caught her in the belly, doubling her over and knocking her back to the ground.

Opening her HUD, Quinn siphoned off stamina and boosted her strength. It came online just in time for her to deflect the follow-up strike. The heavier blade crashed into her Bowie knife, driving down with so much force it almost dislodged the weapon from Quinn's hand.

Rolling to the right, Quinn deflected the sword to the left and gathered her increased strength. She jumped up in a spinning motion that brought a roundhouse kick within a half-inch of the demon-kinder's head.

Red jerked her face away with that preternatural speed the demon-kinder gave their host bodies. The arrogant sneer never left the woman's lips.

Taylor had disengaged from Safka, who still held the hooked silver blade. The two circled each other in the street nearby beneath the streetlight.

Safka drove at Taylor, but the werewolf had anticipated the move. She grabbed Safka's wrist and twisted it.

The blade clattered to the pavement beside the car.

Fighting without her knife didn't faze the demon-kinder. She drove forward and fought Taylor barehanded. Given her strength and speed, it was still an even matchup. Quinn had to get over there and help her friend.

She swung her face to the side just in time to avoid an incoming slash from the other woman's sword. The whoosh of air from the passing blade kissed Quinn's cheek.

She had to stay focused. She couldn't help Taylor if she was dead. The other chick was too good for Quinn to pay attention to Taylor and get away with it again.

Squaring up, Quinn studied her attacker.

Black ooze ran down her leg from where Quinn had cut her earlier. She barely limped, though. Those possessed by demons paid little attention to little things like pain.

The woman's lips curled back in a snarl. "I might let you live if you tell me where your friend is with our little sisters."

"Like I'd tell you anything, even if I knew."

The demon-kinder feinted a lunge, then pulled back to continue circling. "Suit yourself. I'd much rather kill you."

Quinn kept her eyes on the woman while trying to see

everything else around her. There might be others on the way.

"Where are your friends? There's no way you two killed all those people in the social club."

"Those fools are no longer with us. The shifters were more trouble than expected, and our companions failed to live up to the test."

Quinn nodded and smiled. Good to know. Most demons would lie outright but couldn't avoid boasting. They lacked the subtle communication skills to hide important details, like the fact they had no reinforcements coming.

Something the woman had said earlier piqued Quinn's interest. "Why did you call those little girls 'sisters?' I mean, they're obviously not demon-kinder like you. I would think you'd want them dead, not claim them as kin."

"Foolish girl. It takes the collective innocence of several to allow one of our great lords to overcome the barrier that has held us back for so long. They shall be the ones to open the way for us to return to our former glory. Gemma already prepared them for the ritual, melding their minds."

"Maybe I should send you back to hell. You can pass along the message to your masters that the trip back will be delayed."

As she said the last word, Quinn feinted and then lunged to the right, trying to catch the woman partially from behind. With luck, she might be able to get behind the demon-kinder.

With any other supernatural opponent, it might have worked.

The demon-kinder twisted her arm at an impossible

angle, deflecting the incoming Bowie. The heavier sword batted the Bowie away with ease.

Quinn heard Red's elbow pop out of joint as she did it, though. She tried to take advantage of the momentary disability, but the demon-kinder dodged.

She sneered at the Huntress and twisted the forearm back into the elbow joint.

Quinn shook her head. Hunter-trained bodies were perfect vessels for the demons, melding the combat moves Gemma and her supporters had taught them growing up with the speed, strength, and endurance of a demon-kinder. It made for a difficult foe. No wonder Avery was so worried about getting the girls up to Baltimore safely. How many more of these women did Gemma have?

A flicker of movement flashed in her direction. The next few seconds were filled with desperate parries and backpedaling as the other woman went into a full-on assault. The three-foot sword blade, modeled on a Chinese design, seemed to come at her from every direction at once.

Two times, it got past her defenses and drew blood. One was a scratch across her neck that almost opened her jugular vein. The second stabbed into her side, passing through muscle to come out the back.

Quinn fell back from that hit, sliding off the extended blade. She clapped her free hand down to staunch the blood flowing from the wound.

"The vaunted Huntress bleeds just like any other human. Now I move in for the kill."

Red lifted her blade, but Sylvie dove in, raking the woman's eyes with her dragon claws. The attacker shrieked, more from aggravation than pain as she tried to bat the flying dragonling away.

Quinn drew on more stamina and pushed through to overcome the pain in her side.

She backed up a few steps to try to put some space between herself and the demon-kinder, then gathered her will to boost the last of her strength and speed.

The demon-kinder's fist connected at last and sent a screeching Sylvie tumbling through the air to crash into the bricks of a home nearby.

Quinn snarled at seeing the dragon hurt and charged at the woman.

Red was ready for her.

The sword came at Quinn again, and again, and again. All three strikes connected despite the Huntress' best efforts. All were minor cuts compared to the puncture in her side, but the combination sapped her remaining power.

The woman raised her sword as Quinn stumbled over a raised crack in the sidewalk. The Bowie was out of position to stop this attack and Quinn fell to the pavement, wondering what it was like to die.

Then her opponent wasn't there above her anymore.

In a blur Quinn had a hard time following, a hairy, snarling form slammed into the demon-kinder from the side. The impact carried them both into a wrought iron fence across the tiny plot of garden in front of the row home beside their battle.

The demon-kinder shouted once in alarm. The cry cut off in a gurgling rush of black ichor as the powerful wolf's jaws closed on her throat.

Like a true predator, the wolf shook its prey by the neck and snapped the spine, killing her instantly.

Quinn sat up, wincing at the pull on her stomach muscles around the wound in her side. The wolf backed away from the nearly decapitated corpse and turned to Quinn. In an instant, it was Taylor again.

The tech witch huddled into a ball, nearly naked after her full transformation destroyed the clothes she'd been wearing. What little of her clothing remained hung on her in torn strips. She vomited twice on the sidewalk and started sobbing.

Quinn pressed a hand against the wound in her side and crawled over to her friend. Pulling off her leather jacket, she draped over Taylor's back.

"Hey, T, you did good. We're okay. Put your arms into the jacket so we can cover you up some."

"I can't get the foul taste out of my mouth." She spat blackened phlegm into the puddle of vomit.

"Come over here to the car. Maybe they had a water bottle or something in there to rinse with."

Taylor stood, shivering in the early-morning chill. Quinn walked with her over to the SUV. It was still running. On the other side, lying in a heap in the middle of the street, was Safka. Her throat torn open like the other demon-kinder's.

Quinn sat Taylor in the passenger seat while she searched the front and back for something to drink. The SUV was empty, aside from a printed rental agreement in the glove compartment. Quinn wondered which of the dead women was Anna Conchat. It didn't matter. It was probably an alias, anyway.

"I found nothing, T. Sit here. I need to check on Sylvie, then we need to get out of here. Close your door. I'll be right back."

Quinn winced as she twisted to search for the fallen dragon. She smiled when she found her.

The little youngling waddled across the pavement toward the SUV. She looked a little battered but otherwise fine.

"Eeeep?"

"I'll be all right." Quinn glanced down at the hand pressed against her side. "This'll heal soon enough. I just need to get home. How are you?"

"Eeeep."

Quinn nodded. "I guess we are both a little battered. Thanks for fighting so hard."

The little dragon's head bobbed once in reply. Quinn bent and scooped her up in her free hand. "Come on. You can sit with Taylor while I drive."

She returned to the vehicle and got behind the wheel. "We'll take the SUV for now. We can ditch it later so it isn't tied to either of us when the police find the two bodies."

"I hate killing, Quinn. I don't know how you do it."

"I don't like it either. If it's them or me or to save one of my friends, I'll do it, though. That's what you did tonight. *You* saved *me* for a change."

Quinn glanced over to catch Taylor's eye. She wasn't looking. She sat in the passenger seat with her knees drawn up, staring out the window. Sylvie nuzzled her, but Taylor didn't seem to notice.

When they got to a stoplight, Quinn dialed Clark.

"What's up?" he asked. "You get home? The cook from

O'Malley's stopped by the club and said you weren't out at the curb."

"A case of mistaken identity," Quinn replied. "I found the women responsible for the attack. One of them picked us up. I'm not sure if they knew someone was coming to get us or if it was just dumb luck. She drove us to a neighborhood near Hopkins and ambushed us with her partner."

"Text me the address, and I'll get the cleanup crew to go there next. You two hurt?"

"I'm a little dinged. Taylor's not hurt, but she's messed up. She went through a full shift during the fight."

"She hasn't done that since the beginning. Should I call someone from the local pack to come and chat with her?"

Quinn glanced at her friend. "I can do that if it's needed. For now, I'll try to handle it."

The light turned green and Quinn drove through the intersection, then pulled over and texted the cross streets where the attack happened. "Sending the address now. I'll text again when we get home. Can you have the cleaners come and get their SUV? That's what I'm driving now. I'll park it in the alley by O'Malley's."

"I'll let them know. Get home and take care of Taylor. I'll wait for your text to make sure you got there safely."

Quinn disconnected the call.

Taylor said, "You don't have to coddle me. I need to get used to this, I guess."

"No, you don't. You're not a mass murderer or something, T. You did what you had to do to save yourself from a demon-possessed woman with Hunter training. It's a miracle both of us aren't dead right now. You sit back, and we'll get you home. I'll brew hot tea for both of us, and we can talk some more up in your apartment."

Taylor just nodded and went back to watching the city go by outside the window. Quinn's thoughts cycled between worry for Taylor and worry for Avery.

After running her mind ragged with a series of what-ifs about her girlfriend, Quinn turned her attention back to Taylor for the final time. She was here and now, and that made her priority one. If Avery reached out, Quinn would shift her concern.

Until then, she would focus on Taylor.

CHAPTER EIGHT

Quinn opened her eyes and stared at the unfamiliar ceiling. She blinked, still exhausted from the night before. It took her several seconds to remember where she was. She glanced around, taking in the disassembled computer spread all over a small kitchen table. She looked down and realized she was on a couch, not a bed.

Her memory flooded back.

It was Taylor's couch. At least, it was the couch the last resident had left in the apartment.

A clink of silverware in the small kitchenette and the smell of coffee brought a smile to her lips. A familiar voice hummed a pop song as she worked.

"Morning, T. I hope you made a mug for me."

"It's not morning. It's afternoon," Taylor came over to the sofa holding a steaming mug of coffee. "And I remembered to make you some."

Quinn sat up. Sylvie moved from her waist and settled

onto a pillow, curling up again and going back to sleep as she reached out for the mug. A twinge of pain in her side reminded her again of the night before. She took a sip of the coffee, ignoring the injury for now. "I'm supposed to be taking care of you, remember? You were pretty upset last night. How're you feeling this morning?"

Taylor shrugged. "No lasting damage. One benefit of being a shifter: I regenerate most injuries. How about you? You insisted on bandaging that hole in your side by yourself last night."

"It's fine. Huntress genes will help me heal fast. I don't regenerate, but I should be well enough in a day or so. If there's a problem, I can draw in healing from the ley lines nearby."

Taylor chuckled, then a wry smile crossed her lips. "We're a pair, aren't we? I'm emotionally scarred, and you? Well, you're just a bundle of them, aren't you?"

"That's why we're best friends, T. We're perfect for each other."

Quinn's phone buzzed. There were four messages from Clark waiting to be read. "Typical. He tells me to sleep in, and then he hits me up with a bunch of messages starting at eight in the morning."

"At least he didn't come up here looking for you and bang on the door. He knew we were home. If it was an emergency, he could've gotten us easily enough."

Quinn sipped her coffee and stood to get something to eat. "What do you have that's good? I'm starving."

"Nothing in the fridge worth mentioning. I suggest we head down to the pub and get some proper food unless you like cheese puffs and diet cola."

"No thanks on that," Quinn said, closing the door on the empty fridge. "Let's go downstairs. I need fuel for my body to quick-heal. I also need to find out how my mom did, watching Tadpole last night. She wasn't supposed to stay with him all night like that."

At the mention of downstairs, Sylvie launched off the sofa and settled in her usual spot on Quinn's shoulder. The Huntress laughed. "You hungry too?"

"Eeeep."

Taylor hurried to catch up with Quinn and the dragon as they headed for the door. "I'm hungry too. Honestly, I want to return to normal so I can forget about last night."

"It doesn't work that way, T. You know that. You'll have to talk it all out with someone. It doesn't have to be me. It can be another werewolf. Clark offered to reach out to the pack for you."

"I can reach out to the pack on my own if I need to. Let's just go eat."

Quinn shrugged. She pulled the door closed and followed Taylor down to the pub. Along the way, she made a mental note to keep an eye on her friend.

The usual lunch rush was still going on, even though it was close to 1:00. O'Malley's was popular with the supernaturals in the city. Quinn and Taylor ordered their sandwiches directly from the bartender to take the load off Juni and the other two waitresses. He entered it into the computerized system as they grabbed a table to wait for their food.

Quinn texted her mom, telling her where they were. If Naomi wasn't in a vampire's regenerative trance, she could join them. She sent a copy of the text to Clark.

He and Naomi arrived a few minutes later, just ahead of the sandwiches Quinn and Taylor had ordered.

The dark circles around Clark's eyes told Quinn he hadn't slept much, if at all. She wondered how things had settled out the night before.

"Clark, what's going to happen in the city's shifter community now that their leadership has been taken out? This has to play into Gemma's plans somehow."

"She might have thought the attack would disrupt any support we'd get from the local supernaturals, but the effect is only going to be short term. Most supernatural shifter types work under a pack structure, and they have long-standing traditions for replacing leaders. Before I left the club this morning, most of the pack betas had contacted me to let me know they'd stepped into the alpha position."

Quinn's eyebrows lifted in surprise. "That's it? They just take over?"

Clark ran a hand through his graying hair and scratched the back of his neck. "I'm sure there will be a few internal power struggles. Luckily for us, most of them will be just that: internal. I'll keep an ear to the ground to make sure none of the shake-ups that do happen spill over into the rest of the community. If Gemma makes her move soon, we won't be able to count on the packs for a lot of support, but that should settle out after a few weeks."

Quinn was glad the effects were only temporary. She returned to working on her meal. Sylvie hopped down to sit on the arm of the chair and stared at Quinn until she slid a small plate of fried fish over. The long neck snaked out, and she tore chunks off the cooked fish and gulped them down.

Naomi chuckled. "Did you forget to feed her?"

"Nah, we just slept through breakfast."

The vampire reached down to stroke the dragon's head. Sylvie whipped around, snapping at her.

"Hey," Quinn said, reaching out to push Sylvie's head away from her mother's outstretched hand. "That's not nice."

Naomi checked her fingertips after the close call and shook her head. "You really need to get her some obedience training. Have you set up a time to take her out to meet Chessie?"

"Mom, I'm sorry, I—"

She cut Quinn off. "You haven't taken her to meet the big mama dragon, and I think it's time you did."

"I'm sure she's just out of sorts because she's hungry."

"We can't have that happen every time she's eating. Sylvie needs to learn manners, Quinn. Take her to see Chessie. You promised the old dragon you'd do it."

Clark nodded. "She's right. I can understand if you're afraid of going back there. It's got to be terrifying to face something that ancient and powerful."

Quinn began objecting that she wasn't scared. She stopped because it wouldn't fool anyone at the table. They all knew she'd be lying.

"Of course I was scared. I'm just not sure what benefit can be gained by going there. Chessie could have changed her mind. Then what do I say when I show up with Sylvie?"

Naomi said, "Start off with, 'I told you I'd come back, and here I am.'"

"Chessie could decide to keep her, Mom. I'm not sure I could give her up if that happens."

Clark laughed.

"What's so funny?"

"You know the issues we're having raising Sylvie. Imagine being an eighty- or ninety-year-old woman and going through all this. That thousand-year-old dragon will not have the patience to do everything you're doing. She doesn't want to raise a youngling. My guess is Chessie only wants to assure herself you're treating Sylvie right."

His argument made a little sense, but it didn't mean she wasn't still nervous. The last time she was in the dragon's cave, Chessie had commented she might eat Quinn at some later date. Of course, that could be part of Chessie's ordinary bluster. The Huntress only knew a few dragons.

Quinn sighed. "I guess I need to reach out to Jori and see if I can get a ride out to Chessie's island."

"Do you want one or two of us to come along as far as the boat trip goes?" Taylor offered. "It wasn't an awful trip. I could do it again."

"No, you all have your own things you have to get done. I'll have Sylvie with me for company."

Sylvie looked up from the half-eaten plate of food. "Eeeep?"

"Don't play innocent. You know you're in trouble for snapping at my mother. Now you have to face Chessie for it."

Sylvie ignored the comment, returning to her fish.

Quinn glanced at Clark. "How did it go last night after we drove home? Were you or the cleaners able to identify those women?"

Clark shook his head. "I'm pretty sure they were both from outside the country. I had a contact at the airport check recent arrivals. They were both seen coming through the international terminal on the way to the rental car desk."

Taylor asked, "Maybe they're an advance team here to prepare for Gemma's arrival?"

"You could be right, T. Avery warned me about the attacks on her and the girls. If Gemma is turning her trainees into demon-kinder, it has to be part of a larger plan. The fact that four of them turned up in Baltimore can't be good news."

"Clark and I will look into that," Naomi said. "You focus on Sylvie for now. You helped us deal with Tadpole. He was perfectly fine last night. He kept wanting to show me his latest weapons restoration projects. Go do the same for that little dragon."

Quinn nodded. She stroked the smooth scales of the dragon seated on the arm of her chair. Sylvie turned her tiny head around, gulping down another mouthful of fish. Emerald green eyes stared up at her.

Her connection to Sylvie was hard for Quinn to explain, even to herself. It had begun before she hatched, when Quinn used to talk to the egg when the two were alone in her apartment.

She wondered what went on in that little mind. Quinn longed for the time when Sylvie could communicate beyond a simple "Eeeep." Someday she would learn to speak to her mind to mind. That was how the other two dragons talked to her. She guessed it would come in time. Quinn decided it was enough to feel the sliver of the dragon's presence in the corner of her brain. She felt it there whenever Sylvie was close to her.

"I'll contact Jori right after we finish our food." Her stomach gurgled at the mention of her lunch. Quinn leaned forward to grab her sandwich. The motion tugged the edges of the wound in her side and she winced.

"You're hurt?" Naomi asked. "Where? Let me see."

"I'm fine. I'll take care of it after I call Jori."

"She's not fine," Taylor said. "She took a sword through her side."

Quinn glared at her friend. "It just needs some meditation and a little time."

"A sword through your side?" Naomi said. "That's not just a scratch. Where is it?"

Quinn reached down and lifted the edge of her shirt a little to show the bandages. "It went right through the muscle. No vital organs. I'm not spitting or peeing blood. I'm fine."

Clark shook his head. "Your mother's right. I'll call Jori for you after lunch. You go with her when you finish eating and let her look at it. We all need to be in top condition. If Gemma's coming here in force, they could outnumber us, which will magnify every advantage or disadvantage."

Clark had that "I won't take no for an answer" look in his eyes.

"Fine, but you'll see that it's already healing on its own."

"It might be," her mother said. "But you definitely shouldn't be swimming until the wound closes. After I check it, we'll do a directed meditation. You can tap into the ley lines if that doesn't work."

"I thought you and Clark didn't want me doing that too often?"

"If Gemma and her Hunter demons are coming, you need to be at full strength. Maybe you can try to just tap enough to facilitate the healing. It'll be excellent practice for you to learn control."

"I wish Avery were here. She could do it for me."

Taylor smiled and murmured, "That's not all she could do for you."

"I heard that," Quinn said. A flush of heat rushed across her face, and everyone started chuckling.

She looked around at her friends. "Hey, we haven't seen each other in a while. Long-distance relationships are hard."

"No argument there, Quinn," Clark said. "Finish your food. I'll tell Jori to set up the trip for two nights from now. That'll give us enough time to make sure you're fully healed. I want you to get it over with before Avery shows up. I get the feeling a boatload of trouble will come along with her."

"You think Avery might be here that soon?" Taylor asked.

"I'm not sure, but it's possible. According to Quinn, two days ago, she was just south of Mexico. If she gets passports with the money we sent, crossing the border into the States should be no problem. If she has enough left over, she could even bring the girls here by plane. We don't know."

Quinn shook her head. "She won't come by any mainstream travel route. She said Gemma's Hunters had tracked her somehow. Avery will try to lose them by going off the major roads. It's what I would do. Even with passports, she'll probably still try to sneak across the border in case they compromised the immigration system. Someone could alert Gemma."

Clark stroked his chin. "Hmmm, given all that, they could be another week or longer. It would be helpful if we knew for sure. Let's hope she contacts you again. We could use an idea of her route and arrival time."

Clark left them at the table. Naomi kept staring at Quinn's side as if trying to see through her shirt to the wound underneath.

Quinn gulped down the rest of her sandwich. She stood. "Come on, Mother. You're driving me crazy. Let's go so you can check me out up close."

Naomi nodded, a satisfied smile on her face. Quinn reached for the last few fries, shoving them in her mouth. "Come on, Sylvie. Time to go."

The dragon hopped onto Quinn's shoulder.

Quinn asked Taylor, "What are you doing for the rest of the day?"

"I've been working on getting a spare VR rig online, in between working on the new app. Now that the app system is on indefinite hold, I'm back to working on that. I'm always worried that a tech problem could put the system offline for an extended time. We have all that extra gear from the VirSync group. I figure it's stupid not to use it."

"Cool. Maybe you can add racing stripes and flames to the headset while you're souping up the gear."

Taylor laughed. "I'll see what I can come up with."

Quinn thanked Juni as she came over to help the busboy clear their table, then followed Naomi and Taylor back into the tunnels. She had a date with a meditation mat.

CHAPTER NINE

Quinn had to wait three days to head out with Jori. He was out of town when Clark reached out the first time. It took the extra day to heal up the rest of the way, so she was glad.

It was late afternoon when she got a mysterious text from Jori.

Meet at the dock tonight at nine for your ride.

Quinn didn't think a lot about it. Jori was a shady character. She expected he had a habit of sending cryptic texts with as little information as possible. It was probably a necessary skill for a smuggler.

She asked her mom to drive her to the marina and come back later to pick her up. Quinn and Sylvie met Naomi outside O'Malley's. She'd already started Clark's beat-up sedan and sat waiting for them.

"Thanks for the ride, Mom. I appreciate it."

Naomi pulled out of the alley and started across town to the backwater marina where Quinn had met Jori with Clark before.

It was a quick trip. They arrived a few minutes early for the meet-up.

"I know where he keeps his boat, Mom. You can drop us here."

"I can wait."

"No, it'll be several hours out and back. That doesn't take into account the time meeting with Chessie. Go back to O'Malley's, and I'll call you when we're on the way back."

"Sounds good."

Quinn hopped out. "Come on, Sylvie."

The dragon flew out after her and did a circuit around the car before landing on Quinn's shoulder.

Naomi said, "I'll come back to get you if it's before dawn. Otherwise, it'll be Clark or Taylor."

Quinn laughed. "It won't be Taylor. She hates driving anywhere. Hopefully, we're back before then."

"Be careful, Quinn. Don't antagonize the dragon."

"I have no intention—"

"I know you don't plan on doing it, but sometimes you decide without thinking things through."

"If you saw this dragon, you'd realize I will not do anything to get on her bad side. Honestly, it's terrifying just thinking about going back."

"Good," Naomi said. "That's exactly the right attitude. I can't wait to hear how it goes."

She watched her mother pull away and leave the marina parking lot.

"Eeeep?"

Quinn reached up and scratched the scales behind Sylvie's little eye ridges. "It'll be all right. I'll be there with you, but you'd better be on your best behavior. Chessie'll eat you and me both if you're rude."

"Eeeep!"

"You know what I mean," she said. "Just be good."

Quinn started winding her way through the maze of boats. Most of them were in various states of disrepair. They were all one sort of working boat or another. This marina served the watermen who worked out on the bay every day. They brought in the fish, crabs, oysters, and other seafood for the city of Baltimore.

As she got closer to the place she'd met Jori before, she realized there was no boat tied up in Jori's spot. She wondered if he was running late or if she'd misunderstood the text message.

Pulling out her phone to check the message again, Quinn looked around. She jumped and reached for her Bowie when Jori's voice sounded directly behind her.

Spinning, Quinn leveled her blade at Jori's throat. "What are you doing sneaking around like that?"

"Easy, girlie. I didn't realize you hadn't seen me sitting over there."

"Where's your boat? We got the time right, didn't we?"

"Um, yeah. I owed a guy for something, and he, uh, borrowed my boat without telling me about it."

"Why didn't you call to tell me? I could've saved the trip out here."

"It's okay. I didn't want to let you down, so I called a friend. They're on the way now."

"I don't want someone else knowing about this, Jori. That's the reason we called you to begin with."

"It'll be fine. I personally vouch for them."

"Who's going to vouch for you?" Quinn asked.

Jori laughed. "Good one."

"Seriously, you're not the greatest character reference. Clark filled me in on everything you're mixed up in. That's just the stuff we know about. I'm sure there's more."

"That's me. My friend is much more reliable than me. You'll see. Ah, here she comes now." Jori pointed into the channel.

A sleek motorboat cruised around a bend in the channel, moving at a much slower speed than Quinn would have expected from such a flashy vessel. It looked like it could win races. Even at this slow pace, she could hear the power in the idling engines.

A young woman stood behind the wheel in the open cockpit. She was a stunning figure at the helm. Her dark flowing hair looked midnight blue in the moonlight, and she had perfect milky skin covered by just a t-shirt and shorts. The woman steered the boat over when Jori waved. As it nudged the pier, the woman tossed the Selkie a line and held on while Quinn jumped into the rear.

The monogrammed cushions on the seats behind the cockpit spoke of a good deal of money. Quinn wondered what Jori had offered the woman to afford such an expensive ride.

Quinn turned to confront the smuggler. Before she could ask him what he'd gotten her into, he tossed the rope back to the woman and waved as the boat pulled away from the dock.

"Hey, aren't you coming?"

Jori cupped his hands to his mouth so she could hear

him as the engines grew louder. "You're in excellent hands. Trust me. She'll get you back in one piece."

Quinn wanted to yell a few choice words at Jori, but they were already too far away for him to hear. Instead, she walked up to stand beside the woman at the controls. Sylvie hopped from her shoulder and stood on the low windshield, leaning forward into the wind as the boat picked up speed.

"I'm Quinn. I guess you know where you're going?"

The woman smiled. "Yeah, my family has been dealing with Chessie for a long time. Way before the Selkies arrived, for sure." She reached over to shake Quinn's hand. "I'm Ariel, and yes, it's spelled just like the cartoon mermaid. My parents have a sense of humor." The woman laughed as she continued to guide the sleek craft down the channel to the bay.

It took Quinn a second to catch her meaning, then it hit her. "You're a mermaid?" She glanced down at the woman's ordinary though very shapely human legs.

"We only have tails in the water. That old movie *Splash* had it mostly right. We can control the change if we're careful and don't get too wet, but immerse me in water, and my bottom half goes fishy fast."

"You don't sound as if you like it much."

Ariel shook her head and shrugged. "To be honest, there's not much going on down there. Things are more exciting up here on land. In that respect, I'm a little like my namesake." She flashed Quinn a huge grin. "What can I say? I wanna be where the people are."

Quinn groaned. "That's how it's going to be, huh?"

"Sorry, it's my standard greeting. It does a good job breaking the ice, don't you think?"

Quinn smiled back at her. "I guess it does, yes." She reached out to steady herself, grabbing the rail as Ariel gunned the powerful engines. They cleared the marina area and headed out into open water. Quinn's black hair flew behind her as the cool night air rushed past. She couldn't help but notice the way her host's equally dark hair waved in the wind.

Chill, Quinn, she told herself. Avery will be here in just a few days. You don't need this kind of complication. Besides, the mermaid's probably not into girls.

Ariel raised her voice to be heard over the roar of the wind and engines. "I'm glad Jori reached out to me to give you a ride. I've been wanting to meet you for a while."

"I'm not all that hard to find nowadays," Quinn replied. "I'm at O'Malley's in East Baltimore most of the time. Paddy can usually track me down if someone needs me."

The woman glanced at Quinn and then looked away. "Yeah, well, I didn't want to go all fangirl on you. I just wanted to see what was up with the person who has everyone talking."

"And?"

Ariel smiled and scanned Quinn from head to toe. "Not bad, for a human."

"What's that supposed to mean."

"Nothing. Sorry. Just a poor attempt at humor. I'm not like most mermaids. When they say things like that, they're looking down on land-borne folks. They think because you all can't swim, at least not like we can, you're not as beautiful as we are."

Quinn smiled. She liked a challenge. "Wait until you see me in the water. Maybe you'll change your mind."

Ariel stared at Quinn for a long, awkward moment, then a broad grin crossed her face. "I can't wait. Who knows? Maybe this trip will turn out to be more than just a taxi ride." She laughed and turned back to watch the black water ahead.

Quinn smiled and looked forward as well. Inside, her emotions boiled in competition with each other. She was flirting, but she worked to convince herself there was no harm in it. As long as nothing else happened, things were fine. Avery would be home soon, and it would all be good. No one would know anything about this.

Sylvie craned her long neck around and stared up at Quinn. Her emerald eyes glittered in the moonlight. "Eeeep?"

"Mind your own business, squirt. This is grown-up stuff."

It took half the time to get out to the hidden dragon's lair. Quinn planned to swim on the surface to the island with Sylvie flying above, hoping they'd find an entrance to Chessie's cavern from above. She wasn't sure the young dragon could swim.

She needn't have worried.

As Quinn stripped down to the tankini she'd put on earlier beneath her street clothes, Sylvie launched from the boat. She soared out over the black water, the moon reflecting off her glittering green scales. Then she twisted in mid-air, folded her wings, and dove into the dark, choppy waters of the bay.

Quinn gasped and leaned over the rail. As she stared at

the place where Sylvie had entered the water, she wondered if she should dive in after the little one.

Relief flooded Quinn when, a few seconds later, the dragonling rocketed back out of the water, a tiny fish in her jaws. She flapped her wings twice and landed on the rail beside Quinn.

Sylvie flipped up her head and gulped down the fish. The bulge moved along her neck until the fish disappeared into her stomach.

The youngling shot a jet of flame into the air and let out a triumphant, "Eeeep!"

"I guess you know how to swim just fine. Good, you can follow me underwater as we head out to meet Chessie."

Quinn sat on the boat's edge, ready to dive overboard. She stopped when she glimpsed Ariel out of the corner of her eye.

The woman stood beside the stern with Quinn, having returned from dropping the anchors. She had stripped out of her jeans and underwear and stood on the deck stark naked.

"Ariel, what are you doing?"

"You let on that you had a surprise for me waiting when we got in the water. Did you think I wasn't coming with you after that invitation?"

Quinn stammered a reply, then tore her eyes away from the naked mermaid and stared at Sylvie instead.

"Uh, look, Ariel. Maybe we got off on the wrong foot here. I have a sort of…" Quinn trailed off.

Ariel laughed. "Were you going to say, 'girlfriend?' It's okay, I get that reaction from many people. It's a mermaid magic thing. We create a field of attraction around us."

"Oh, good," Quinn said.

"Don't get me wrong. If you weren't attached, we could definitely have a thing, but I'm not the type to get jealous. You know what they say."

"No, what?"

Ariel stepped up on the side of the boat. "Plenty of fish in the sea." She dove into the cool waters of the Chesapeake Bay and disappeared under the waves.

Sylvie dove in right after the mermaid, leaving Quinn alone on the boat. She swung her legs over the side and slipped into the water, annoyed she was the last one in.

She dove deep while activating her wild magic icon, letting the power inherent in the water transform her. There was a split second of uncomfortable resistance, and she worked to control a moment of panic. The wild magic might decide not to work this time.

Then the magical shift to aquatic form happened, and Quinn took in a full breath of water. She shoved it down into her lungs, expelling the oxygen-depleted fluid from the gill flaps that had appeared beneath her arms.

A warm, melodious voice filled Quinn's mind. "Wow, you weren't kidding. I've never seen anything like that. You sure you don't have Selkie in your background or something?"

"I have a connection with the natural wild magic in the water, that's all. It wasn't easy to learn, but it works rather well."

Quinn kicked her flippered feet with calm purpose, searching the blackness ahead. Sylvie swam up beside her, wings folded tight against her side, undulating through the water by using her tail to propel her along.

Ariel appeared ahead of them. Her long legs were gone, replaced by an even longer tail covered in iridescent blue scales with flecks of gold. Her black hair floated around her head. Somehow, when she moved, it didn't seem out of control. Quinn figured it must be a mermaid thing. If she didn't have her hair back in a ponytail, she'd end up with a tangled mess.

The mermaid smiled, giving Quinn a fresh shock. Instead of the normal human teeth she'd had on the boat, Ariel now had a double row of teeth on the top and bottom. For a moment, Quinn felt like a shark had smiled at her. There was no doubt Ariel was a carnivore.

Quinn sent, *Are you planning on swimming with us all the way to the dragon's lair?*

I haven't seen Chessie since I was little. I guess it would be rude to come all this way and not extend my family's greetings.

Suit yourself. Let's go.

Quinn kicked, Ariel flicked her tail, and Sylvie snaked along between the two. It was time to visit the dragon and fulfill a promise Quinn had made before the youngling hatched. Hopefully, all three would return to the boat. Quinn was still worried Chessie would want to keep Sylvie with her.

Too late to do anything about it, though. They were almost there.

CHAPTER TEN

As Quinn, Sylvie, and Ariel approached the rocky island, she once again felt the sudden aversion to getting any closer. All she wanted to do was swim away and ignore this place.

Quinn focused her mind and pushed past it. It helped that she'd done this once already. Soon, she'd crossed the boundary where the spell of avoidance was strongest. The feeling left her as she kept swimming. She glanced at Ariel and Sylvie. Neither of them showed any negative effects. Maybe true supernaturals like them were immune to the spell's effects. Maybe most supernaturals had the common sense to let a sleeping dragon be.

Through the underwater gloom ahead, she saw the cave opening at the base of the island. Quinn dove to the rocky floor, then angled upward as she swam inside. She followed the smooth rounded tunnel up at an angle as she'd done before.

Sylvie swam beside Quinn. Ariel was right behind. The youngling and Quinn popped out into open air inside the cavernous lair. With just their heads showing above the water, Quinn shifted back to human form.

No light filtered into the cave from the moon outside. Quinn could see nothing.

She whispered, "Dammit, I need to see," and her night vision ability engaged. This time she knew what to look for. She spotted the dragon coiled around the cave's perimeter, blending into the rock walls.

Quinn climbed out of the pool and stood on the rocky ledge beside the water. Sylvie launched into the air, circled Quinn twice, and landed on her shoulder. The little body quivered and pressed against her cheek and neck.

"It's okay, Sylvie." Quinn scratched the dragon's head. "I won't let anyone hurt you. We're here to meet a friend." Quinn hoped Sylvie couldn't detect the fib. The dragon was neutral at best toward Quinn and other humans.

"Eeeep."

A voice echoed in Quinn's brain. *Why do you call the youngling Sylvie? Younglings are not named until we are certain they will survive to maturity. It's far too early to know that.*

My apologies, Great One. Human babies are most often named at or near their births. That was the standard I had to go on, and I decided her name was appropriate.

A slight wave of positive amusement rolled into her mind just ahead of, *Sylvie is appropriate. The youngling is a Sylvan Green Dragon. I suppose I find it acceptable.*

Naomi's earlier words of caution came to mind. Quinn took a deep breath, swallowing her initial response. *I'm glad it meets with your approval. She seems to like it.*

And you brought one of the daughters of Poseidon with you, too. Who are you, young one?

I'm Ariel. I met you first when I was tiny. My father, Marlin, brought me with him on a visit to pay you homage.

I remember it well. How is your father? It has been many years.

Busy with business and keeping track of his many wives.

That is why dragons only mate once in our lifetimes. It avoids all the bother of trying to make someone else happy for eternity.

Polyamory is our way, Ariel said. *Merpeople aren't a fertile race.*

Quinn was learning all sorts of things. She was glad Ariel remained in the pool, though, bobbing about in the middle of the water. If she'd climbed out into the cavern, Quinn would have had to deal with that distraction on top of everything else.

Mistress Chessie, I wonder if we might discuss what you wanted to know about Sylvie. I promised to bring her here to you when the time came for her to hatch. It's been a few months, but as you can see, she is doing well.

Well? Chessie said. *If that was the case, why isn't she talking?*

Um, I'm not sure. Was there something I was supposed to teach her?

Ariel spoke up from the water. *I think what the Great One means is, why didn't you teach the dragon to mindspeak?' I wondered about that, too. All the dragon does is make strange little sounds in reply to things you say.*

A happy "Eeeep" punctuated Ariel's words.

I didn't know that was a thing, Quinn replied. She realized she was out of her element here and knew what she had to do. *Perhaps Sylvie should live among her own kind.*

What? Here with me? I have no desire to have her here, making a mess of my cave. It would take weeks to teach her at this point. You have bonded with her, so you must teach Sylvie to mindspeak.

Quinn hid her relief at not having to leave Sylvie here, but problems with what Chessie had said soon replaced the feeling. She raced through her objections. She didn't know what to do. She never learned an ability, it just appeared when she needed it. The only other person she knew who could mindspeak was the lake dragon Gil out in western Maryland.

She pulled up her HUD and tried to see if she could concentrate on learning mindspeak as a skill. If she could turn it on and off, she might be able to figure a way to teach it to the little dragon.

Nothing happened.

Ariel cleared her throat. "I might have an idea, Quinn. If you're both open to it, that is."

Before she thought it through, Quinn replied, "Sure, anything."

Ariel smiled. "Excellent. I figure I could come by your place two or three times a week. Together, we could try to teach Sylvie. I'm sure if we put our heads together and worked with her, she could learn. I learned from birth, and I think I could translate what my parents did into a plan to teach the dragonling."

She squirmed a little inside at the thought of spending a lot of time with Ariel. Quinn regretted her earlier flirting on the boat. That little harmless interlude couldn't be allowed to go farther, though. Now, they would see each other several times a week for who knew how long.

Quinn's stomach churned. Avery could show up any day. Having Ariel around could make things awkward if anyone got the wrong idea.

"Come on, Quinn," Ariel said. "I think it would be fun to spend some time together. You and I are the perfect match for this project." She punctuated her words with a wink.

Chessie's voice rumbled inside Quinn's head. *I accept this solution. You will work with the daughter of Poseidon. When you next return, you will bring to me a youngling who can properly communicate.*

Um, I'm not sure how long it will take. It might be a while.

You and the mermaid have two seasons. I'll expect you back around the time of the vernal equinox. Understood?

Quinn wasn't sure when that was. She looked at Ariel for help.

The mermaid laughed. "The first day of Spring, silly. Looks like I have lots of things to teach you, too. This will be fun."

Chessie's mind voice took on an edge. *Take the youngling and go. I tire of this. Make sure you teach her well, Huntress. You and she are bonded. Mistakes made now will be magnified as she grows.* ·

Quinn started to reply but stopped when the huge, triangular head turned so the great yellow eye stared at her from barely a foot away.

There is one more thing. I have felt a coming upheaval but didn't understand until you came close. It is tied to you somehow. It foretells the coming of significant power coupled with an evil I have not felt in many, many centuries. The youngling will feel it soon too if she hasn't already. Beware, Huntress. Grim times come your way.

Quinn wanted to say, "So what else is new?" but she kept her mouth closed. She had an idea what the great dragon was talking about. It was time to warn the clan to get ready.

As the dragon settled her head once again against her body, blending into the surrounding rocks, Quinn said, "Sylvie, you heard the big dragon. Time to go."

"Eeeep." Sylvie pushed off of Quinn's shoulder and dove into the center of the pool. Clearly the little dragon understood more than she could communicate.

Ariel laughed again and dove too, leaving Quinn alone with the sleeping dragon.

Quinn shook her head and dove after them, clicking the wild magic icon in her HUD as she sliced into the cool water.

The mermaid and the young dragon waited outside the cave's entrance. As soon as Quinn appeared, they both headed back toward the boat. Quinn called out with her mind, *Hey, wait up.* She kicked off the side of the entrance with her powerful flippers and swam after them.

Quinn caught up with the pair after a few minutes. Then they veered to the left, heading for deeper water.

"What's up? The boat's that way."

"But the striped bass are schooling. Come on. We can catch a few for each of us, and Sylvie can have one of her own."

"Aren't they all bigger than she is?"

"That's why she'll need our help. Come on. I'll show you how the big girls fish in this part of the world."

Quinn swam after them and drew her Bowie. She knew how to fish. She'd learned that much from her time with Gil at the lake. This would not be that hard.

Except it was.

Ariel and Sylvie made it look easy. The schooling fish were faster and more agile than the trout she'd gone after in the lake. Ariel and Sylvie seemed to anticipate the school's movements.

Quinn struggled every time she got close to skewering one of the fish, each as long as her arm.

Ariel's pleasant laugh sounded in Quinn's mind. *You're tensing up. Fish in the sea are used to big predators swimming nearby. You have to relax and swim with them so you can be ready for their turns.*

Quinn forced herself to relax. Ariel was right. She swam with the schooling rockfish. Before long, she got the hang of anticipating the movements.

Got one! Quinn exclaimed.

Ariel waved, a fish in each hand. *Outstanding work. I think this is enough for tonight.*

Sylvie had also caught one. She floated nearby, already tearing into it, taking big gulps of the fresh fish.

Quinn swam closer to the others. It looked like Ariel had already taken a bite out of one of them, too. Her stomach churned at the thought of eating fish raw underwater like that. It was one thing for Sylvie, but with Ariel, it didn't seem right. Then she thought about the merpeople and where they lived. It wasn't like they could cook their food underwater.

Quinn shrugged and smiled as Ariel took another bite with her shark teeth.

I haven't had fresh rockfish in so long, Ariel said. *It's so good this way.*

I'll take your word for it. Do you want mine too?

Don't worry. I don't expect you to eat it like this. There's a built-in cooler on the boat. You can take yours home. I'll bet Paddy or one of his cooks can make you a delicious meal out of it.

Quinn nodded. She thought that was a much better idea.

Quinn, Ariel, and Sylvie left the school of fish and headed back to the boat.

When they reached the bobbing hull, Ariel propelled herself up and over the side with a flip of her tail. When Quinn's head broke the surface, she shifted back to human form. She coughed a few times to clear the rest of the water from her lungs, then reached up and climbed up and over the stern using the handholds there. As she stood on the deck, she looked around for Sylvie.

The little dragon was already out of the water. She perched on one of the seat cushions and had her head and long neck buried up to the shoulders in the side of the fish. Her long neck slid out, trailing bits of fish guts she held in her mouth. Sylvie chomped a few times, making quite a mess before swallowing what she'd pulled out.

"Eeeep," was all she said before going back for more.

Ariel sat on deck nearby, drying her tail with a fluffy towel.

"Got any more of those?"

"Sure. They're in the chest beneath the seat cushion over there."

Quinn walked over and lifted the cushion. A lid beneath

revealed a small linen storage full of fresh white towels. Quinn grabbed one and started drying herself. The chilly night air had raised goosebumps all over her, and she wanted to get back into her clothes.

Changing in the open felt weird to Quinn, even with all her experience playing sports and changing in front of other women. This felt different. Ariel still hadn't gotten dressed, and Quinn had to strip out of her swimsuit and into the clean underwear from her backpack.

She persevered, moving quickly and pretending not to notice when Ariel, with human legs now, stood and walked naked past her to the bow.

Ariel, her hair somehow magically flowing and dry now, said, "Let's head back. I put your fish in a chill chest. You can come over to my apartment and fry it up when we get back if you want."

Quinn smiled while she struggled to come up with an answer that wouldn't upset her new friend. She needed Ariel now that she was supposed to help teach Sylvie. At least the mermaid's teeth were normal again.

She played it cool. "The way you finished off that first fish, I didn't think you cooked your food."

"Nah, I was just showing off. I like a good lemon butter sauté as much as the next girl."

"Good to know. Still, I should probably be getting back. Sylvie gets cranky, the later it is. I wouldn't want her to set fire to your drapes."

"Oh, sure. I understand. Maybe another time," Ariel didn't hide her disappointment. Her eyes brightened. "Hey, I do need to catch up with you for those mind-voice classes for Sylvie, though."

"Yeah, we need to do that," Quinn said. "Once I get back, I can get with you to schedule a time to start the lessons. I should call my mom now so she can meet us at the marina."

"Sounds good. I'll bring the bass we caught and make you the best fish fry you've ever had." She flipped her hair around and headed back to the cockpit. Soon, the engines fired up, and Ariel steered the boat back toward Baltimore.

Quinn winced. That hadn't gone exactly as she'd hoped, but at least she'd avoided going home with the mermaid tonight. She stole a glance at her behind the wheel as the boat cruised over the waves.

The moonlight shone on the black curls that cascaded down Ariel's back. Quinn cursed under her breath. Why were things so complicated all the time?

CHAPTER ELEVEN

Naomi waited at the end of the pier as Ariel brought the boat alongside. Quinn took one of the lines and jumped to the dock, leaning back to hold the boat in place. Sylvie leapt into the air and circled overhead.

"Thanks for the lift," Quinn said. "I'll get in touch with you about those lessons for Sylvie."

"I can't wait. It'll be fun to hang out again. Toss me the line."

Quinn did as she asked.

The mermaid quickly coiled it on the deck and returned to the cockpit. She waved as she pulled away from the dock and headed for the main channel.

Quinn glanced at Naomi.

Her mother stood there with her eyebrows raised, then glanced at the boat.

"Relax, Mom. Nothing happened."

"It didn't seem like nothing. She seemed pretty excited to come see you again."

"Chessie suggested she could help train Sylvie. That's all. I think she's up for the challenge."

"She's up for something, that's for sure."

Sylvie landed on Quinn's shoulder, bobbed her head once, and said, "Eeeep."

Quinn rolled her eyes at both of them. Without answering the questions in her mother's amused expression, she started toward the parking lot. Naomi fell in behind, following in silence.

A few minutes later, they were on the road home. Quinn checked her phone to see if there were any messages or even an email from Avery. She needed to talk to her girlfriend. Staying grounded with their relationship would help how Quinn felt at the moment. Ariel had called it some sort of attraction magic, but that didn't make how she felt any better.

Quinn sighed as she put away her phone. Nothing new. She was worried about Avery and the girls. With what Chessie had told her before leaving the cave, that worry had turned into fear.

"Do you want to talk about it?" her mom asked.

"The old dragon said some things that concern me."

"About Sylvie?"

"No, about trouble coming. I think it has to do with the ones chasing Avery. Chessie mentioned evil of a kind she hadn't seen for many centuries pursuing innocence. Doesn't that sound like something coming after Avery and the others?"

"It could be. Did the dragon say anything about when?"

"Only that it was coming from the south and she could sense it now. How far can a dragon sense stuff like this?"

Naomi shrugged. "I have no idea. We should take this back to the group. Miranda might have some ideas on how we could tap into what Chessie detected. You have a tracking ability. That could be enough if we could combine the two."

"Chessie said Sylvie might be able to sense it. Maybe that's a way to narrow our search some?"

"It's late now, or early, depending on which way you view these things. I'm sure the others are in bed. Is this urgent enough to wake them when we get back, or can it wait for morning? Did you get any sense of how close this evil was?"

"Not sure. It felt like Chessie was giving me a heads up to get ready, not warning me of an impending attack happening right away."

"That's good, at least. We'll get you and Sylvie back to get some rest, and I'll spread the word for a clan meeting in Taylor's workshop when you get up."

Quinn nodded. "I need some sleep to clear my mind. It's been a long night."

By the time they got back to O'Malley's, the pub was closed. They used their keys to go in via the kitchen entrance. Quinn could barely keep her eyes open as she trudged upstairs to her apartment. Shapeshifting and all that swimming when they'd hunted the fish had worn her out.

Sylvie was tired, too. As soon as they entered the apartment, the little dragon flew to the bedroom. She'd already curled up on the pillow beside Quinn's by the time she got there.

"Get some rest. I feel like we will be busy for the next few days."

A long, lazy, "Eeeeeeep," came from the pillow. It trailed off at the end, and Quinn glanced down to see the little eyelids closed.

Stripping down, she pulled on a t-shirt and climbed into bed beside the little dragon. She fell asleep nearly as fast.

A loud noise woke Quinn. She sat up and tried to see what it was, except she couldn't see anything.

That wasn't true. She could see grayness all around her. It was like that line on the horizon just before the sunrise started, the point between light and dark.

Quinn put her hand down and pressed on her bed. It wasn't there. The surface upon which she rested had that same gray nothingness quality to it. It yielded a little when she pressed it—not as much as a mattress, but soft. Like the color gray.

"This has to be a dream."

Quinn's voice came across muffled by wherever she was. She had dreams, and some of them were vivid, recalling traumatic situations in which she'd found herself. None of them were like this. This was something else. Some*where* else.

A thundering boom sounded in the distance. Another just like it followed. It sounded like someone was trying to break down a wall or door.

As soon as the thought greeted her, the grayness thinned, revealing a long, unending stone barrier. It extended left and right and up and down for as far as Quinn could see.

The boom sounded again.

As the noise faded, she noticed the massive iron door for the first time. How had she failed to see it until now?

Six tiny figures sat on the gray floor in front of the door. Quinn tried to see more. As soon as the thought occurred to her, her body moved closer to the six.

She didn't walk or run. She zoomed over, like when you blow up a picture on a camera.

Six girls of various ages and sizes sat there, five around a taller redhead.

The boom sounded again. This time, the iron door shook under the impact.

The girls all winced. The redhead noticed Quinn for the first time. Her head cocked to the side as she studied the Huntress.

The intense scrutiny, even from one so young, made Quinn check herself. That was when she noticed she wasn't in her nightshirt. She wore the Huntress garb from her VR persona.

"Hello, Huntress." The redhead held Quinn's gaze.

"You know me, little one? Do I know you?"

The girl shrugged. "It's your dream. Do you know me?"

"I think so. You're one of the girls with Avery, right?"

The girl nodded.

The crash came again.

The redhead winced along with her fellows. None of the others had turned to look at Quinn. All kept their attention on the girl in the center of their circle.

"Why are you all in my dream? Can you carry a message to Avery?"

The redhead paused. "I'm not sure. I think we're here to

tell you something important, something you have to know."

"It's about whatever's trying to open that door, right?"

"Yes. It's almost time, Huntress. You will be called upon to assemble your entire clan. The risk will be great, and you could lose all of them. Would you do that to save us?"

Quinn started to give an automatic answer. Of course she—

Faces flashed through Quinn's mind: Taylor, Avery, Tadpole, Clark, and her mother. Each had the vacant gaze of the dead, their features splashed with blood and gore.

Doubt filled her.

She remembered how Miranda had died. The thought of losing the others the same way filled her with dread. Would she sacrifice the ones who mattered to her most to save six girls she hardly knew?

"I-I don't know." Quinn hung her head in shame. The answer betrayed a weakness she hadn't known existed.

"You must decide, Huntress."

"When?"

"Soon."

The booming crash sounded again, and this time, the iron door buckled. The girls screamed as something reached from the darkness on the far side. Scaly red arms snaked through the open gaps and plucked the little ones from the gray floor. A spray of blood erupted from each body as talons as long as Quinn's forearm pierced them. Their screams cut off as the demon arms yanked the girls into the darkness on the other side of the barrier.

The redhead was last. She didn't scream. Her last words rang in Quinn's ears.

"Choose, Huntress. Choose well."

The scene went gray and then faded into blackness as screams from somewhere else drowned out the little girl's voice.

The screams wouldn't stop. A weight settled on Quinn's chest, startling her. She opened her eyes and realized the screams were erupting from her mouth.

Tiny green glowing eyes stared down at her. Sylvie was perched on Quinn's chest.

"Eeeep?"

Quinn's screams faltered and then stopped as she recognized her bedroom. She wasn't inside the dream world anymore.

"I'm good," Quinn gasped, reassuring herself. She looked at the dragon. "I'm good, Sylvie. Thank you for waking me."

The dragon slid off her chest as she sat up. She raked her fingers through her hair as she tried to make sense of what she'd witnessed in the dream. She didn't think it was an accident. She never remembered this much detail after her usual nightmares. This had almost felt real.

The dread she'd felt as the iron door burst open was still with her. Quinn lay back down, turning on her side and pulling Sylvie close. The gentle vibrations of the dragon's body soothed her some.

"The old dragon was right, Sylvie. Something bad is coming, and I don't think we're ready for it."

The little head nuzzled under Quinn's chin and the vibrations grew stronger. She stared at the wall beside her bed, trying to understand how much of what she'd seen was real and how much was a fabrication of her mind.

Those thoughts swirled as the dragon's vibrating body did its job and drew Quinn into a deep and thankfully peaceful slumber.

CHAPTER TWELVE

The buzzing of the phone on the nightstand woke Quinn. She reached for it, eyes still fuzzy with sleep. She squinted at the screen for a few seconds before anything registered in her exhausted brain.

Taylor's profile picture from Quinn's contacts.

She checked the time before answering. It had to be early in the morning. She didn't feel rested, so she assumed she'd only just fallen asleep after the nightmare.

Her eyes widened. It was just after eleven. She'd slept for almost seven hours, though it didn't feel like it.

"Hey, T. I'm sorry. I didn't mean to sleep so late. What's up?"

"No big deal. Your mom said you were beat. She mentioned that you wanted to talk to us after lunch. I figured you'd want to get up and eat something before getting together. You know, recharge the batteries a bit."

"That's an outstanding idea. Thank you. Have you eaten yet?"

"No. At least not lunch."

"Tell everyone we'll meet in the workshop around one. You and I can get together in the pub around noon. Does that work?"

"Sounds good. See you soon."

Quinn put her phone down. Sylvie hopped across the bed and rubbed her head and neck against her arm.

"Eeeep?"

"Did you sleep any better than I did?"

"Eeeep." The dragon crawled over and curled up in Quinn's lap.

"Oh, no, you don't. We can't go back to sleep. Taylor's meeting us for lunch, then we have to talk to everyone about what Chessie said. I hope we can figure out a way to hone in on what's coming."

Sylvie bobbed her head once and climbed out of Quinn's lap, settling on the pillow again. The young dragon curled into a ball of green scales and closed her eyes.

"I really need to get on teaching you to mindspeak. It would be so much easier to understand you."

Sylvie responded with a single sigh, not opening her eyes. Quinn chuckled and got up. She headed for the shower, checking the time again. She could take her time and soak. Maybe that would wake her up some.

As soon as she got to the bathroom and turned on the water, Sylvie zoomed in and perched on the showerhead.

Quinn laughed. "Ah, you want to clean up too?"

She climbed in and stepped beneath the hot water. She'd been too tired to shower the night before. It felt great to rinse off the brine from the swim in the bay.

A few seconds later, Sylvie hopped down to Quinn's shoulder to partake of the spray. She let the dragon have some time under the water, then started on rinsing her hair while she pondered ways to track Avery down. The dream from the night before weighed on her. She had to warn her girlfriend.

Of course, wishing she could contact Avery and being able to do it were two separate things. Quinn wracked her brain for ideas, mundane and magical, that would allow her to get a message to Avery. None of them held much promise.

By the time she exited the shower, she had worked herself into a ball of frustrated and helpless anxiety. She pulled herself together, not bothering to do more than towel-dry her hair. After putting it back in a ponytail, Quinn left to get food. Nothing else was helping her. Maybe a burger and Paddy's fresh-cut fries would do the trick.

Taylor waited downstairs at their usual table by the bar. Quinn sat down, and Sylvie hopped over to perch on the empty chair beside her. Juni came over as soon as Quinn sat down.

"Hey, what do you want today?" She reached out to scratch Sylvie's head while Quinn glanced at the menu.

"I don't know why I even look. Your pizza burger is just too good to pass up. Make it a double. I'm starving and need to rebuild my energy."

"A double it is. Anything for you, Taylor?"

"Crab cake sandwich and a basket of Old Bay fries for us to share."

Juni nodded. She fished in her apron pocket for a second.

Sylvie knew what was coming and hopped from foot to

foot on the back of the chair, her head weaving back and forth.

Juni's hand came out holding a crispy chicken nugget. "Taylor told me you were coming down, so I brought you a treat. Here you go."

She tossed the nugget to Sylvie. The youngling snapped it out of the air and settled back on her perch to work on the snack.

"You spoil her, Juni," Quinn said.

"Aunt Juni can spoil her niece if she wants," the waitress said. "How many baby dragons do I get to help raise?"

"Fair enough, but if she gets too fat to fly, you're carrying her around."

Sylvie let out an indignant, "Eeeep."

"No, Sylvie," Quinn said. "I do not think you're fat, but you will be if you keep eating everything Juni tosses you."

Juni laughed as Sylvie went back to eating the bit of chicken. "I'll be back with your food soon."

Taylor smiled as she watched Sylvie eating. "She is displaying a little more in the way of manners. Did you learn anything from Chessie we can use to help train her? I assume that's what you want to talk to the clan about."

"It's actually other things, but that too. I'd rather wait to cover it with everyone all at once. Chessie mentioned the training, though. Apparently, we were supposed to be teaching her to speak with her mind."

"How are we going to do that?"

"I have an expert coming to help with it. I just have to line up a time for her to come by."

"That should be fun," Taylor said. "I love learning new things. Maybe I can hang out too."

Quinn perked up. If Taylor was there, it wouldn't be as awkward with Ariel. "Ooo, that's a brilliant idea. Thanks, T."

Something about the way Quinn answered triggered a curious glance from Taylor. "What aren't you telling me, Quinn?"

"Well," she began, searching for a way to tell Taylor what had happened with Ariel the night before. "Her name is Ariel. She arranged to meet with Sylvie and me for a lesson."

"Quinn, you didn't flirt with her, did you?"

"I was just being nice."

"That's what you always say. You flash those pearly whites and drop a compliment or two. You don't even know the effect it has. What about Avery? Did you forget about her?"

"I know, T. Nothing happened, though. I kept it legit, I promise. I even told her I wasn't interested."

"Did this Ariel hear you say it?"

"I think so. She said she did. It's just that after we went fishing with Sylvie, she wanted me to come back to her place so she could cook the fish we caught. I told her it wouldn't be a good idea."

"Quinn," Taylor said, "you have to get this straightened out before Avery gets here. You're horrible at hiding things like this from the people you care about. She'll see it right away, especially if she and this Ariel are ever in the same room together with you."

"Well, we must make sure that never happens. I only need to keep seeing her until Sylvie learns to talk to us, or at least me, mind to mind."

Sylvie finished the last bit of the chicken nugget and snaked her long neck toward Quinn. "Eeeep?"

"No, there's no more. You'll have to wait until Juni comes back."

The dragon's head sank, and she let out a sad sigh.

Juni came out just in time to keep Taylor from asking more awkward questions about Ariel. The double pizza burger looked amazing.

Quinn's mouth watered as Juni set it in front of her. "Thank you! I'm starving."

She didn't wait for Taylor to start on her plate. Quinn picked up the burger in both hands and took a huge bite.

"Mmmmm." Quinn smiled as she chewed. Her body already felt better and more energized.

Taylor laughed. "Wow, you really *were* hungry, weren't you?"

Juni said, "There's more where that came from if you want it."

"This is wonderful. I think it'll be enough, though I might come back in a few hours for a snack."

"Eeeep?"

"I didn't forget you," Juni said. She reached onto her tray and set a plate with three hot chicken nuggets in front of the dragon.

Sylvie hopped from the chair to the table and grabbed one nugget, chomping on her favorite food from the pub.

"Juni," Quinn asked, "you never told me how you knew she'd like chicken nuggets so much."

"When I heard she was going after the pigeons all the time, I figured she was into fowl. After that, it was a simple choice to start with chicken nuggets. I mean, she's a kid, right? It made sense to pick the chicken from the kid's menu."

"I guess that makes sense in a roundabout way," Taylor said.

"Honestly," Quinn said, "I'm glad you figured it out. It got her to stop trying to get at the pigeons all the time."

"I'll try some other things to see what else she likes, but those seem to work for now." The leprechaun girl smiled as Sylvie ate. "You two call me if you need anything else."

Quinn and Taylor nodded. Juni left as the pair dove into their meals with gusto. Quinn checked the clock on the wall. They still had plenty of time before the meeting with the rest of the clan. She slowed down a bit after the first few bites, savoring the burger and fries. Maybe she'd even do dessert before she went to the meeting. She was afraid things would kick into high gear once she explained what Chessie had said and what had happened in her dream.

CHAPTER THIRTEEN

Quinn stared at the assembled clan members as she finished telling them what Chessie had warned her about.

Naomi asked, "So, what's your plan? The warning is so vague that it's nearly useless. It's all right. I understand why you didn't tell the dragon that."

"I was hoping there'd be a way for us to somehow use the VR system to do a preemptive strike or something to help Avery get here safely."

"It's not possible," Taylor said. "We'd need a locus for the magical interface. The VR rig has to have coordinates to send you somewhere that far away. Close to our base, inside the city limits, I can triangulate with the draw on ley lines. Farther away, that becomes dangerous. You could end up in a tree or trapped inside a hill."

Miranda tapped her ethereal chin with a ghostly finger. "If Chessie could sense it, what about Sylvie?"

"The big dragon did say she might be able to sense it. She might have already. It's not like I would know it."

Taylor nodded. "That means we have to find a way to communicate with Sylvie beyond a few simple sounds. Quinn, you have to move forward with helping Sylvie learn to mindspeak."

Quinn winced. "I was afraid you were going to say that."

Clark looked at Quinn. "Why are you reluctant to move forward with this? Isn't that specifically what Chessie asked you to do for the youngling?"

Quinn shrugged. "Yes, but—"

"No buts about it. You have to do it."

Looking at Taylor, Quinn pleaded for help with her eyes.

"I'll reach out to this Ariel chick," Taylor said, jumping in. "I need to talk to her anyway to understand how all this works. If Sylvie is going to provide a locus for transport, I have to adjust the interface so it can read a dragon's mind."

"You'll be there with Sylvie and me for the lessons too, right?"

"Yes, I'll be there."

Clark glanced at Naomi and then Miranda. Quinn could tell all three knew something had been left unsaid. From Naomi's knowing glance in Quinn's direction, she knew what the issue was.

Quinn waited for one of them to press, but they let it drop.

Clark changed the subject. "On a related note, Joshua contacted me. He was able to use his connections to old Keepers elsewhere to keep an eye on Avery's account. Her account had a cash withdrawal a day ago at the bank's international branch in Mexico City."

"What's that mean?" Quinn asked.

"It means she spent the money we sent her and probably has the passports she needs, or she'll have them soon. That probably puts her about to cross the border into the United States soon, if she's not already here."

Quinn smiled. "That means she could be here any day."

Miranda shook her head. "Based on the dragon's warning about what's coming from the south, my guess is she's taking a roundabout route. We can't assume she'll do what we expect. We need to move forward with the plan as it stands."

Everyone nodded.

Taylor said. "I'll reach out to Ariel about setting up the lessons as soon as we're done here."

"Excellent," Clark said. "While you do that, I have some new training ideas for you, Quinn. With Tadpole getting the armory shaped up, we found additional training gear we can use."

"Like what?" Quinn asked.

"Climbing gear, for one. Your mom is going to take that particular lesson. She's found a good wall in the caverns below. That'll be a great place to start the basics of free-climbing."

Naomi smiled. "I always loved climbing. It'll be fun to teach you."

"I can't wait." Quinn knew what her mother meant when she referred to training as fun. The only people who enjoyed it were Naomi and Clark. Still, it would take Quinn's mind off worrying about Avery, and about Ariel. The group separated to their own tasks. Sylvie stayed with

Taylor as Quinn followed her mother and Clark down to the training room and armory.

Four hours later, Quinn finally got to set her foot on the cave floor again. It was the first time since Naomi had started the training. Quinn's arms and shoulders ached. She rubbed her sore muscles with fingers roughened by the jagged stones of the cavern.

"That's a good start," Naomi said, noticing Quinn working at her tired muscles with both hands. "You're going to be sore for the next day or so. Climbing uses muscles in combinations you're not used to."

"Great. Something else to look forward to."

"You want to tell me what's bugging you? You've been in a mood since the meeting earlier. I thought you'd be happy about finding a way to help Avery and get her here faster?"

"I am. It's complicated, though."

"By the cute mermaid?" Naomi asked.

"Is it so obvious?"

"It is now that you confirmed my guess is right. You told me when I picked you up at the pier that nothing happened."

"Nothing did happen. It was just very charged with awkward energy."

"That's why you wanted Taylor to come along on the lessons." Naomi smiled. "Inviting a third wheel might not be enough to break the tension. You should probably just tell Ariel you have a girlfriend. Once she learns about Avery, I'm sure she'll understand."

"I sort of already did, but she still invited me over. What if she decides not to teach Sylvie and me to talk to each other? We need her to come, no matter what. We can't afford for her to lose interest in coming here."

"That's a dangerous game, Quinn. I've found that when you give people a chance to step up and do the right thing, they follow through. But it's your life. I just hope it doesn't blow up in your face."

"Me too." Quinn finished stowing the climbing gear back in the canvas bag and handed it to her mother.

Naomi slid it over her shoulder. "Come on, let's go take this back, and then you can go check on Taylor."

Quinn nodded. She followed her mother into the tunnels leading up to the training room and armory. Tadpole had already left. The heavy iron door to the armory was locked. The big orc had probably gone to get something to eat. With Quinn's help, he'd made up with the cooks. He'd resharpened all their knives for them, apparently putting an edge on the blades that amazed everyone.

Dropping the gear bag by the door to the armory, Naomi said, "He can put these away when he gets back in the morning. I don't want to do it by myself. He doesn't like anyone to mess up his organization system in there."

"It's funny how quickly he took to that job. I'm so glad we found it for him."

"I know Clark's glad to have the armory back in shape again. I don't think he cared who did it as long as it wasn't him. That it turned out to be the orc warrior was a bonus for everyone concerned."

"Yeah," Quinn said. "Who knew orc warriors learned to care for and repair weapons as part of their training?"

"Not me."

A distant "Eeeep" from up ahead in the long underground passage materialized into Sylvie flying down the tunnel toward them.

As the dragon landed on her usual perch on Quinn's shoulder, the Huntress said, "What are you doing out and about? I thought Taylor was keeping an eye on you for me?"

The dragon swayed her long neck and pointed her head back up the tunnel. "Eeeep."

Quinn laughed. "Who says we can't communicate with her? She just told me where Taylor is."

Naomi shook her head. "It's a long way from that to finding Avery's location on a map."

Sylvie launched, flew about ten yards down the tunnel, and then turned, hovering as she looked back at them. "Eeeep."

"I think she wants us to follow her," Quinn said.

"I think you're right."

The two of them continued up the tunnel until they got to Taylor's workshop door. It was open, and Sylvie darted inside, then came back out to hover by the entrance.

"We're coming," Quinn said. "You fly a lot faster than we walk, remember?"

Ariel stepped out into the hallway to stand beside the hovering dragon. "Hey, you're finally back." She leaned in and hugged Quinn, ignoring the way the Huntress stiffened in the embrace. "How'd the climbing thing go? Taylor told me what you were up to. I'm glad it was you and not me. I don't like heights at all."

Quinn initially balked and moved back a step, but recovered quickly. "Once you've been pushed off a cliff and survive, you kind of get over the whole fear of heights thing."

Ariel shuddered, shaking her head. "I'm sure there's a story there somewhere, but I have no desire to hear it. I'm happy with my feet on dry ground or swimming in open blue water."

"I'm, uh, surprised to see you here," Quinn said, following Ariel inside. "So soon, I mean."

"Taylor called me and told me you all had a deadline or something. I grabbed the cooler and the ingredients for dinner and came right over."

Naomi asked, "A cooler and food? Is that for training Sylvie?"

"Oh, no, not for Sylvie." Taylor fixed Quinn with a level stare from across the room. "Apparently, she and Quinn were supposed to fry up the fish they caught on their little expedition last night."

Naomi hid a smile behind her hand. "Oh, I see."

"Honestly, Ariel, I forgot about that part."

The mermaid's smile deflated. "Oh. I just thought we could…"

"No, of course we can make dinner. I just want to make sure we focus on training Sylvie. We think this is important and might be a way to keep some bad stuff from happening to someone I—we care about. I figure there'll be time for other stuff after the emergency passes."

Ariel seemed puzzled. "So, is dinner on or off?"

"We can do both," Quinn said, trying to cover her discomfort. "Taylor's going to join us, though."

"Just for the training," Taylor said. She held Quinn's gaze and cocked her head to one side. "I didn't know about dinner. I guess you two have a lot to discuss before the training starts. Right, Quinn?"

"Uh, I guess so." It was clear Taylor wasn't going to help with this part. "Let's go cook the fish. Taylor, why don't you come up to my apartment in a half-hour?"

"I'd make it at least an hour," Ariel suggested. "We have to cook and eat the fish, after all."

"Okay, an hour. Got that, T?"

"I heard you. Hopefully I won't get distracted by my work and forget."

It was Quinn's turn to glare.

Taylor adopted an angelic smile and said. "I'll be there. Don't worry."

Quinn nodded, relieved. "Okay, grab the fish, and we'll go get dinner done."

Ariel picked up a cooler with a handle on top. "Lead the way."

Quinn steeled herself for the pending awkwardness and led her guest up to her apartment. Sylvie perched on Quinn's shoulder and snaked her neck around Quinn's so she could look back at Ariel.

CHAPTER FOURTEEN

Q uinn opened the door to her apartment and led Ariel inside. "You can put the cooler on the table over there. I don't have a lot of counter space, sorry. I'll see what I have."

Ariel chuckled. "You don't know what pans you have? This is your apartment, isn't it?"

"I sort of inherited it from the last owner after they suffered a sudden accident. I don't do a lot of cooking for myself. We eat for free down at O'Malley's, so there's not much need. We stay here because the tunnels leading down to the old Hunter chambers connect to the pub."

"Really? My father told me he and the others in our tribe used to work with the Hunters all the time. I think he mentioned there was a secret water entrance through which they smuggled people or magical gear they didn't want others to see. It might be fun looking around some time to find it."

"That might be fun," Quinn said. "Uh, what kind of pan did you need? I've only got a few here."

"See if you can dig up a twelve-inch frying pan. We can do it all in there." Avery started pulling small plastic containers from the cooler. "I prepped everything before I came, so it'll go fast."

Quinn nodded and bent down to rummage in the cabinet beside the stove for a frying pan. She was sure there was one down there. She spotted one near the back and reached all the way in with one arm to grab it.

Ariel's sudden voice in her ear and hand on her back made Quinn jump. She bumped her head on the cabinet door.

"Need any help with that?"

A little puff of air blew in Quinn's ear from the way Ariel emphasized the final "t" in her question. A chill ran down Quinn's spine.

"Uh, no," Quinn said, pulling her head out of the cabinet and standing. "I've got it, see?" She held up the frying pan.

"You've got goosebumps up and down your arm, Quinn. Did I do that? I'm sorry." Her smile said she wasn't sorry at all. Ariel spun with a flip of her hair to get the fish and other ingredients. "Good thing I brought oil, too. I'll bet you don't have any, do you?"

"I don't, so good call," Quinn said. She turned to the stovetop. "How hot do you want it?"

"I like it plenty hot," Ariel giggled. "Oh, the pan? Yes, medium-high heat will do on the burner. Here's the oil. Pour a nice long drizzle into the frying pan and let it heat up."

Quinn blushed and took the small bottle of oil from her. She set the frying pan over the gas burner and turned it on, then poured oil in the pan until a shallow layer covered the entire bottom.

"How's that?" Quinn asked.

"Perfect. Let me bring the rest of this over, and I'll show you how people who really know seafood cook."

After Quinn moved aside, Ariel took over, and soon her apartment smelled like a fine dining restaurant. Fifteen minutes later, the two of them sat down to eat the fish and sautéed green beans the mermaid had prepared.

Quinn glanced at the time on her phone. She hadn't realized dinner would be done quickly. They'd have a good half-hour alone before Taylor arrived. She decided to slow down and eat like she savored each bite.

Luckily, she didn't have to pretend. The fish was amazing, cooked to perfection. The beans were good, too, though she rarely liked veggies.

As she chewed the last bite, Quinn checked her phone again.

Ariel laughed. "I've never seen anyone take so long to finish a meal. Was it so bad that you had to choke it down?"

"No, I was savoring it. I swear. Look, Avery, I thought we had worked this out on your boat last night. I told you about my friend."

Ariel threw her head back and laughed. "I knew it. You didn't believe me when I said I was good with it."

Quinn's confused expression drew another chuckle from the mermaid. "Quinn, I was just messing with you. I couldn't resist. You were so nervous about everything, and then the way you reacted when I hugged you. I just had to have a little fun. Don't be angry with me."

Ariel met Quinn's eyes. After a few awkward seconds,

Quinn nodded. "It's all in good fun, I guess. You had me going, though."

"Sorry, it surprised me that my mermaid attraction thing worked on someone like you. I would have thought you'd be immune."

Quinn's hand drifted up to her amulet. It hadn't warned her, but then, she was never in any actual danger, was she?

"I guess because you didn't intend me any harm, my natural Huntress protections never triggered. You have a way with turning on the charm, though, don't you?"

"You have your protections, I have mine." Ariel flashed an enormous grin. "Now, tell me about the ones we're trying to save, especially this girlfriend of yours. I love a good romance story."

"Avery is her name. They trained her as a Huntress like me, some evil people who had other plans for her skills. Together we freed her from their control. She went out looking for others like her. She found some little girls being trained by these same people and she rescued them." Quinn's brow furrowed as she continued. "Now she's on the way here with the girls. The ones who used to control her have already attacked her at least twice. That was what Chessie meant by evil to the south chasing innocence."

"Little girls in danger, huh?" Ariel said. "You know how to get folks on your side, don't you?"

"So you'll stay? You'll help me learn to talk to Sylvie?"

"Of course. I'd do it just for the city's sake. It makes sense to have a way to communicate with a young dragon if only to keep her from hunting in and around Baltimore."

Quinn laughed. "That's not far off. She's already thinned out the pigeon population around here."

Ariel laughed, too.

"What are you two laughing about?" Taylor asked from the door. She cast a suspicious glance at Quinn.

"We've worked things out, T. Ariel is up to date on all things Avery."

"Oh, so you warned her about your stealth flirting? Seriously, Quinn, you should come with a warning label."

Ariel smiled. "Actually, I think this particular magical effect was my fault, Taylor." Ariel explained about the mermaid's ability to charm potential partners.

Taylor nodded as she listened, then adopted a movie-announcer voice. "Once you get sucked in, you can't escape."

"Something like that," Ariel replied. "Quinn here didn't believe me when I told her I was okay during our boat trip last night. We've got it all worked out now."

"Eeeep?" the dragon asked from across the room where she was curled up on the sofa.

Quinn held out her arms. "Come here, Sylvie. Ariel is going to try to teach you to speak with your mind."

The youngling flapped her wings, lifting off the back of the sofa and flying to land on Quinn's shoulder.

Ariel smiled. "It's clear she understands you. Their vocal cords don't make sounds like ours do, so she can't imitate our speech. It's a cute little sound she makes, though."

"Eeeep!"

Ariel held up a hand. "Sorry, Sylvie. I meant, 'majestic roar.'"

Sylvie puffed up her chest and raised her head high.

Ariel whispered, "Dragons are known to be vain, in case you didn't already know."

Quinn and Taylor chuckled as the little dragon preened, oblivious that they were still talking about her.

"So, what do we do?" Quinn asked. "I can talk to people who talk to me in my mind, but I do not understand how to reach out to someone else like that."

Ariel closed her eyes. As she did, her voice sounded in Quinn's mind. Judging from Taylor's expression, she heard it, too.

Sylvie, can you hear me?

"Eeeep," the dragon replied aloud.

Try answering me the same way, but just inside your mind.

Ariel opened her eyes and looked at the youngling.

Sylvie stared at Ariel, her emerald eyes drilling into the mermaid's.

Quinn felt a ripple of something go through her mind. It was intangible, like a faint breeze.

"Very good," Ariel said. *"Almost got it. Try again."*

Sylvie's body grew rigid as if every muscle in her body tensed at once.

Ariel nodded and smiled. She beckoned to the dragon to keep going.

Then Quinn heard it.

It sounded far off, but it was there.

Eeeeeeep.

Very good, kiddo, Quinn projected at Sylvie. *Try again.*

Quinn once again heard the far-off projection from the dragon. She looked at Ariel. *What's wrong? Why isn't it louder?*

I'm not sure, Ariel thought. *She might just need to practice. How did you learn when you first did it underwater?*

Quinn shrugged. *I'm not sure. I gained the ability through wild magic. It worked out of the box.*

Taylor said, *I had to learn something like this when studying magic with Miranda. Some of what I do is using my mind to tell the magical energy what to do. I think her ability to transmit and be heard will grow with time.*

That's true, Ariel projected. *But we still have to work on the most important thing, which is words.*

How do we teach that? Quinn asked.

I will have to work at getting her to form the thoughts into pictures first. When I was younger, before they allowed me on land, we used to use images of our favorite fish.

Quinn nodded. *Sylvie enjoyed fishing with us. Maybe we can teach her to share her memory images of those fish she caught?*

Excellent idea.

Taylor smiled. *Sounds like fun. How do I get invited on a fishing trip?*

Quinn projected, *First, you have to be able to shift into an underwater werewolf with fins.*

They all laughed. Quinn noticed the humor was more genuine in mind speech. You didn't just hear the laughter; you soaked in the raw emotion behind it.

Ariel projected, *Let's try that fishing idea, Quinn. You and I think back to what we can remember of Sylvie underwater with us. Focus on the times we remember her catching fish.*

Quinn did as Ariel asked. Soon, Ariel started picturing moving images of Sylvie, too. They kept at it for a while, sending the images back and forth, trying to entice Sylvie to join in. Other than an occasional distant *Eeeeeep*, there was nothing from the dragon.

After they'd been working at it for an hour and a half and Quinn was starting on the mother of all migraines, a grainy, blurred image floated into view. It took Quinn a few seconds to realize it was a fish just in front of Sylvie's jaws. It flickered and then disappeared as quickly as it had come.

"Sylvie, you did it," Quinn shouted aloud. She reached up, pulled the dragon off her shoulder, and hugged her tight.

Excellent job, Sylvie, Ariel projected. *Try again with a different thought. Quinn, use your mind so you don't confuse her.*

Oh, right. Sorry.

Taylor nodded as the next picture appeared. It too was out of focus and in poor definition. *I can help with the image quality she's sending. Hopefully, she'll understand what I want her to try. Sylvie, when you send the image, try thinking of the brightest sunshine you can at the same time. Think of it lit up like the middle of the day.*

The image faded, and another floated into view. It was the same swimming fish, but this time, the scales shone in the colors of the rainbow, and the water was a deep ocean blue all around it. As Quinn concentrated, she realized she could see other fish swimming in the distance, too.

Wonderful, Sylvie, Quinn thought. *Great idea, T.*

I remembered something about making the colors brighter when I was working with magical energy flows. Miranda explained it to me as the brightest color on the brightest day. She'll be happy it worked here too.

Let's keep going, Ariel projected. *Let's work on more complex images for a bit longer. Then we should take a break. We can reconvene tomorrow night if that works for you both?*

Quinn and Taylor nodded. Sylvie nodded too, showing she'd heard the conversation. Despite her headache, Quinn pressed on for another half hour. By the time they were done, Sylvie was showing images of their friends in the clan and even folks who worked in the pub, Juni and a few other waitresses who spoiled the little dragon.

Ariel leaned back in her chair and stretched. "It's amazing how using your mind like that is such hard work. I'm totally beat."

Quinn smiled. "I'd offer you a place to stay for the night, but I'm afraid it would be the wrong thing for both of us."

"Agreed. I need to go home. I sleep better in my own bed, anyway." The mermaid stood, gathering her things. "You did well, Sylvie. You keep working with Quinn and Taylor on sending your pictures. We'll try simple words tomorrow night when I come back."

"Thanks again for being so understanding, Ariel," Quinn said.

"Hey, not a problem. I want to meet this woman, though. She must be quite something if she's hooked you so completely."

"She definitely is. I'll arrange a meeting once she's settled in." Quinn escorted the mermaid to the door. "Do you need someone to walk you out to your car? It's late."

"No need. I can take the stairs to O'Malley's and go out that way, right?"

"Yes. See you tomorrow."

Ariel smiled and headed down the hallway. Quinn shut the door as Taylor said, "Quinn, you never stop amazing me. Even when you screw up, you still manage to charm your way out of trouble."

"I was honest with her. She's a pleasant girl, and she deserved that much."

"Good for you. Okay, I'm out, too. I need to rest. I feel like I've been casting spells all day, and my mind is mush."

Quinn nodded. "Me, too. Get some rest. I'm going to lie down, too."

Taylor left for her apartment, and Quinn shut off the living room light before heading to her bedroom. Sylvie followed her. The image of a toothbrush and toothpaste appeared in her mind, followed by a closeup picture of a pillow.

Quinn laughed. "Yes, I'm going to brush my teeth and get ready for bed. I think we could both use some sleep after that session with Ariel."

Ariel's face floated through her mind.

"Yes, I like her too. But Avery's my number one. Understood?"

The dragon's little head bobbed, and she flew to the bedroom. Quinn finished brushing her teeth. By the time she got to her room, Sylvie had already curled up on the second pillow and gone to sleep.

Quinn smiled. "Beat me to it. Good for you."

She climbed into bed and settled in next to the sleeping dragon. She fell asleep almost before she'd closed her eyes.

CHAPTER FIFTEEN

Quinn shouted for Avery to duck. The other Huntress was locked in a fierce fight with a tall woman. The opponent's short-cropped pink hair was a sharp contrast to Avery's long strawberry-blonde hair, which was pulled back in its usual ponytail. Swords clashed again, and magical sparks flew from the two weapons.

Despite her shouts of encouragement and warning, Quinn's cries went unheeded, and Avery took a vicious slash across her shoulder.

Fresh cries of alarm in the corner drew Quinn's attention away from the fighting. Six girls huddled on the far side of the compact motel room. They crouched behind the second bed. There was nowhere for them to go. The pink-haired attacker blocked the door to freedom.

As Quinn watched the girls, they all turned her way, saying in one communal voice, "Huntress, you must help us. She cannot fight them all."

Quinn looked back at Avery. The opponent had

changed. This time she fought a woman with long dread-locks and ebony skin. The newcomer wielded a broad-bladed weapon shaped like a spade with sword grip. There was no sign of the pink-haired woman, not even a body on the floor.

That was when Quinn noticed the line. There were other women behind the fresh attacker. Each lined up behind the others, waiting for their turn at Quinn's girlfriend.

"Avery, I don't know if you can hear me, but I'm coming. Hang on. I'll be there soon." She turned to the six girls. "Tell her I'm on my way. Hang on and keep fighting. It won't be long."

Without responding, the girls looked back at the fight. Avery had a new opponent, and the line was even longer now.

Quinn kept repeating, "I'm coming," as the scene faded into mist. Screaming in anger and frustration, she clawed at the mist in a vain attempt to get back to Avery. Nothing she did worked, though. At last, exhausted, Quinn collapsed in tears on the hard ground.

She woke with a gasp.

Quinn lay on her back in bed. Sylvie sat on her chest, staring down at her. Sunlight streamed through the bedroom window around the edges of the blinds.

"Eeeep."

"Was that you? Did you send me that message from Avery and the girls?"

The head bobbed once.

"Have you seen them before?"

Sylvie bobbed again.

"Do you know where they are? Can you take me to them?"

Another bob of the tiny head, slower this time, followed by a tentative, "Eeeep?"

"Okay, I get it. You're not sure, but I'll take that over not having any way to get to her. Come on, let's get up and go tell Taylor. She needs to figure out how to get their location out of your head. We need to get me there in VR before it's too late."

Quinn raced through her morning routine and was down in the pub, heading back to Taylor's workshop in a half hour. The tech witch wasn't there, though.

Pulling out her phone, Quinn tapped a text.

Where r u?

Still in bed. Why?

Sylvie found Avery. We r down in the workshop. Meet us there.

Let's get breakfast first. I need coffee.

I'll get the table and coffee.

Be right down.

The mention of coffee reminded Quinn she'd skipped her morning cup. She'd been so energized by her excitement at having a way to locate Avery, she'd raced out with no coffee of her own.

"Eeeep?"

"Use your mind. You have to practice. I'll talk aloud to get you used to going back and forth with other people."

A pause, then Taylor's face floated in Quinn's mind.

"Good. Yes, Taylor's on her way. We're going to eat first. You're probably hungry, too. How about a big plate of maple bacon sausage?"

A plate of steaming sausages appeared in her mind, followed by a small pitcher. The pitcher flashed with a light of its own several times.

It took Quinn a second to realize what the thing with the pitcher meant. Then she smiled. "Yes, you can have a *little* syrup on them. They already have maple syrup in them, you sugar fiend. Come on, Taylor will be on her way down."

Taylor soon met them in O'Malley's, and they ate breakfast with the regular morning pub crowd. Clark and Naomi showed up and joined them, along with Miranda. Tadpole wandered in last and pulled a stout barrel over to sit beside Quinn.

With everyone gathered around, Quinn repeated what she'd told Taylor about the dream and what she hoped to do.

Naomi looked at Miranda and Taylor. "Is that even possible?"

Miranda shrugged. "It would be risky, although it is theoretically possible."

Taylor smiled. "I'm pretty sure I can do it. We've already used Quinn to localize a target site. I think we can modify the magic in the VR system for our little dragon. After working with Sylvie last night, I have a few ideas that could work. It'll depend on how well I can interface the magic for the targeting system with Sylvie's thoughts. I think if you hold her and she sends you an image of the location, I can use the VR headset rig to draw off the GPS coordinates."

"How long, T? It's urgent. Avery's in trouble, I can feel it."

"I'll go as fast as I can. Come down later this afternoon.

If Miranda and I get it figured out sooner, we'll contact you. This is a big ask, though. It will probably take a while."

"I know you'll do the best you can. If you need us to come down and test anything, let me know."

Taylor got up. "I will."

Miranda floated over to her. "I have some ideas about guided visualization of magical energy that might translate into this adaptation of the spell."

The two of them headed back to the workshop, deep in conversation about the magical theory involved in what Taylor wanted to do.

Tadpole said, "Will it be dangerous, Quinn? Maybe I should come with you."

"I wish you could, buddy. You'd be a welcome addition to this fight. I think there will be a lot more fighting later, though. We'll need you then. For now, you can help by making sure the armory is ready to go. We might all need to arm up, and maybe get others to take up the fight. I get the feeling this will come to a head faster than we expected."

Clark asked, "You think Gemma's got what she needs to put Filippa's and Aurora's plans into action?"

"I do. Why else would she spend so much energy chasing Avery and a few little girls? There's something about them or what they know that's important. If we can figure it out, it might give us the advantage."

"You think they'll even come here?" Naomi asked. "They have to know how strong the clan has become."

"I think they were always coming here. This is where the Crystal Well is located. This was where they kicked off the purges. And this is where I am."

"You?" Clark asked.

"I don't think any of this is accidental. I think I'm here in Baltimore for a reason. I think that's true for each of us. We'll need all of us for the fight that's coming. Bet on it."

"I've learned not to bet against you, Quinn," Clark said. "You've managed to get out of every situation I've ever seen you encounter. If you say there's a fight coming, we'll get ourselves ready for it." Clark looked around O'Malley's. "I need to find Paddy and have a chat about what protections he's got around this place."

Naomi said, "Is it a good idea to let him in on what we're doing like that?"

"I won't tell him everything, but leprechauns have tricks up their sleeves others don't know about. How else would they have been able to protect their gold all these years? I think giving him a heads up that trouble is coming that could affect him might get him to tip his hand. I'll tell him we could supplement his existing wards and cover any gaps or weaknesses in his perimeter."

"Isn't the pub neutral ground? I received sanctuary here."

Naomi shook her head. "I don't think they will honor it this time. They honored it before, thinking they had the advantage by having you fight Tadpole. This time, I think the old rules are off the table."

Clark asked, "What will you do this afternoon while you wait for Taylor to get ready?"

"I'm going to work with Sylvie some more. I have to get her to communicate more than just images. She understands words, but she doesn't think in them. If I can change that before we track Avery down, I might have a better idea of what's waiting for us when we get there."

Clark stood. "I'll see if Taylor and Miranda need anything."

"I'll join you," Naomi said.

After the others left, Quinn sat alone with Sylvie for a while, nibbling on the scraps on her plate. Sylvie was curled up on the table beside her. The little dragon's belly bulged after finishing an entire plate full of sausage. She stared up at Quinn through glazed eyes.

A picture of flame engulfing a pile of sausage links until they charred to ash floated across Quinn's mind. It kept repeating like a GIF. Sylvie let out a soft groan as the image replayed.

"Of course you have heartburn. Serves you right, stinker. You should have thought about how stuffed you'd feel after eating all that food. Are you going to be okay?"

The little head lifted and bobbed once before descending to rest on her tail again.

"Come on," she said. "Let's take you upstairs and work on the lessons from last night some. It'll get your mind off your stomach."

Quinn picked up the bloated dragon and carried her in her arms rather than on her shoulder as usual. The two of them headed up to her room to work on improving their communications.

By the time late afternoon rolled around, Quinn believed Sylvie would never get the hang of transmitting words. All the dragon could do was send images and brief video sequences. The only good news was that Quinn was better at understanding what Sylvie wanted. That was a plus, but it wasn't the same as having a proper conversation.

Quinn glanced at her phone and sighed. It would have to do. They were out of time. It was after four, and Taylor still hadn't reached out to them. She didn't want to put too much pressure on her best friend, but the thought of Avery being in danger drove her.

Gathering Sylvie up, Quinn headed down to check on their progress. When she entered, Taylor was bent over the wooden worktable, wisps of smoke rising in curled tendrils past her head. Miranda hovered beside her, intent on the tech witch's progress.

"What's that you're working on, T?"

Without looking up or turning around, Taylor said, "I'm soldering the last few connections. It's the new VR interface for Sylvie."

"Cool! You got it working?"

Miranda said, "We won't know for sure until we try to use it. Now shush and let her work."

Quinn stopped and waited until Taylor straightened and set the soldering iron down on its holder.

"That will not hurt Sylvie if it doesn't work, will it?"

"Not any worse than it hurts you," Taylor said. "I think that's it, Miranda. I can't think of anything else that doesn't require spellwork and magic. Honestly, Quinn, I don't know what it'll do, but the worst case should be that it won't work. I don't know enough about the way a dragon thinks to know if the parameters are even right. I made way too many educated guesses based on what Miranda and I came up with."

Miranda smiled. "It's an amazing piece of hybrid

magical technology. If it wasn't such a secret that we can do this, I'd want her to publish it in one of the magic journals. It's huge what she's done to learn and adapt existing tech the way she has."

"I've had a lot of help," Taylor said. "If this ever gets published, I will give you top billing on the author list."

"As long as it works," Quinn said, "I don't care what you do with the ideas. We need to help Avery before it's too late."

Taylor started clearing up the work table, unplugging her soldering iron and gathering bits of wire and insulation she'd snipped off to put the rig together. Quinn wandered over with Sylvie perched on her shoulder and looked at what Taylor had devised.

It looked like she'd taken one of the spare headset rigs and turned it upside-down to form a bowl. Then she'd attached another wiring harness around the perimeter to match the wires running across the top.

"So, how will this work?" Quinn asked.

Taylor picked up the inverted rig. "She likes to sleep curled up, which was what gave me this idea. We'll let her curl up in here next to you, then we'll use a modified version of the software's magic interface to interpret her mind signals in a way that tells us which direction and how far away her visions of Avery are. That should give us good coordinates. I've also made this little collar with a GPS transceiver from a cellphone on it. We'll have a lock on her location, just like we would with your comm unit. The rest is cake. We immerse you both in the system and send you down to help Avery."

"Cake, huh?" Quinn said. "Why don't I think it'll be that easy?"

Miranda said, "From your end, it should be. Taylor will have to do all the heavy lifting magically. It should be seamless as far as you're concerned."

"Okay, when do we go?" Quinn asked.

"As soon as I get something to eat. I'm going to burn a lot of magical energy on this one, so I need to top off with food first. Then we can get going."

Quinn nodded, and the four of them, plus Sylvie, headed back to O'Malley's for food and some last-minute planning.

CHAPTER SIXTEEN

Quinn lay back on the table after settling the VR headgear in place. She turned her head to the side and saw Sylvie curled up inside the rig Taylor had made for her.

Holding up a thumb, Quinn said, "I'm ready when you are, T. Are you getting coordinates from Sylvie?"

"Something's coming through. Sylvie, keep thinking about Avery and her charges. I have to fine-tune things."

Taylor tapped a few keys, then began a chant coupled with elaborate motions of her hands as she cast a magical spell of some sort.

Thirty long seconds later, Taylor said, "Got it! You two ready?"

Quinn nodded and reached up to drop the goggles into place. Taylor began chanting again, weaving her spell into the complex VR computer code. Quinn took a breath as the magic took hold. An instant of disorientation set in, then Quinn felt herself tumbling backward into darkness.

The last thing she remembered was seeing Sylvie tumbling beside her into the VR matrix.

Quinn woke up staring at the nighttime stars. She lay outside a small, run-down shack standing amidst a grove of tall pines. A blue minivan with Texas plates was parked a few yards away.

"Eeeep?" the dragon said as she spread her wings and launched into the night sky. Sylvie disappeared into the darkness of the surrounding forest.

Quinn muttered, "Dammit, I need to see." Instantly, the entire area brightened as her night vision ability kicked in. She stood, searching for signs of Avery and the girls.

A crash of cracking wood preceded the shack's door splintering outward. A body flew through the opening, landing on the ground outside.

A woman with long dirty-blonde hair stood. Her face was bruised, her nose bleeding, and her eyes glowed red in the darkness when she turned to look Quinn's way.

"Come back here, demon," Avery shouted as she stumbled into view.

The other woman looked from Avery to Quinn and bolted into the trees.

"Damn!" Avery took two stumbling steps in pursuit and fell to the ground. Even from several feet away, her many wounds were clear.

"Avery!" Quinn yelled, running to the woman collapsed on the ground.

"Quinn? How did you get here?"

"Just a little VR magic wizardry from our tech witch."

Avery started to rise. Quinn pushed her back down.

"You stay put. You're bleeding from several places, and I can't stop them all at once."

"We have to follow her. The others took the girls just now. That one and another stayed behind to keep me from going after them. She's the key to finding out where they took them. I killed one of them, but I needed the other alive."

A quick glance around told Quinn the escaped demonkinder wasn't skulking nearby. "The woman's gone. Maybe Sylvie can find her."

She whistled. Sylvie swooped out of the trees and landed on Quinn's shoulder.

Pointing into the woods, Quinn said, "Follow that woman who ran away. See where she goes. Hurry."

The dragonling jumped into the air and flew into the forest, disappearing into the darkness. Quinn turned her attention back to her injured girlfriend.

"Avery, I need to do something. I'm going to draw in energy and try to heal the worst of your wounds."

"There's no time. Save them."

"I'll find them. Sylvie will track them down. She found you here. Now lie still so I can concentrate."

Quinn rested her hands on Avery's shoulder and stomach while she reached out with her mind, pulling up her HUD map overlay. A ley line ran underground about a quarter-mile away. It wasn't the most powerful one she'd seen, and it was a stretch for her to siphon energy from it, but she had to try. If it didn't work, she'd have to get Avery into the van and try to get closer to the power.

Reaching out, she stretched her senses to the limit and brushed the edges of the magic coursing through the natural energy source. She tried many times to pull in some energy, but it was like trying to grab paper streamers flapping in the wind. She'd hold on to a tiny piece, but it would break away from the rest, leaving Quinn with only a tiny amount of magic to absorb.

After trying for several minutes, she finally peeled the thinnest of magical strands away and pulled it in her direction.

As the trickle of power filled her, Quinn watched her mana bar in the HUD. She waited for it to fill, then directed that energy in a healing flow as Avery had taught her months before. Though the magic filled the bar, it wasn't powerful enough to do everything Quinn wanted for her friend's wounds. It was enough to stabilize her, though. At least Avery wouldn't die now.

The thread of power dwindled to nothing, and Quinn let go as the final bit passed through her to Avery.

Avery's eyes fluttered open.

"Feel better?" Quinn asked.

"Yes, but you should have left me."

"Never. I only just got here."

Avery smiled. "You're not thinking like a Huntress, Quinn. Those girls are more important than me."

"I've got my dragon on it. Sylvie will let me know when she finds something. In the meantime, I've got to get you real medical attention. You're still severely injured. Can you get up?"

Avery tried but sank back to the ground. "I'm no good for anything right now. You should go."

"Not a chance. Not until I get you someplace to rest."

Quinn tapped her earpiece to activate her comm unit.

"Taylor here, what's going on?"

"Avery's hurt. Too hurt to travel on her own or come with me to rescue the girls."

Clark's voice came on. "The girls are gone?"

"Yes, taken before I got here. Clark, I need you to drive to—" Quinn looked around before continuing. "Well, wherever here is and pick up Avery. She'll need medical attention."

Clark asked, "Taylor, do you have a fix on their location?"

"It's in North Carolina, near the Virginia border. It's about six hours away."

Clark asked, "Will she be able to hold out that long?"

"I used healing magic to stabilize her. It'll have to do until you get here."

"Okay, I'm leaving now."

"Taylor, do you still have tracking data on Sylvie?"

"Yes, I show her about a half-mile away from you right now. How'd she get so far away? Did the VR system screw up?"

"No, I sent her to follow someone. As soon as she stops moving, tell me so I can go after her."

"What are you going to do in the meantime?" Naomi asked over the comm.

"I'll get Avery as comfortable as I can so I can leave her for Clark. I'll call later when I'm ready to go. Ping me if Sylvie stops."

"Will do," Taylor said.

The comm clicked off, and Quinn looked at Avery. "You are a mess. Let's get you inside and see if we can make you more comfortable."

Avery tried to object again, but she slipped into unconsciousness before she could say anything. Quinn picked her up and carried her into the shack.

The fighting had overturned most of the furniture inside. There was an old single mattress on the floor in the corner. Quinn set Avery on it and keyed her comm again.

"I've got Avery in a shack at these coordinates. She's resting and should be all right until Clark gets here."

Taylor said, "He just left. I'll keep track of his progress. What are you doing?"

"I'm going after Sylvie. You're still tracking her location, right?"

"Yes, She's about a mile away to the south and moving fast. She has to be in or on a moving vehicle. I don't think she can fly as fast as a car."

Quinn searched Avery's pockets but couldn't find the keys. She checked the floor, moving the overturned chairs and table, and spotted them by the door.

"I have Avery's keys. I'm going after Sylvie now. Send her location to my phone, and I'll hone in on her. You can update it on the fly, right?"

"Yes, but Quinn, maybe you should wait for Clark."

"No. I have a feeling if I do that, it'll be too late to rescue the kids. Gemma needed them for something, or she wouldn't have gone to all this trouble. Whatever it is, we can't let it happen. Avery said they're special, and I believe her. I have to go after them now. Keep track of my location, and send it to Clark when he reaches Avery."

"Got it. Be careful, Quinn. I've sent the tracking info for Sylvie to your phone. Do me a favor and don't just go rushing in. If it looks like you're outnumbered, wait for Clark."

"Taylor, outnumbered is my favorite way to fight. Gotta go. I'll check in later."

Quinn cut the connection before Taylor could argue further. She checked on Avery one more time, then headed for the van.

She drove down a country road, following the phone's directions to wherever Sylvie was. The data updates shifted the dragon's location regularly. She was still moving south.

Quinn focused on the road ahead, squeezing the best speed from the van, given the winding roads on which she traveled. As she drove, her mind drifted back to concern about Avery. It took a lot to knock out a Huntress. She was every bit as tough as Quinn, so the injuries were severe. She hoped Clark got there in time. Quinn hated leaving her there alone.

As she shifted her attention back to the route displayed on her phone, a ping sounded. Quinn slowed as she read the notification. Taylor's message said Sylvie had stopped moving. Quinn pulled over and stared at the map. A switch to satellite view displayed a cluster of buildings set back from the road amidst trees and hills. It was the perfect hideout. That was where Gemma's demon-kinder had the girls.

Quinn sped up again and concentrated on the road. She could be there in fifteen minutes if she hurried.

CHAPTER SEVENTEEN

Quinn pulled off the road onto the grass and shut off the lights. She could make out a narrow track leading into the woods. She glanced at the phone again. The long driveway to the cluster of buildings was still about a quarter-mile down the road. The dirt track didn't show up on the map or satellite view.

Quinn decided it was a perfect place to park the van out of sight. She'd walk the rest of the way. She hoped this track led to where the girls were being held. It started heading the right way, at least.

For a while, the narrow lane angled to the left, then it ended abruptly at a tall cell phone tower surrounded by a chain-link fence. Using the cleared space around the tower, Quinn turned the van around so it faced back the way she came. If they pursued her on the way out, she could drive away in a hurry.

Checking her phone to make sure the dragon was still around the buildings, Quinn started into the woods.

She tapped her earpiece and said, "Hey, T, you still there?"

"Always. What's up?"

"I'm at the location. Still no change in where Sylvie is, right?"

"Nope, she's still somewhere in or around those buildings. I can see you're about five hundred yards to the north of them. What's your plan? I know it seems like a long time, but Clark will be there in about five hours. You know how fast he drives. Wait and watch."

"No, I have to go in. I have an awful feeling about this. I can't shake the thought we can't let them do anything to those little girls."

Taylor paused for a long time. "You will not listen to me, so be careful and try not to get caught."

"Who, me? I'm like a shadow."

Taylor laughed. "Sure you are. I'm signing off, Ms. Shadow. Like I said. Be careful."

The comm clicked off, and Quinn kept moving toward the buildings. She could make out lights ahead through the trees. As she continued walking, the lights grew brighter until she reached the perimeter of a large circular clearing with a house and four small barns and storage sheds.

Crouching behind a tree, Quinn scanned the area, trying to see if there was any security other than the bright lighting. It would negate her shadow-hiding ability, so she wasn't going to sneak up to the house if anyone was watching. She'd have to race across open ground to get to any of the structures.

Realizing there was no other option, she resigned herself to making the dash when something brushed her shoulder. Quinn whipped around and drew her Bowie in a single motion.

"Eeeep?"

"Oh, my God, Sylvie. You scared me. Did you see the girls? Are they here?"

An image appeared in her mind. It showed an aerial view approaching the home and flying up to one window on the second floor. The girls were huddled in a plain unfurnished room with a wooden floor.

Quinn looked at the home, studying the outside. She thought the window Sylvie had shown her was the second-floor window closest to her position. A small detached garage with a covered breezeway was just below the window. If she could get up on that garage roof, she could cross the breezeway's roof and be just outside the girls' room.

"Outstanding job, Sylvie. Now I need you to keep watch and tell me if anyone is coming. With all the floodlights, once I'm on that roof, anyone in the yard will see me instantly."

Sylvie's head bobbed and she took off, circling high above the yard beyond the lights.

Quinn moved around the wooded perimeter until she reached the point closest to the garage. A metal drainpipe at the corner might help her climb up to the roof. She was worried the downspout might not be sturdy enough for what she wanted, but she could boost her speed and strength too. It might be enough for her to leap, grab the garage's coping, and pull herself up.

Taking one last look around at the yard for sentries, Quinn ran across the open space to the garage.

Pressing her back against the wall, she listened for an alarm. Hearing nothing, she reached up and tested the downspout. The aluminum creaked and pulled out of its mount almost instantly. It was far too flimsy to support her weight. She'd have to find another way up.

Peeking around the corner to make sure the coast was clear, Quinn took four steps back. She drew off some of her stamina and boosted her strength.

Quinn ran at the side of the building, pushed off, and jumped with everything she had. Reaching up, she gripped the roof's edge and pushed off with her toes against the siding. She pulled herself up with ease and settled onto her stomach across the pitched roof's edge.

The asphalt shingles still held some of the day's residual warmth. It radiated through her clothes and helped to dispel the chill of the night air. She waited there, pressed flat against the roof, while she listened for any reaction from below. She glanced up and sent a message to Sylvie, circling above in the night sky.

Is it clear?

An image of the whole clearing seen from above entered her mind. She studied it and saw no one anywhere on the grounds. It was odd. Gemma wasn't dumb. She should have put out sentries to watch for a rescue or other intruders.

Quinn looked back over her shoulder at the trees. Maybe she *should* wait for Clark. After a few seconds, she shook her head. She was committed now. She couldn't go back and risk being seen running away.

Quinn got to her feet and ran to the other side of the

garage roof and the covered breezeway beyond. The girls' window was right there. She had a clear path to it.

As she reached the edge of the garage and stepped down onto the breezeway roof, a flash of movement below caught Quinn's eye.

A man stepped out from under the breezeway roof, raised a crossbow to his shoulder, and pulled the trigger.

Quinn had built up too much speed and momentum to do much. She twisted her torso out of the way a little, but that was it.

It was enough that she avoided the killing strike from the crossbow bolt. It coursed past her ribs, scoring a grazing wound before passing into the darkness. The wound wasn't serious, but the evasive move had pulled her off-balance.

Her arms windmilled as she teetered on the edge of the roof. She tried to think of something, even calling upon her connection to wild magic to stabilize her.

Nothing worked.

Realizing it was a losing battle, Quinn pushed off the edge, trying to control some aspect of her fall.

She tried to angle enough that she would land atop the man now frantically working at reloading the crossbow.

He looked up at the last instant. Seeing her coming, he stepped aside just in time to avoid her.

Quinn landed hard and it knocked the wind out of her, delaying her rise.

Gasping for air, Quinn struggled to her feet and turned to face the man who'd attacked her. He'd reloaded and stood barely five feet away.

There was no way he'd miss from that range.

Behind him stood three women, each holding a sword.

The woman in the center pointed her blade at Quinn. "Surrender, or I'll tell the mortal to fire." Her voice had the otherness of the demon-kinder.

Quinn straightened and pulled her hand away from the hilt of her Bowie. If the bolt didn't kill her outright, the three demon-kinder Hunters would finish her. She might have been able to take two of them on, but not all three, especially while injured.

"Toss your blade onto the grass over there, Huntress."

Quinn did as she was told, feeling naked without her weapon.

An image of fiery explosions entered her mind.

No, Sylvie. Stay up there. I'll call you when I have a way for you to come help.

The youngling sent a flurry of images too rapidly to understand. Quinn didn't catch all of it, but what she saw conveyed annoyance and disappointment.

To the three women, Quinn said, "I surrender. I won't attack. I came to make sure the girls you kidnapped still live."

"You cannot kidnap that which belongs to you," a familiar voice said. Gemma stepped into the breezeway between the house and garage. "I'm not sure how you got down here so quickly. My agents reported you were still in Baltimore."

"It's hard to find good help these days. People are so unreliable."

"It matters not. Since two of my Hunters are missing and you're here, I assume you killed the ones I left to finish Avery?"

"Oh, yes. Avery's fine, too. She sends her regards."

"I doubt that, or she'd be here with you. That means she's either dead or sorely injured. Good. I'd rather only deal with one false Huntress at a time."

Quinn refused to rise to the bait. She let the smile remain on her face and held Gemma's gaze.

Gemma waved a hand. "If you three want to have some fun with her first, I'm fine with that. Just make sure she's alive when you bring her inside. And make sure you restrain her. She's a very resourceful girl."

The three women sheathed their swords and ran at Quinn with a blinding speed she hadn't expected. She blocked only a few of the incoming blows before they took her to the ground. They kicked and punched her for a long time before they stopped.

One retrieved some rope from the man with the crossbow and they restrained Quinn, tying her arms behind her at both the wrists and the elbows. Then they marched her into the house.

The house and the property around it seemed to be abandoned. There was little furniture in sight as they took her in through the kitchen to an adjacent room.

A folding card table sat in the center of the room, along with four folding chairs. Carryout and delivery bags were piled in the corner. Gemma occupied one chair and stared at the screen of a tablet propped on the table. It looked like she was checking messages or email.

"What should I do with her?"

"Remove her phone and any other electronics she has on her. Make sure you get that thing in her ear." Rough hands pulled at her belt, removing the comm unit along with the earpiece. The shortest of the three dug into Quinn's pockets, removing her phone.

"Now take her upstairs and put her in one of the empty bedrooms. Tie her securely. We don't want her getting free. We might be able to use her for the rites once we arrive in Baltimore."

The three women tugged at Quinn but stopped as Gemma said, "Oh, and while you're up there, tell those brats to stop crying. I can hear them from here."

Quinn concentrated and caught the faint keening of a child. Her anger boiled over. "Gemma, you're the one who brought those girls together. Perhaps you should treat them a little better."

"Quiet, Huntress. If I want your opinion on how to deal with children, I'll ask for it. Crying will be the least of their problems once they've served their purpose in a few days."

"What do you have planned?"

Gemma smiled. "You'll die in ignorance. Just know that everyone and everything you ever cared about will be utterly destroyed. Take her away."

A demon-kinder, this one with red hair, asked, "What are you keeping her alive for? No rite is worth the risk. Kill her now."

"No. She has power, just like the girls upstairs. Her life sacrifice will open the portal even wider than we planned." Gemma stood and picked up the tablet. "I'm going out for a bit to complete plans with my colleagues. Once that is finished, I'll send for you. Bring her and the little ones and come meet me."

"Leaving so soon?" Quinn quipped as the lanky demon-kinder yanked her by the arm toward the stairs. "Afraid of what I will do to your last three lackeys here?"

"My last three?" Gemma laughed. "Oh, no, my dear, there are many more where these came from. Our operation has been ramping up for over a year, waiting for what is coming. You'll see soon enough."

The demon-kinder yanked again at Quinn, and she stumbled up the stairs. They'd beaten her pretty badly, and she had trouble staying on her feet. She stopped at the top of the stairs to catch her balance. The crying from the bedroom was clearer.

Quinn raised her voice. "Help is close, girls. Don't lose hope."

"Shut up."

The fist that slammed into the side of her face left her seeing stars. She smashed into the wall, teetering dangerously close to the stairs.

The woman planted a foot in the small of Quinn's back and propelled her into the bedroom across the hall.

Quinn stayed on her feet for a few steps, then crashed to the hardwood floor. She rolled onto her back and grinned up at the woman standing over her with her hands on her hips. "It will be fun killing another of your kind. I know my friend Avery has finished off a few, but I'm the expert. Do you know how many I sent back to the netherworld the night I took back the Hunter chambers?"

"Gloat if you want. We will have the last laugh. I'd relax and enjoy your last days on this plane, Huntress." The woman knelt and tied Quinn's feet and legs, checked Quinn's hands to make sure the ropes were still tight, and then stood.

Quinn kept the grin on her face as the woman left her lying there. After the door's lock clicked and the footsteps receded down the hallway, her smile faded. It was important to bluster in situations like this. She couldn't let them see her give up.

Rolling over, Quinn grimaced. The hard landing on the floor felt like it might have dislocated her shoulder, and the pain was extreme. No time to worry about that. She had to get free and figure a way to warn Clark so he didn't rush into a trap too.

She closed her eyes and tried to call Sylvie. To her surprise, the dragon answered her with a hazy image of herself lying bound on the floor.

Quinn turned to stare out the window. She snapped her eyes shut as a brilliant flash of white-hot fire melted a one-foot circle in the center of the glass. The wood around the sash charred a bit from the intense heat, but luckily, it didn't catch fire. Quinn made a mental note to talk to Sylvie about fire safety.

The melted glass pooled on the windowsill, and she heard a triumphant "Eeeep" as Sylvie flew straight at the window. At the last instant, she folded her wings and shot through the circular hole like an arrow. Her wings unfurled as soon as she cleared the gap. The dragon landed in the center of the room, right in front of Quinn.

"That was impressive, squirt."

"Eeeep!"

"Shhhh, they'll hear you. No one knows you're here." Quinn rolled over so her back was toward Sylvie. "Can you cut through these bonds without using fire?"

Sylvie walked over to where Quinn sat. The Huntress

craned her neck to try to see what the dragon was doing. Something tugged at the rope tying her elbows together. Then Sylvie moved down to the ropes around her wrists.

"What's wrong? Can't you chew through them or something?"

"Eeeep?"

"Use your teeth."

An image of teeth sinking into her bloody arm flashed in her mind.

"No, you will not bite me. Just be careful and take your time. I trust you."

The tugging on the bindings on her elbows began again. Sylvie's fiery breath tickled the little hairs on her upper arms as the pulling continued. Quinn held still, especially when a few pinches from the youngling's razor-sharp teeth probably meant the dragon had scratched her.

Suddenly the ropes parted, and she could let her shoulders relax from the awkward angle her bound elbows had forced on her.

The tugging started anew on her hands, and Quinn waited patiently for that to end. A minute later, her wrists popped free as Sylvie chewed her way through the last bit of rope. Quinn swung her arms around to the front. She rubbed at her wrists and elbows where the tight binding had cut off the circulation. Thankfully, her shoulder seemed to have escaped dislocation.

While Quinn did that, Sylvie moved on to chew through the rope binding her legs. Soon she'd chewed through all the ropes.

Quinn got up and shut off the bare overhead lightbulb at the switch by the door, then went to stare out the window. Gemma walked to a car parked on the lane by the front door and climbed into the passenger side. The man who'd held the crossbow on Quinn got in to drive. The car started and drove down the lane.

"Eeeep?" Sylvie asked as she landed on her usual perch on Quinn's shoulder and watched Gemma drive away.

"No, we're not escaping. We wait until Clark comes to rescue me. Then we'll hit them from behind like vengeance from heaven."

Quinn grinned in the darkness and sat down by the door to wait in the dark for the right moment to spring her trap.

CHAPTER EIGHTEEN

"Avery, can you hear me?"

Avery opened her eyes, instantly blinded by the flashlight's beam. She brought her hands up to shield her face from the brightness. The voice was familiar, even if she couldn't make out the shadowy face. Her mind raced as she tried to place the voice.

"C-clark, is that you?"

"Yeah, I just got here." He moved the flashlight so it didn't shine right at her. "Sorry about the light. It's dark in here, and you were so still, I was afraid of the worst. How are you feeling?"

"Better. Quinn healed me a little. The sleep helped, too." Avery sat up, looking past Clark. "Where is she?"

"We think they captured her. Her comm went dead a few hours ago. What did she tell you when she left you here?"

"The last thing I remember was her talking to you and Taylor on the radio. I think I passed out."

"You look better than I expected, given how Quinn described you."

Avery stood, reaching out to steady herself against the wall with one hand. "We have to find her, and the girls, too. They're important, but I haven't figured out why."

"There's no 'we' here, Avery. I can help Quinn, but even with the healing, you're in no shape to go into a fight right now."

"You'd be surprised what I can do, even injured. Besides, we don't have time to sit here and argue. We can talk on the road."

Clark chuckled. "You two are a perfect match. That sounded just like something Quinn would say."

"Good, then you're used to it." Avery started for the door, stopping to pick up her sword from the floor. "Let's see if we can find her. You're in touch with Taylor?"

"Yes." He followed her outside and got in the car while she climbed in the passenger side. "Let's get on the road. She's got a lock on Sylvie's location. The dragon has to be somewhere near Quinn."

Clark started down the twisting lane. He keyed the comm so it played over the car's speakers. "Taylor, I've got Avery. We're headed south toward Quinn's last location. Any updates?"

"How's Avery?"

"I'm well enough, thanks to Quinn."

"I'm glad. It's good to hear your voice. I'm trying to locate Quinn, but her comm is still dead. Sylvie's basic location is the same as before. She's in the center of that cluster of buildings."

Avery thought about Brea and the others. "Any way you can monitor the activity live at that location? I'd love to know if the girls are there with Quinn."

"I can't access a live satellite feed if that's what you mean. I've got enough going on without trying to hack government video access right now."

"I had to ask," Avery replied.

"Better to just in case."

Taylor nodded. "Any more ideas about what makes these six so special?"

"They are all connected to each other somehow. All their minds and senses are linked."

Taylor said, "That sounds kind of creepy."

"I know it sounds like it would be, but they're like normal kids from what I can tell. I don't have all that much experience. Gemma and other adults raised me alone, remember."

Clark glanced at his phone's map directions. "I think we're close. I'll reach out when we get there and look around a little. I have to figure out a way to breach whatever defenses they have. Quinn must have triggered them to get herself caught, so we have to be extra careful."

"I'll monitor the location beacons and let you know if anything changes. Be careful down there." Taylor cut the connection.

Clark handed Avery his phone, opened to a maps app. "You can be my navigator. It looks like we'll be on back roads most of the way there, so give me plenty of notice if there's a turnoff coming up."

"I can do that." Avery took the phone and studied it as

they drove. It wasn't difficult working with Clark. He had always been professional when she'd had her limited inter- actions with him the last time she was here.

After several turns onto twisting back roads, they reached the lane that led to the cluster of buildings on the satellite map. Bright lights glowed over the trees.

Avery looked from the phone to the trees. "It looks to be about a half kilometer down this lane. Given how lit up it is, should we drive all the way in?"

Clark shut off his headlights. "No. We'll go until we run out of cover. Then I'll go the rest of the way on foot."

"I'm coming with you, Clark. If you leave me in the car, I'll just follow. Having two pairs of eyes are better than one, and you know it."

Letting out an exasperated sigh, Clark said, "Fine, but let me lead. You're still injured, no matter what you want me to think."

"Fair enough. I'll stay back to start."

Clark held her gaze, but Avery didn't back down. He sighed, turned down the lane, and drove until they could see the bright lights and buildings through the trees. The two of them got out and proceeded on foot the rest of the way until they crouched behind a broad tree trunk at the edge of the forested area.

Clark pointed at the house. "See, there in the front room. There's movement. I've seen two people pass the window. When they came and took the girls, how many were there?"

"Four or five. I think three took the girls and left while I fought the other two. One was the body you saw back at the shack. Quinn chased off the second one when she showed up."

"So we can count on at least three. Were all of them demon-kinder?"

"The one I fought was, so I assume the others are. I can't be sure, though."

"This'll be a tough fight if they're all Hunter-trained like you are. They'll be just as fast as you and me, and stronger. I wish Quinn wasn't missing right now. We could use her boosted strength and speed."

Avery shook her head. "No sense worrying about that right now. Maybe if we get to her first, we can free her, and she can join the fight."

"If she's here."

"The little dragon of hers is still in there, right?"

Clark reached into his pocket and pulled out his earpiece. "Forgot to put this in." He inserted it and tapped it once. "Taylor, can you hear me?"

Avery waited while Clark nodded in response to Taylor's answer.

"Avery and I are at the house. Is Sylvie still inside?"

Another pause.

"Good," Clark said. He nodded at Avery. "We're coming up with a plan now. We'll let you know how it goes."

He reached up and cut the connection. "The dragon's still inside as far as Taylor can tell. I don't like how lit up that place is, though. There's no way to approach without them seeing us."

"There would be for one of us if the other distracted them."

"What did you have in mind?"

"You swing around through the woods to the opposite side. There must be a rear door. When you've had long enough to get in position, I'll step out and announce my presence to get all of them looking this way."

"That might work, but, Avery, it's risky. We could end up with them taking or killing you before I can hit them from behind. I could sneak in and find Quinn. Then all we'd have to do is hit them while they're dealing with you. Are you sure you keep them busy long enough for me to do all that?"

"I can do my part. You focus on what you have to do. Will fifteen minutes be long enough for you to get in position?"

"It should be."

"Good, then get going. I'll start the countdown now. You'll hear me when I announce myself. Be ready to go."

Clark nodded. "Be careful." He started through the trees to the left.

Avery stared at her phone, watching the clock while he got into position. It seemed like a long time, but eventually, the clock ticked over to show fifteen minutes had passed. She stood, checked the windows and grounds one last time, and, taking a deep breath, walked onto the lighted lawn in front of the house. She moved across the grass until she was halfway there and stopped.

"You in the house," she shouted. She waited until she saw a face peering out the window at her. "I'm here to take back the girls. Come out and face me if you dare."

Several figures moved past the window toward the

front door. Avery leaned forward on the balls of her feet, ready for anything. She pushed down the residual aches and pain from the earlier fight. She would hold them off as long as she could. All that mattered was getting the girls and Quinn out safely.

CHAPTER NINETEEN

Quinn's head popped up from where she'd been dozing by the door as the first shouts reached her.

"You in the house, I'm here to take back the girls. Come out and face me if you dare."

"Sylvie, that's Avery." She moved to the window, testing the floorboards to avoid any unnecessary creaks that might alert the women downstairs. Quinn didn't want them to know she was up and moving.

Sure enough, Avery stood in the yard outside the front door, shouting at the house's occupants.

"She's still injured. They'll kill her for sure this time. Sylvie, go help her."

"Eeeep?"

"Don't worry about me. I'll break out of here and come at them from behind. Just keep them busy and off her. Got it?"

"Eeeep."

Quinn lifted the dragon so she could climb through the

circular hole in the window. She dropped to the roof outside and lifted into the inky sky.

Avery called out again. "Don't just stand there in the doorway. Come out here and face me if you dare. I've already killed one of you." She lifted her hand, and her sword appeared in it. She beckoned toward the house with her free hand.

Two women armed with swords ran out into the yard. One was the lanky girl. The other was the shorter redhead.

Quinn cursed. The time for quiet was over. She dialed up her strength in the HUD, drawing down her stamina bar, and ran at the flimsy interior door.

She hit it with her shoulder, bursting through into the upstairs hallway. The frame splintered and the door's hinges pulled free so the slab hung at an angle.

Quinn paused for an instant, staring at the door where the girls were being held, then shook her head. They were safe enough for now. Priority number one was to deal with the remaining demon-kinder downstairs.

Moving to the top of the stairs, Quinn leaped over the railing, landing in the entry hall. The final demon-kinder stood in the doorway, watching the fight outside. She spun as Quinn landed.

The woman sneered and raised her curved sword. "You escaped. Good. I never liked the mage's plan to bring you along. Now I can kill you without crossing her."

"You can try."

The woman smiled. "Your puny knife is with Gemma, girl. How do you expect to beat me without a weapon?"

It was a good question, but Quinn didn't let on. Instead, she pointed past the woman at the fight outside.

"Maybe I'll just let my dragon kill you."

The woman opened her mouth to reply, then heard the screaming in the yard behind her. She twisted to stare slack-jawed at one of her companions stumbling around in the yard.

Flames engulfed the woman's head. Her hands beat at the fire, trying to put it out.

Sylvie flew in for another pass, shooting another jet of blue-white flame at the burning woman.

Quinn didn't wait to see what happened next. Dialing her speed to maximum and spending the rest of her stamina on strength, she charged at the demon-kinder's back.

The unnatural swiftness of the attack caught the woman by surprise. Quinn tackled her as she turned back to the Huntress.

Wrapping her arms around the woman's torso, Quinn dragged her down. They tumbled out the door and down the steps onto the front walk.

The sword clattered across the concrete path. The demon-kinder grabbed Quinn's wrists to break free.

Her demon-enhanced fingers dug in and wrenched Quinn's hands apart. She rolled free and bounced to her feet.

Quinn rose to face her. "Let's finish this."

The pair circled each other. In the center of the yard, Avery crossed swords with the other demon-kinder in a flurry of steel on steel. She was holding her own for now. A burning heap on the ground was all that remained of the third demon-kinder.

Quinn knew Clark must be around somewhere, but she

couldn't take the time to find him. He and Avery must've had a plan to get the girls out.

The demon-kinder, possessing all the training of the Hunter woman she controlled, charged at Quinn. She led with a rapid series of punches and then tried for a kick at Quinn's head.

The entire sequence came at Quinn so fast, the woman's hands and feet were blurs. She blocked only two of the three punches and barely ducked away from the kick.

This other woman had some of that hunter super speed Naomi possessed. Even with Quinn's speed boosts, it would be a close fight.

Sylvie buzzed by the woman's head, distracting her for a second. Quinn launched a roundhouse kick, catching her distracted opponent on the shoulder. The blow knocked her several feet away to roll across the grass.

"Thank you, Sylvie. Go help Avery. I've got this."

"Eeeep."

As the dragon flew away, Quinn raced to get to her opponent before the woman got back up.

She failed.

The demon-kinder timed her attack perfectly and launched up at Quinn just before she got there.

The move caught the Huntress by surprise. Before she could react, she found herself on her back, fending off punch after punch at her face and head.

The woman straddled Quinn's waist as she rained blows on her.

Bloody and dazed from the headshots, Quinn tried to buck her hips to dislodge her attacker. It didn't work.

She tried punching back.

None of the shots landed, and they left her face and head unprotected. The dizzying array of punches continued to come at her.

Quinn realized she should probably call Sylvie back. She needed help.

The punching stopped.

Quinn moved her arms from in front of her face and peered up through swollen eyelids. The tip of a sword blade had appeared in the center of the woman's chest. As it withdrew, a wisp of smoke curled up from the hole in her shirt as black ichor oozed from it.

The woman fell to the side. Clark stood behind her.

Quinn rolled over and forced herself to her feet. She swayed a little but steadied herself. She searched the yard for Avery. The other Huntress stood in the center of the yard, pulling her katana from the throat of the final demon-kinder. Scorch marks striped the demon-kinder's back and shirt where dragon fire had burned away the fabric.

Avery spotted Quinn staring at her and ran toward her, pulling her into a tight embrace. When they finally let go of each other, Quinn laughed. Avery had fresh wounds atop the partially healed ones from earlier. "Aren't we a mess?"

"Your face," Avery said, reaching up to trace a finger down Quinn's bruised cheek. "Are you all right?"

"I'll be fine. A little healing, either from a friend or a nearby ley line, will do the trick. How about you?"

A fresh gash in her arm still trickled blood down to Avery's elbow. It didn't seem too deep, though.

"I'm still feeling the effects of the earlier beating, but with your little friend's help, I held my own."

Sylvie came around and landed on Quinn's shoulder. "Eeeep?"

"Sorry, Sylvie. Let me formally introduce you. Avery, this is Sylvie. Sylvie, this is my girlfriend Avery."

Avery smiled. "Nice to meet you, little one. You showed up just in time."

"Eeeep," Sylvie crooned, lifting her head high and puffing out her chest.

"Yes, you're the best dragon around for sure," Quinn said, laughing. She scratched Sylvie's brow ridge. A smooth vibrating hum emanated from the dragon as she leaned into the attention.

Clark came over. "I don't mean to interrupt your reunion, but we still have work to do. Any idea where the girls are?"

Quinn pointed at the house. "They're locked in a room at the top of the stairs. The demon-kinder were to keep them here until Gemma sent for them. Then they were to bring them all to her, presumably somewhere up in Baltimore."

Clark said, "You still think that's where she's headed?"

"I do."

Avery said, "She'll have to go there either way now. I assume we can take the little ones back to your place at O'Malley's?"

"That's where we can protect them the best," Clark agreed.

Quinn nodded. "Let's go fetch them. I heard one of them crying earlier when they locked me up."

"Oh." Avery frowned with concern. "Let's go. They must have heard the commotion. We should let them know they're safe now."

"Wait a sec," Quinn said. She searched the pockets of the demon-kinder who'd taken her upstairs and found what she looked for. She held up an old iron key.

Avery nodded, and they all headed into the house. Clark remained at the bottom of the stairs, keeping an eye out for trouble as Quinn unlocked the door.

Avery pushed past as the door swung open.

As soon as she entered the room, a chorus of little voices shouted as one. "Avery!"

Six figures rushed at her from the far corner, wrapping her in hugs from all sides.

"Girls, I'm glad to see all of you, too. Are you all okay?" Avery leaned down to check each of the girls.

The redhead, who looked like the oldest of them, nodded. "We're fine. They didn't hurt us. We're just hungry. Do you have food?"

Quinn chuckled. "Typical kids. Always hungry."

Avery laughed. "How would you know?"

"Fair enough. We'll get them food soon. First, we need to get them out of here."

"Clark's got his car. Where's my van?"

"It's parked in the woods nearby."

Avery nodded. "We'll need it. It has all our things. Before you go get it, though, let me introduce you."

Quinn smiled as Avery introduced her to Brea, Kami, the twins Margie and Jordi, and finally Ola and Suko. "It's very nice to meet all of you. Now let's go downstairs and get ready to leave. Then you can stop for food."

Cheers erupted, bringing more smiles to Quinn's and Avery's faces.

Clark was still at the bottom of the stairs. "What's the plan?"

"I'll go fetch the van. See if you can find my comm gear and the Bowie. They took them from me in the front room off the kitchen. The one demon-kinder made a comment about Gemma taking my knife, but she might have been lying."

Clark nodded. He started searching while Avery corralled the girls by the front door. Quinn ran toward the woods where she'd parked the van. Sylvie flitted along in the air behind her.

Ten minutes later, Quinn pulled the van in front of the house. Clark had retrieved his car too. Avery and the six girls came out right away.

Clark came over and handed Quinn her phone, her comm gear, and the Bowie. "They were all there on a card table. It looks like they are all fine."

Quinn sheathed her knife, clipped the comm pack on her belt, and put the earpiece in place. She tapped it once and said, "Taylor, can you hear me?"

"Quinn, thank God you're all right. How are the others?"

"All good. We got the girls, and Clark's here to help escort them back to Baltimore."

"Good. I'm ready to bring you and Sylvie back when you're ready."

"Let me get them on the road, then you can send the recall."

Quinn helped Avery get the girls settled in the van and nodded to Clark as he went to his car.

"Avery, Clark will shadow you in his car. He'll keep an eye out for Gemma or any other trouble. I'll see you in a few hours."

Avery nodded and pulled her close. "It'll be nice to be with you again, Quinn. Thanks for coming when I needed you."

"Always, you know that."

Avery smiled and gave her a quick kiss. A chorus of "Oooooos" came from the girls in the van. Avery and Quinn started laughing as their lips parted.

Avery winked at Quinn. "More of that when I see you in Baltimore."

"I'll hold you to it. Be careful. You're almost there, but don't let your guard down."

Avery nodded. She started the van and followed Clark's sedan down the lane.

Quinn watched them drive away until they were out of sight, then called Sylvie to come land on her shoulder.

As the dragon landed, Quinn tapped her earpiece. "Taylor, we're all set here. Bring us home."

CHAPTER TWENTY

Quinn, Taylor, and Naomi had their hands full as soon as Quinn and Sylvie returned via the VR system. It only took a few minutes of chatting as Quinn and her dragon recovered from the VR trip to realize they had six little guests coming. They would need a place to stay, somewhere they would be both comfortable and out of sight.

Their normal apartments were too exposed and easy to assault if Gemma came to take them back. It was Naomi who suggested the solution.

"We could put them in rooms down in the Hunter tunnels. There are only a few ways in, and they'd be out of view if Gemma or the Fae sent spies into O'Malley's to see where they were. Plus, we can use Tadpole's help to get everything ready."

"It's kind of creepy down there, isn't it?"

"It doesn't have to be. You've never seen the rooms I use."

"I'm sorry," Quinn said. "I figured it was a vampire crypt thing."

Naomi laughed. "I see I should have invited you down sooner. I have two fully furnished rooms with rugs on the floor, and even a bed."

Quinn's eyebrows shot up. What her mother described was the opposite of what she'd envisioned. "Okay, I guess I owe you an apology."

"Nonsense. It's my fault for not inviting you down to hang out. The important thing is, there are a series of rooms off the hall linking the training room and the ceremonial chamber."

Quinn nodded. "I know the ones. I've never opened the doors to see what was inside, though. You're sure they'll be suitable?"

"They have power, and they're close to the bathroom off the training area. Tadpole stays in one of them. He took the largest room for himself. There are three others, though. They're a little smaller than his, but I'm sure we could put two girls in each of them. Plus, there is the ceremonial vestments room. We could clean that out for you and Avery so you could be nearby. That way, you'd be close enough to keep an eye on them."

Taylor smiled. She started typing on the keyboard behind the computer screens. "That means we have work to do."

"What do you mean?" Quinn asked.

"I mean, we have to shop for furniture for six kids. This will be so much fun."

"Easy does it, T. We don't have all that much time—five or six hours at the most."

"Then we'd better get started." Taylor clapped her hands and rubbed them together as she ticked off the things they had to get done. "Naomi, go find Tadpole and clean out the rooms. I'll order what we need online, then Quinn and I will borrow Paddy's catering van and run to the Swedish Furniture Store for pickup. By the time I finish here, it'll be time to leave. They open in an hour. We'll need beds and other stuff for everyone, including you and Avery."

Quinn shrugged. "I guess we have a plan. Taylor, you will be in charge. We have to hurry. All that furniture has to be assembled, and they'll be here before we know it."

Naomi said, "I'll get things ready and figure out how we will assemble everything. Let me make some calls and see if Juni and Paddy can lend a hand. Maybe some other servers will come in early to help, too. Hurry back."

Naomi headed down the hall, already talking on her phone. Taylor continued shopping online.

Quinn left the workshop to get the keys for the van from Paddy's office. It was early in the morning, and it wouldn't take Taylor long to gather what they needed online.

Taylor met Quinn as she came out of Paddy's office. "Done already?"

Taylor shook her head. "No, but I can finish on here." She held up a tablet. "We can finalize the order in the parking lot while we wait for them to open."

Quinn and Taylor were standing at the doors when the manager unlocked them. Taylor showed him the order she'd put together on the tablet.

Seeing the number of items they were ready to purchase all at once, the manager called for several sales associates to assist them in gathering it all from the warehouse. That left Quinn and Taylor time to shop for a few fun items to help it feel more like a home for the girls.

An hour after they walked into the store, they left with a fully loaded catering van and a hefty credit card charge. Quinn pulled up behind O'Malley's a half-hour later and checked the time on her phone. Avery and the girls would be here in three hours.

"I don't know if we will get all this unloaded and assembled in time, T."

"We can at least get started. Come on."

The two of them went around back and opened the doors. As they did, the kitchen doors to the pub opened. Naomi stood inside, staying well out of the sunlight streaming into the alley. Tadpole, Paddy, Juni, and a bunch of the pub's staff came out and started loading the heavy boxes onto carts. As soon as each cart was full, someone rolled it down into the tunnels.

Before long, all three rooms had teams inside who worked at assembling two beds and dressers in each one. They also had room for a small table and two chairs. Tadpole roamed around, cleaning up empty boxes and helping with heavy lifting to put the items into position.

They finished getting the last room ready with five minutes to spare. Quinn and Taylor were making the final checks on the freshly made beds when her phone chirped with a message from Avery.

We're out back. Come help us bring the kids in. They're beat from the drive.

Quinn smiled and called, "They're here." She texted a quick reply and went into the hallway.

Everyone who'd been helping them get ready waited for her.

"Thank you all for helping with this. You've gone a long way toward making this place a home for us over the last few months. Now you've done even more for people you don't even know."

Paddy grinned. "Never let it be said I don't know how to extend hospitality to people in need. Juni and I'll go up with the others and put some food together. Kids are always hungry, and I'll bet your girls will want to eat once they're settled in."

As the pub staff headed back up to O'Malley's, Tadpole reached out and tugged on Quinn's sleeve. "Uh, Quinn, what should I do? Little kids might be scared because I'm so big."

"Oh, right, that's an outstanding idea." She hated making him feel like that, but she was worried about their reaction, too. "You hang back in your room or the armory. Stay hidden until I can introduce you to them at the right moment. It might overwhelm them at first."

Naomi nodded. "I'll stay down here with him and double-check everything. You and Taylor should go up and greet them."

Taylor bounced on the balls of her feet, excited to meet the girls. "I can't wait to show them all the stuff in their rooms."

Quinn knew her best friend liked kids. She'd done a lot of babysitting in high school, and she probably missed it.

The minivan with Avery behind the wheel had pulled up behind Clark's sedan in the alley as Quinn and Taylor arrived. Avery smiled as soon as she spotted Quinn. The girls waved as the doors opened.

Quinn said, "Hi, ladies. Welcome to O'Malley's. This is our home, and we hope it becomes one for you, too."

The youngest of the group, Kami with the pixie-cut brown hair, walked over to Quinn, her eyes wide. "A home? Really? I've always wanted a real home."

The Huntress' heart melted. She'd been an orphan and a foster child most of her life. Now she got the chance to provide a home for girls who were special in that way, just like her.

Crouching so her eyes were level with Kami's, she nodded. "Yep, this can be your home for as long as you want to stay here. You and all your sisters."

Little arms wrapped around Quinn's neck, catching her by surprise. It took her a second to return the hug. She stood, holding onto Kami and shifting her into piggy-back position.

"Come on," Taylor said. "We have a surprise for all of you."

The other five girls scampered along behind, following Taylor and Quinn into the pub, with Clark and Avery bringing up the rear. After leading them through the bar and restaurant area, Taylor opened the door to the store-rooms and the tunnel down to the Hunter chambers.

As the hallway transitioned into a true tunnel, the girls stopped chattering to each other. There were only a few excited whispers.

Noting the change, Quinn said, "We're going to a super-secret place that only a few people have ever seen. We've made a special place for all of you there."

Brea, the red-headed leader of the six, caught up with Quinn in the hallway and walked beside her. She reached out to hold Kami's hand as she rode on Quinn's back.

After taking the stairs down to the ceremonial chamber, the group turned the corner to the area made up just for them. Naomi waited for them. She'd made sure all the lights were on, so it looked bright and cheerful.

Quinn stopped and said, "Girls, this is my mom, Naomi. Maybe Avery can come forward to help me with introductions the other way since I'm still learning your names."

Avery smiled and started with the eldest. "Naomi, this is Brea. She's the oldest and is smart and resourceful."

Motioning for the blonde twins to come forward, she said, "These two young ladies are Jordi and Margie. Behind them with the long black hair is Suko, and behind her with the dark brown hair is Ola. Last but not least is our fiercest little warrior girl, Kami."

Quinn set Kami down beside Avery and smiled. The six-year-old puffed out her chest and stood with hands on her hips in a heroic pose.

Naomi nodded a greeting to each girl as Avery introduced them. Then she said, "I have rooms for you. You'll each have to share with someone else, so I hope that's okay."

Ola smiled. "You mean, we don't have to all sleep in the same bed anymore?"

"No, sweetie," Naomi replied. "You each get your own bed, two to a room. Is that okay?"

"It's wonderful!" Ola spun like a dancer. "Can we see?"

"You sure can." Naomi waved her hand. "Come on. The rooms are right down here."

The girls ran to catch up to Naomi, leaving Clark, Taylor, Quinn, and Avery in the hallway. They peeked into the rooms as the girls got situated in their new home.

Avery shook her head. "This must have been a lot of work. Thank you. They've been through so much."

"Your room is right down there," Taylor said. "It has a queen-sized bed in case you want some company."

"Taylor," Quinn grumbled, "that's enough. Avery, I'm sorry."

"I'm glad she said something. I was wondering who would watch the girls if I snuck up to your apartment."

"Well," Quinn said, "we can't have you sneaking around like that. This is your home, at least for now. I'll move down here with you if you don't mind."

Avery laced her fingers with Quinn's. "I'd like that."

Taylor nudged Clark. "Come on. Let's go see if we can help Paddy with the food."

Clark nodded, and the pair of them left Quinn and Avery alone in the passage. The hallway wasn't silent, but they were by themselves for the moment. The background murmur of children's voices filled the space with a joyful sound Quinn had never heard down here.

Quinn tugged at Avery's hand. "I'll show you to your room."

They walked down the hall to the room prepared for them. A few minutes later, as Avery admired the quilt Quinn had chosen for her bed, Naomi came to the door.

"What is it, Mom?"

"Is Kami in here?"

Avery said, "No, why?" Her brows furrowed with concern.

"She was in the room with Brea and me. I turned around, and she was gone."

Brea came to the door beside Naomi. "She's not in the rooms with the other girls. I should have kept an eye on her. She's always wandering off."

Avery stood. "It's easy to get lost down here, especially if she wanders into the labyrinth maze."

Quinn said, "Come on. She can't have gone far in just a few minutes."

They all headed into the hallway and froze as they heard a loud shriek at the far end of the hall where the armory and training room were located.

"Oh, no. Tadpole's there."

"The orc warrior?" Avery asked. "Is he safe?"

Quinn started running. "He's safe, but I was afraid he might scare the girls if we didn't introduce him to them the right way. He lives down here too."

Avery ran after Quinn as another loud shriek sounded.

Quinn reached the training room first and skidded to a halt. Kami sat in the middle of the room, giggling. At the other end of the training mats sat Tadpole. He had his enormous green hands over his face.

He dropped his hands, revealing his tusked visage. He'd screwed up his face so his tongue lolled out the side of his mouth, and he crossed his eyes.

Kami shrieked again and rolled on the floor, clutching her belly as she laughed.

Across the room, Tadpole spotted the newcomers and said, "Hey, Quinn. I stayed here just like you told me. Kami found me, though. I hope it's okay that I played a game with her."

"It's perfectly fine, buddy. I'm glad you made friends."

"She's great. You should see the funny faces she can make."

Kami turned around on cue. She pulled up on her nose with one finger and down on her cheeks with the other, contorting her face while she made pig noises.

Tadpole burst out laughing. "See what I mean? She's awesome."

Quinn glanced at Avery and shrugged. "I guess meeting Tadpole won't be a problem after all."

Behind them, the other girls surged into the room to see what was up. They all began laughing and sharing their own silly faces until everyone was giggling along with them.

Quinn smiled. She, Taylor, and the others had pulled it off. They'd made this place a home for these girls. In the process, it had become a little more of a home for them all.

She pulled a smiling Avery over and the two stood arm in arm, watching the girls and the giant orc play games.

CHAPTER TWENTY-ONE

Quinn woke staring up at the stone ceiling, confused until she remembered she was down in the tunnels. A smile crossed her face, and she turned to her right. She studied Avery's face, relaxed in peaceful sleep.

Their reunion the night before had been awkward, partly because they'd been apart for months, partly because they both had bruises from the fight the day before. Avery had taken the worst of it. Even with Quinn's healing efforts at the shack, there were signs of her injuries in the fading bruises and residual swelling on her face.

Avery's eyes opened, catching Quinn staring her way. "Hey, you. Have you been awake long?"

"No, I just woke up a few seconds ago. I didn't wake you, did I?"

"No, I've been rising early out of habit since I've been on the road."

"Do you think there are any more girls out there she hasn't turned into demon-kinder?"

"No, these six were at the last location on the list I uncovered. All the others were vacant. Sometimes, it looked like the occupants had left, or been taken, just before I got to them."

"At least you saved these six. That's something."

"It is, but they're not safe yet. Gemma still wants them for something—probably the ritual we were told about. I'm sure it has to do with their collective sight and senses. Until we defeat her, they'll be at risk."

Quinn knew Avery was right. It irked her that they wouldn't have more of a break before the two of them dove back into the fray. The quest to stop Gemma and the Dark Fae plot came first, though.

A tiny head popped up on the other side of Avery, beside her shoulder. The long scaly neck curled over until the little dragon's chin rested on Avery's chest. A sensation of gentle love flooded Quinn's mind as she gazed into the little emerald eyes.

"She likes you," Quinn said.

"Well, she's been curled up against my back all night. Maybe she just likes a warm body."

"She is a hedonist."

"Eeeep?"

Quinn laughed. "Sorry, kiddo. I'm just telling the truth."

A distant flurry of giggles outside their room brought an eye roll and a sigh from Avery. "They have so much energy in the mornings. I need to get out there and see what they're up to."

"Stay," Quinn urged. "I'm sure they're fine."

"You don't know the trouble they can get into. I've spent the last two weeks with them, and it feels like I've known them my entire life. Believe me when I say it's better if we get up."

The giggling girls ran past their door, heading down the hallway toward the training room.

Quinn groaned. "We'd better make sure they don't get into the weapons in the armory."

She and Avery dressed and opened the door. Laughter echoed down the hall. Avery pushed past Quinn and started in that direction.

When they arrived in the training room, they found all six girls tugging on Tadpole, trying to pull him down to the mats. He walked slowly around with a girl wrapped around each leg, one tugging at each arm, and Kami perched on his shoulders with her hands wrapped around his head from behind so she could cover his eyes.

Brea stood to the side, pointing at the center of the mats. She shouted, "Pull him down. We must defeat the invader."

The giant orc warrior dropped to his knees and then rolled slowly over onto his back, laughing as the giggling mass of children climbed onto his chest.

Quinn glanced at Avery. "If we'd known Tadpole was watching them, we could have slept in."

"I'm still not sure about him, Quinn. Are you positive he's safe?"

"To those he considers friends, he's as gentle as a butterfly."

Avery looked back at the pile of giggling bodies on the floor. "They seem to have taken to him."

"And he to them. I was afraid he'd scare them and I'd

have to find another place for him to stay. This is a much better outcome, don't you think?"

"I do," Avery said. She clapped her hands together. "Ladies, ladies, who wants breakfast?"

A chorus of cheers sounded.

Quinn laughed. "I guess that's a yes." She nodded at the six girls, now lined up in front of her. "You all get cleaned up, and I'll bring you food from the kitchen upstairs."

They all scampered toward the small bathroom beside the training area.

Avery said, "I'll stay down here and make sure they don't make a mess. You okay getting the food by yourself?"

"I can go with Quinn," Tadpole offered.

Quinn nodded. "Come on, big guy. Let's get everyone fed, including you."

She left with Tadpole lumbering behind her. In the halls and tunnels leading to the pub, he had to bend a little to avoid bumping his head. Quinn slowed down so he could keep up.

"Tadpole, the girls aren't bothering you, are they? You've been very nice about playing with them."

"Oh, no. It's lots of fun having friends around. I enjoy having someone to play with. It's been a little lonely down here, especially on the days when you and the others don't come down to train."

Quinn hadn't considered that, and she realized she had to pay more attention to him. She didn't want him to feel like he didn't belong in the clan as much as the others. She wanted him to know he belonged as much as any of them did.

"I'm glad you told me that. I'll come and hang out more often."

"You don't have to, at least not now that they're all here. I never had friends to play with growing up. My brothers always worked, training me to fight. There wasn't any time to play."

"I'm glad you have someone to play with now. Promise me that if you tire of playing with them, you'll come tell Avery and me right away. Got it?"

"Yes." His face split in an enormous grin. "I won't have to, though. They're my friends now."

Quinn smiled. It made her happy that he'd found a place to be his normal, gentle self. The clan's newest member seemed to have settled in just fine.

The regular busy breakfast crowd buzzed with conversation in the dining room when they arrived. Most stopped when Quinn entered, accompanied by the giant orc. Tadpole smiled and waved at everyone. Eyes turned back to their meals and companions, and the conversations started up again.

"I think you should come up here more often, Tadpole. It's important for people to see you as a normal guy and not a threat."

"I'm used to it. It's okay. Besides, the cook doesn't like me coming into the kitchen for food. I'm supposed to wait for someone to bring it down to me."

"They should trust you. You know the rules now. I want you to come up here and order from Juni or one of the people who works here. You don't have to bother the cook. Let Juni do it. She'll fetch your food and bring it out here, then you can eat up here with everyone else. I'll tell Paddy we've changed things so you can order like a normal person."

Tadpole's grin broadened. He wrapped Quinn in a tight bearhug.

"Easy does it." Quinn groaned. "I'm still sore from the fighting yesterday."

The orc released her, and his face took on a serious expression as he stared down at her. "You should take me with you when you know you have to fight. I won't let anyone hurt you."

"I'm fine. Just a little bruised, that's all. Avery and Clark were there to help me. Besides, I need you here now. Watch over the little ones. There are awful people like the two Fae princesses who want to hurt them. We can't let that happen."

His face grew deadly serious. "No one will hurt them, Quinn. I'll die before I let that happen."

"Let's hope it doesn't come to that, but I'm glad to hear it. Come on, let's order breakfast. I'm as hungry as you are, and those young ladies need to eat, too."

A half-hour later, back in the training room, Quinn and Avery watched as the six girls and Tadpole ate. They all sat in a circle atop the central training mat.

Clark tapped Quinn's shoulder. "I brought the others down to the ceremonial chamber. I think we need to plan our next steps. Can Tadpole watch them for a bit?"

Avery nodded, and he headed back toward the ceremonial chamber.

Quinn and Avery followed Clark into the open circular chamber. The rectangular panels around the walls marked the tombs of past Hunter clan leaders. Naomi, Taylor, and Miranda were already there.

Taylor said, "From the sound of it, they're settling in well."

Avery nodded. "They are. You and Quinn went above and beyond. You all did."

"We did what we would have done for anyone who is part of our clan, Ave," Quinn said.

"Well, I'm glad I'm part of it, then." Avery looked at Clark. "What now?"

Clark shook his head. "I'm not sure. We know that Gemma, along with Filippa and Aurora, will assume we have the girls. They have to make a play to attack here and try to retrieve them. Avery, are you sure you have no idea what their purpose is in Gemma's master plan?"

Avery shook her head. "I wish I did. Then maybe we'd have a way to leverage it for our own use."

"They're coming to Baltimore," Quinn said. "We know that much. Besides trying to get the girls back, they'll also head to the Crystal Well. That has to be their ultimate destination. It would be the logical choice as the magical center of power for an opening to the netherworld."

Miranda asked, "How do you know? There are other centers of magic energy around the city or just outside it. Heck, this chamber is a power center of sorts."

"Think back to all the times we've been there," Quinn said. "I first met Filippa above the hidden entrance to those tunnels. Gemma worked to dig a passage to get down there. They even brought the Fae court to hold their trial there. It has to be the location."

Taylor stared into the air, lost in thought.

"What're you thinking, T?"

"Well, I don't know how good an idea this is, but what if we used their own methods against them?"

Clark asked. "What methods?"

"I'm talking about the Fae Court. Quinn, you said before when you were on trial that the magistrates seemed to be impartial. They didn't side with Filippa and Aurora, even when the princesses tried to pressure them."

"That's true. Why?"

"What if we go to the court and ask for an injunction against them coming here?"

Miranda looked at Naomi and Clark. "Would that work?"

Naomi shrugged.

Clark thought for a second and said, "I don't think any human has ever used the Fae court against the royals. At least, I've never heard of it."

Quinn smiled. "There's always a first time. It might buy us some time to discover why they want the girls."

Naomi said, "It's worth a try. Quinn, you might even have an advantage, given that they tried to have you killed. I think that makes you the logical choice to present the case."

Clark nodded. "You and Avery should go together. She's a witness to the attacks on the girls while she had them. You make the case with her as your evidence."

Quinn wondered if it was just far-fetched enough to help them. "I suppose I could do that. Where do we find the magistrates? Do they have a website or something?"

Naomi and Miranda laughed.

Clark smiled. "Petition them in person. There's a Fae

legal hangout on the south side of the city near Camden. I'll give you directions. Go there and plead your case."

Quinn nodded. As strange as the idea sounded, it felt right somehow. The court had been fair to her. They hadn't forced her and Tadpole to fight to the death. After hearing all she and Avery had to present, maybe they'd side with her again.

"Give us the address. We'll go there this afternoon."

CHAPTER TWENTY-TWO

Quinn checked the address on her phone again. Avery leaned forward in the passenger seat to look at the line of boarded-up row homes along the street.

"Are you sure this is where Clark told us to come?"

Quinn nodded. "See, this is the right address. It's that house with the blue door right there."

"But the windows are boarded up. There are boards across the front door, too. There's no way in."

Turning off the car, Quinn said, "Let's get out and look around. Maybe there's another way in. Remember, not everything is as it seems.."

The pair left Clark's old sedan. Quinn pointed to a gate blocking the narrow gap between two of the homes. "We can get around back through there."

Quinn led the way. She had to yank hard twice to get the stubborn wooden gate to open. She held it for Avery, and they walked through the gap between buildings. It emerged into an overgrown yard full of knee-high grass.

Broken furniture and old tires littered the small rectangular patch of ground.

"This doesn't look much like the home of the Fae court," Avery said. "Maybe there's another place with a similar address."

"You could be right. Let's just check the back of the house with the blue door before we go."

Quinn walked through a gap in the broken fence between the two yards and over to the back steps of their building. The paint flaked and peeled from the door in front of her. She reached for the knob. To her surprise, it was unlocked and opened easily. She waved Avery over, and the two of them walked into the home together.

The transition between what the outside appeared to be and what they encountered inside took them to another time and place. The room had the feel of an old Victorian pub with complex custom ironwork around the room, coupled with fine woodwork and carving. Lamps with colorful stained-glass shades provided muted illumination for the small round tables spread along the wall opposite the bar.

A tall Fae woman stood behind the bar. She dried a glass mug with a white linen cloth and set it on the shelf before turning to greet the newcomers.

"Don't get many humans in here anymore. The neighborhood discourages sightseers. Are you lost?"

"No," Quinn answered. "I came looking for the chief magistrate of the Fae court. Is she here?"

A gruff male voice interrupted the bartender before she could answer. "What would someone such as you have to say to a person from the high court?" Darkness shrouded the area where the voice came from. Quinn hadn't noticed anyone sitting there when she came in. Now that she stared at the area, she could make out a tall form in the shadows.

Quinn turned to the shadows. "That's between the magistrate and me. I ask again, is she here?"

"I don't think we want to bother her with the trivial concerns of a human girl who hasn't yet seen, what, twenty years?"

"I'm going to have to insist." Quinn moved her right hand, pulling back the front of her leather jacket. The move revealed the inverted Bowie slung in the shoulder holster.

"Are you threatening me, girl?" The Fae man stood. He wore a long black overcoat over a dark brown business suit. He reached into his coat and slid a foot of bare steel from a sword sheathed beneath it.

Avery laid a hand on Quinn's arm. "I think we all need to take a breath." She turned to the bartender. "Miss, please tell the magistrate that the city's Huntress clan leader is here to see her. I'm sure she'll meet with us."

The bartender nodded to the man in the corner. "That's her chief clerk. All requests go through him."

"Great," Avery muttered. She cast a glance at Quinn. "Did you have to threaten him?"

Quinn shrugged. "I didn't know." She returned her gaze to the man, who was still standing, although he'd sheathed his blade. He had the smile of someone who knew he held the upper hand.

"Sir, I think we got off on the wrong foot. As my friend said, I am the Huntress, clan leader here in Baltimore. We have urgent business with Her Honor. Please advise the magistrate we are here."

"I will not. Nothing you have to say is important enough to interrupt her duties."

Quinn steeled herself to fight the guy if that was what it took. She had to speak to the woman who'd overseen her trial. She was the closest thing to a fair-minded Fae she'd ever met.

She opened her mouth to tell the man what she thought of his assessment of the importance of her mission, but she never got the chance to speak.

"Stop," a woman shouted from the door at the end of the bar.

All eyes turned in that direction. An old Fae woman in a navy blue velvet robe stood there.

Quinn recognized her and bowed. "Your Honor. We have asked to speak with you on a private matter of some urgency."

"So I hear," the woman said. "My clerk is sometimes overzealous in the way he protects my time these days. He knows I do not have the energy I had a few centuries ago. Still, he should have come to me with your request, given your unique history with the court."

The clerk's eyes darkened at being admonished in front of mere humans.

The magistrate beckoned to Quinn and Avery. "Come with me. I will hear what you have to say."

The clerk glared at Quinn. She returned it with a sickly sweet smile and followed the magistrate into the back room. Avery was right behind her.

The room behind the bar looked like an old-school

legal office, with rows of books lining shelves on all four walls. Above them were rolls of what Quinn assumed were scrolls stacked to the ceiling. The magistrate walked behind the desk to a worn leather chair.

"Sit, please."

Quinn and Avery sat in the two chairs facing the desk and glanced at each other, nervous now that they were here.

"Tell me what's so urgent that you risked angering a man who belongs to one of the oldest Fae dynasties."

Quinn swallowed hard and took a deep breath. "Your Honor, I remembered your fair and even-handed treatment during my recent trial."

"I did nothing but follow the law."

"I understand, and that is why we have come to you today. We believe two members of the Fae royal families have joined a plot to open a gate to the netherworld."

If Quinn expected surprise to show on the woman's face, she was disappointed. The magistrate didn't even twitch.

"That's a serious charge. How do you know such a thing to be true?"

"It is information my associate and I have put together over time."

The magistrate nodded. "That doesn't have the sound of convincing evidence. Still, you made the effort to see me. Tell me what you have discovered."

Over the next twenty minutes, Quinn and Avery took turns laying out the entire plot as they understood it. Avery talked about her discovery of notes belonging to Gemma. She told how the notes discussed the plans to use Hunter-trained women to assist with ancient magic to remove the barriers between the worlds and open the gateway.

Quinn testified to her discovery of the Dark Fae plot while she was out with Gil and Terrence in western Maryland. She even mentioned the things she learned during her talks with Chessie, the ancient dragon in the bay.

When they both finished, the old woman nodded. She stared at her hands, clasped on the desk, for some time before she answered. The silence weighed heavily on Quinn, making her fidget in her chair.

Finally, the magistrate spoke. "Your accusations are serious. Do you have the names of the royals you lay them against?"

"I do, Your Honor," Quinn said. "They are Princess Filippa and Princess Aurora. I do not know their house names."

"I see." Once again, the magistrate was silent for a time. When she spoke again, it was with sadness in her eyes. "You have laid out an interesting and compelling case against the two princesses and this human woman, Gemma Beckingsly. At another time, it might even be a firm case."

She paused again and then sighed. "However, in this situation, since you accuse two who are not just members of the royal Fae lines, but princesses of their houses, I must decline to rule."

Quinn couldn't believe what the woman had said. "What do you mean, 'decline?' You said our case was strong."

"I said it *might* be strong. It is the ones accused who cause a problem for your case. For those so highly placed in their families, we must have incontrovertible evidence." She looked at Avery. "You mentioned notes and letters linking one of the princesses to Miss Beckingsly. Do you have them to submit as evidence?"

"Uh, no, Your Honor. I do not. They were destroyed in the fight to reach Baltimore with some precious cargo."

"What about the other things you both have testified about? Do you have any proof beyond your own words and memories?"

Quinn's jaw dropped. "Like what? Isn't our testimony enough?"

"No, I'm afraid it is not."

"So, you don't believe us or any of this?"

The woman shook her head. "I did not say that. I fear every word you say is true, and that there is indeed significant danger on our doorstep. Unfortunately, your evidence is not strong enough for me to take direct action against their highnesses or their agents. I'm sorry."

Quinn's fury burned deep inside. "You refuse to do anything to help us?"

"I cannot, Huntress. You must find the solution yourself. That is the calling of the Hunters of old. They joined together to fight that which was outside the law. Now that ancient calling falls to you."

Avery put a hand on Quinn's arm before she said anything more. "Magistrate, ma'am, you're aware that if we cannot stop them, this world as we know it will end and demon Fae will once more roam this land?"

"I am aware of the consequences. That does not mean I'm free to bend the law to make it fit the evidence. It is the evidence that must meet the standards of the law, not the other way around. For everything else, it falls to those such as you and the clan to stop what might happen."

Quinn shifted her arm out from under Avery's quieting hand and stood. "Come on, Avery. This was a complete waste of time. I thought we'd find justice. Instead, I find a reason to kill every suspected Dark Fae I see. At least that way, some of them will be bad guys." Quinn glared at the magistrate as her hand shifted to reach for her Bowie.

Avery stepped in front of Quinn, meeting her eye to eye. "No. That's not the answer. She's been honest with us about what she can and cannot do. She is not our enemy. There may be others who deserve our blades, but not this woman."

The old magistrate nodded but said nothing.

Quinn and Avery headed for the door.

As Quinn was about to pull it open, the magistrate said, "The test of tests is laid before you, Huntress. May you find strength in the members of your unique clan to see it through to the end."

Quinn glanced back at the woman. "The blood from what is coming is on your hands."

Sadness filled the old woman's eyes. "That is my charge, girl. In the end, the blood is always on my hands. Be true to your calling. May you find the path that leads to the light."

Quinn had had enough of the cryptic words for one day. She stormed into the bar, with Avery right behind her. They left without saying another word, walking straight to the door.

The Fae clerk talked on a cell phone in the corner, watching as they left. His following gaze didn't escape Quinn's attention.

Back in the car, Quinn pulled away from the curb and started cursing. "That woman as much as admitted the princesses were about to end the world, and she didn't do a thing."

"She did do something. She gave you permission to do whatever you need to do. You've got a pass to fight and kill two princesses if you want. That's a huge deal, Quinn. She really was on our side."

"Maybe, but did you see her clerk, Avery? When we left, he was talking to someone and watching us closely. That old biddy might be on our side. Her clerk wasn't. I'm willing to bet he was talking to Gemma or one of the princesses, reporting on our failure to stop them."

"You think he's a Dark Fae?"

"I think it's worth looking into who he is. Maybe Clark or Naomi can help us figure it out. He might lead us to the center of the plot here in Baltimore. Track them down through him, and we stop the entire thing before it starts."

"You want to follow him? That could be dangerous to do alone, Quinn."

"Yeah, ordinarily that would be true, but they've screwed up because they think they're only facing me. There are two angry Huntresses in the city now. I think it's time to show them what that means."

Avery smiled. "Okay, I'm interested. What did you have in mind?"

"You'll see. Let's get back and talk to the others first, especially Taylor. There are some things we need before my plan will work."

CHAPTER TWENTY-THREE

"So that's the plan," Quinn said to the assembled clan members sitting in straight-backed chairs arranged in a circle inside the ceremonial chamber. "Avery and I go into VR together and track this guy back to Gemma and the two princesses."

Taylor said, "Avery's never been in the VR. I'm not sure I can put together a rig for you both soon enough."

"Don't let me down now, T. You put together a rig for a baby dragon in a day. I'm sure adding one for a person will be easier than that. You have all that spare VirSync gear. It's time to use it."

Taylor shook her head and stared at the ceiling as if she were counting something in her mind.

Miranda said, "It takes a lot of power to activate the magic in the VR system, Quinn. The dragon was a smaller creature, which made it easier. Two full-sized adults might be a problem even for Taylor. She's become a powerful mage, but this might be too much for her to manage. You said it took one or two spellcasters and their magic per candidate when you both worked at VirSync. There might be a reason for that."

"I need you two to figure it out. I need Avery there with me on this. If I get into the mess I think I will, it's going to take both of us to fight off the demon-kinder and others Gemma has with her."

Avery smiled. "We'll show them what the two of us can do together. I'm looking forward to fighting side by side with you again."

Naomi leaned back in her chair. "If you will take Avery, why not take me instead? I'm Hunter-trained, too."

Taylor shook her head. "It won't work for you, Naomi. You're undead. The negative energy of your being would cancel out the additional life energy infusing the system. At best, you'd stay on the workshop table and not go anywhere. At worst, you'd end up dusted into your component atoms as soon as I cast the first spell."

"Well, we can't have that," Quinn said. "Besides, I need you and Clark to be ready to come in as backup if we need it. We know they're somewhere in the city, or at least close by. We'll make our move at night and track the guy to the others. You and Clark can come to our location as soon as we know where we're going."

Naomi did a poor job hiding her disappointment, but she nodded to accept the assignment as part of the backup team.

Quinn nodded. "Then it's settled. How soon can you figure out the details, T?"

Taylor and Miranda exchanged glances. Judging from the doubtful expression on the ghost's face, she didn't think much of Quinn's idea. Taylor seemed more determined.

"If it'll work at all, I'll know as soon as I wire in the second rig for Avery." She glanced at her phone, checking the time. "It will take me at least a day to get the new rig online. Check with me tomorrow afternoon. I should know more by then."

Avery smiled. "Good. That'll give Quinn and me a chance to figure out someone to watch the girls and help them get to bed on time. Miranda and Taylor will be tied up here. Clark and Naomi will be on the road tracking us."

"What about Tadpole?" Naomi suggested.

"What about him?" Avery asked. "He gets along well enough with them, but you think he's up to watching all six by himself?"

"Why not? He's watching them now while we have this meeting."

Clark said, "That's different, Naomi. We're just down the hall from them. We left them watching a movie projected on the wall in the training room. The movie's doing the babysitting right now, not the orc."

Naomi shook her head. "Have you seen him with them? They adore him, and he's been very gentle and beyond careful with them. He'd never let them come to any harm. You know that."

"I don't know, Mom. Clark's right. Social services would have a cow if they knew we were using a trained killer to babysit those kids."

"Well," Naomi said, "what about a blood-sucking vampire? Or a ghost? Or a werewolf? I mean, we don't have a lot of options here. It's not the optimal answer, but we should consider it."

Quinn did. She thought about asking Juni or some of the other waitresses at O'Malley's to help. That idea was shot down right away. They were too busy to spare anyone during the evening shift.

She leaned back in her seat and craned her neck so she could see down the hall to the training room. The flickering light of the projector was the only illumination coming down the corridor. It was quiet, which Quinn found strange. Usually, when they played with Tadpole, they ran around making a lot of noise, even when a show was playing.

She leaned forward again. "How long have they been back there watching the movie?"

Taylor said, "I set them up with a playlist and showed Brea how to click on the movies on a tablet to stream them to the projector. They've been there for about two hours, maybe longer."

Naomi smiled. "See, not a peep. They're fine."

"I guess so," Avery said. "What are they watching? Usually there's laughter or something. I've learned that silence is not a good sign unless they're asleep."

Taylor shrugged. "I downloaded the top twenty kid shows from an online service. They're all cartoons or shows that are appropriate, I assure you."

"I'm not questioning that. I'm wondering if it's a little too quiet." Avery stood. "I'll be right back."

Quinn stood too. "We're done here. I'll come with you. Maybe they're all asleep."

Avery nodded, and they walked down the hall to the

training room. The projector sat in the middle of the room on a cardboard box. The images on the screen were from an animated movie. It wasn't one Quinn was familiar with.

Quinn didn't study the screen for long. She was more concerned about the fact that the room was empty.

"Where are they?" Avery asked.

"I'm sure they're fine." Quinn looked around. "Listen. I hear voices."

The murmur came from the other side of the stout armory door.

"What are they doing in the armory?" Avery wondered aloud.

"Let's find out."

When Quinn opened the door and looked inside, her jaw dropped. A fully armored Tadpole stood at the far end of the room. He held the gold spear from the Crystal Well in his gauntleted grip. In front of him, arrayed in appropriately sized armor, stood all six girls. They also held various weapons. Brea held a staff topped by a long-bladed sword-spear. Kami hefted a tomahawk that looked more like a battle axe in her small two-handed grip. The others carried weapons of their own.

"What the hell is going on here?" Avery asked, not bothering to hide the anger in her tone. "Girls, put those weapons down now, and be careful while you do it. I don't want to have to take any of you in for stitches. I know how sharp those things are."

"Hi, Quinn," Tadpole said, lifting the visor on his helmet. "We were just trying on the armor I found to fit the girls. You said to take care of them and make sure they were safe."

Quinn rolled her eyes. "I meant *you* were supposed to protect them and make sure they did nothing dangerous. I didn't want you to hand them every sort of sharp object in the armory and deck them out in metal shirts."

None of the girls had put down the weapons. They all held them in grips that looked like they knew exactly how to use them.

One of the twins—Quinn thought it was Jordi—said, "We trained with weapons all the time at the *estancia*. We never had cool armor to wear, though. It's heavy, but I can see how it would help in an actual fight."

"That's not the point," Avery said. "If you're going to handle dangerous things like this, we need to know about it first. Now, give the weapons back to Tadpole so he can put them away. Then you can help each other get out of the armor. Got it?"

"Yes, ma'am," the six said in unison.

Tadpole's shoulders slumped as he took off his helmet and set it on the floor. The girls handed their weapons to him one at a time.

Quinn went over to him as he returned the various blades, axes, and spears to their racks along the walls.

"Tadpole, what were you thinking? These things are for training warriors."

"I didn't know it was wrong, Quinn. I'm sorry. Is it because they're so young? I don't understand since I started training at three, and Kami is already six. I've seen them practice. They're all very good; better than I was at their ages."

"I'm not angry with you. I wish you had asked permission first, though. I know you were only doing what you thought I wanted. I have to remember to be more careful when I ask you to do something."

"You're really not mad?"

Quinn put her hand on his massive forearm. "No. We're all still learning. We were just talking about whether we could leave you alone to watch the six of them."

Tadpole's eyes brightened. His head bobbed up and down in an enthusiastic nod. "You absolutely can, Quinn. I would be extra careful and make sure nothing happened to them, I promise."

"It's something we still need to think about, bud. After this, Avery will be hard to convince you're the man for the job."

"I won't do this again. I always follow your rules. All we will do is watch movies if that's what you want. You can give me a list with everything to do, and I'll follow it."

Quinn laughed. "You can't read, buddy."

"You could draw pictures for me."

"I could." She shook her head, chuckling at the thought of what that list would look like. "I'll think about it. Go change out of your armor. I need to talk to Avery."

The other Huntress stood at the far end of the armory, having a stern talk with the girls. Judging from their expressions, they were as clueless about what was wrong as Tadpole had been.

Quinn walked over. "Avery, send them into the other room to watch the rest of the movie. I want to talk to you."

"You heard what she said. Go into the other room and stay there. Don't go anywhere else until I get there." She glanced at Quinn. "Are you going to tell me to relax?"

"No, but they are all doing really well. No one got hurt,

and they told you they've had weapons training. I'm not saying we should make this a regular thing, especially unsupervised by anyone but Tadpole, but if they're staying here and will be part of the clan, we'll have to train them eventually."

"What did you tell the orc?"

"I told him I wasn't angry with him." When Avery made a face, Quinn added, "He's sorry, Avery. He takes things very literally. It's my fault for not being more specific. I have to remember to ask him questions to make sure he understands what we want him to do."

"I'm not sure, Quinn. I don't want to screw this up, but I'm learning as I go too. I just know I can't let anything happen to them."

"Hey, me either. It looks like you've done a decent job so far, though. They seem like good kids. Let's just do the best we can. In the end, that's all anybody can expect."

"I guess so." Avery shrugged. "I want to sit with them for a while to make sure they're settled."

"I'll come with you. We can watch the movie together."

Avery reached out, her fingers intertwining with Quinn's. Quinn gave a squeeze, which brought a brief smile to her girlfriend's face. The two of them went back into the darkened training room and sat on the mat behind the girls as they watched the show. Soon all were laughing at the antics on the screen. For a moment, Quinn thought things were almost normal. She knew it wouldn't last, but she savored it while it was happening.

CHAPTER TWENTY-FOUR

I t turned out Quinn's belief in Taylor's magical and technical abilities wasn't unfounded. Not only had the tech witch been able to bring the second full-sized VR rig online faster than expected, but she also got a hit on a standard facial recognition bot she'd deployed to search for Gemma.

With Clark's and Naomi's help, they were able to confirm the face on the convenience store surveillance video was Gemma. She was definitely hiding somewhere in town near the Fae quarter. Now it was time to see if the Fae magistrate's clerk would lead them to her.

In the workshop, they had set a second table up for Avery beside the one Quinn used. Both women now sat on the edge of the tables facing each other. Taylor's desk was between them, with her triple computer monitors displaying program readouts. She had the system ramping up for both rigs.

"So, what's this like?" Avery asked.

"It's a little disorienting the first time you go in. Don't

worry, I'll be there right beside you. Just remember to call in on the commlink if you need anything or we get separated."

Avery's hand dropped to her waist to check the comm system belt pack. Her earpiece was in place, and they'd already verified everything worked.

"Relax," Quinn said. "This is just a recon mission. We follow the guy and hope he leads us to Gemma. If it looks promising, we can investigate further. If not, we can return and work on another plan."

"Easy for you to say. You've done this how many times?"

"Enough. I'm interested in what your experience is like in there. There are things I bring back to the real world from inside. Maybe you'll be able to do that too. If we get into a fight, remember what I told you about the HUD. It might help you access extra power and abilities."

Taylor looked up from her computer screens. "I'm all set. You two ready?"

Avery and Quinn both nodded. Avery added, "Let's do this."

Quinn shifted so she could lay back on the table. Avery did the same. Quinn settled the headset goggles in place and stared at the workshop's stone ceiling, waiting for Taylor to begin.

The tech witch started chanting.

The familiar tugging began at the back of Quinn's mind. She relaxed and waited for the transition. The process seemed to take longer this time. Instead of the quick drop she expected, Quinn fell backward into the blackness in slow motion. The last thing she heard was a gasp of surprise from Avery.

Quinn woke in the alley on the block next to the hidden Fae bar. She knelt in place and gathered herself, tamping down the headache that always accompanied the transition. It was worse than the last trip, but it was nowhere near as bad as it had been the first few times.

"Oh, my God," Avery said. "It worked."

Quinn glanced to the right. Avery knelt there, twisting her head to get her bearings.

"I'm right here."

"This is amazing." She raised a hand to her forehead. "Except for the headache."

"Taylor is still trying to iron out the kinks on that one. It has something to do with our Huntress genes or something. It gets a little better every time she dials it in."

"You mean, it was worse?"

Quinn nodded. "I used to throw up as soon as I landed. It was bad." She changed the subject. "Bring up your HUD and check the icons and options."

Avery went through the process as Quinn walked her through the system. She didn't have any icons other than the map overlay. She had a stamina bar, but no blue mana bar. Quinn wasn't sure what to do to make the other icons appear for Avery. Taylor had said they might be unique to her. They didn't have the luxury to sit and play with it right now.

"Okay, time to get on with the mission. We'll see if you can at least dial up your strength the way I can next." Quinn pointed at the nearby roof of a row home. "I'll jump up to that ledge and then leap from there onto the neighboring rooftop. Draw on your stamina and try to follow me."

"I don't understand."

"Try this," Quinn said. "Say to yourself that you need to be stronger."

Avery looked doubtful, but she stared into space and said, "I need strength."

Quinn waited for a few seconds. "What happened? Anything?"

Avery shook her head. "You said the stamina thing lowered and gave you strength, right? Nothing happened to mine."

"Damn, I'd hoped all this would work for you the same way."

"At least it got me here. Remember that I trained as a Hunter growing up. Maybe this only works on latent powers."

Quinn shrugged. "Okay, we go with Plan B. I'll jump up there and find somewhere else you can jump up."

"I can push myself and jump almost that high normally."

Quinn remembered how fast Avery was in training bouts. Her Hunter abilities were fully realized. Maybe they'd work here, too.

"Okay, follow me."

Quinn drew on her stamina and boosted her strength and speed a little. She ran at the house across the alley, leaping at the last second. She planted a foot on the wall ten feet up and used it to spring the last bit to the ledge. It was an easy leap to the rooftop from there.

She turned in time to see Avery blur into motion, using her innate abilities. She got almost as high as Quinn did.

She had to stretch out to reach for the ledge with her fingers. Avery gripped the edge and pulled herself up the rest of the way. Another running leap brought her onto the roof with Quinn.

"Not quite as graceful as you, but I managed it."

"We'll get Taylor to work on it from her end. Maybe it's in the magic she uses."

Avery shook her head. "I prefer it this way. My abilities seem to be working normally. This way, I won't be stumbling around trying to figure things out."

Quinn couldn't argue with the other woman's logic. "Okay, let's hide and head across the rooftops until we can see the back of the home with the Fae bar."

Leading the way, Quinn muttered "mist" to slip into the shadows. Beside her, Avery did whatever she did to activate the same ability. Quinn had given Avery the amulet she now wore, but she'd developed her skills without it.

Studying the rooftop beside her, Quinn could still see Avery's shadowed outline, but no one else would notice the shifting shadows running above them.

The two of them leapt from roof to roof until they reached the home next to the Fae bar. They settled into place behind a brick chimney, where they could see the rear door.

Quinn tapped her earpiece. "We're in position, T. Everything worked pretty well. Clark, Mom, are you there?"

"We are," Naomi answered. "Just tell us when you locate the eventual destination. We'll start that way as soon as you have it."

"Will do," Quinn said. "One of us will let you know if

anything strange happens outside of the plan. Until then, we're out."

Quinn shut down the commlink and glanced at Avery. "You still good?"

"I am. I'm still amazed at how this system works. You could go just about anywhere with it."

"The farthest we've tried was when I came down to help you with that attack in North Carolina. In theory, though, you're right."

Avery nodded at the door as they watched. "You want to settle in and take turns? That way, one of us can get some rest."

"That works. You want to go first?"

Avery nodded again. "I'll tap you on the shoulder if anything changes."

Quinn shifted until she was fully behind the chimney and settled her back against the bricks. She relaxed and let her mind wander as she stared at the lights of the Baltimore skyline.

She must have dozed a little because she started when Avery tapped her shoulder.

Avery held a finger to her lips and pointed down.

Quinn dialed in her shadow-hiding again. It had lapsed as she dozed. She moved from behind the chimney to look down. The clerk and the bartender walked through the tall grass in the unkempt backyard and into the alley. Once there, the bartender turned one way, and the tall Fae clerk went the other. He strode away from their position.

"We need to keep up so we don't lose him," Quinn whispered. She pointed to the adjacent roof leading to the next set of connected row homes. "Follow me."

She drew some more strength, ran for the roof's edge, and jumped the gap without a problem. Avery was right behind her, so Quinn kept going. Wreathed in shadow, the two Huntresses followed the clerk to wherever he was headed next.

He stopped at the corner store and came out with a small paper bag. He stuffed it into the pocket of his short overcoat and continued down the street.

Soon the neighborhood turned into better-kept homes, and then they entered a small industrial district. Quinn and Avery had to drop to street level to follow him.

He led them to a large two-story building with metal siding. It looked like a painter's building, though the sign on the side of the building had faded and was in disrepair.

The clerk knocked on the door twice and waited.

The door opened and he entered, letting it close behind him. She brought up her map overlay. The HUD filled with a view of the building and the immediate surroundings. Inside the building was a collection of moving red dots.

"That's got to be the place," Quinn said.

"How do you know?"

"I can see enemies when I'm this close. It's on the map overlay. Bring yours up."

Avery stared into space for a second and shook her head. "Nope. I see you and me on the map and the surrounding buildings, but nothing else."

"Well, take my word for it. That place is chock-full of baddies."

"How many?"

"At least ten. That's more than we can handle alone. Let me call Clark and Mom."

Quinn tapped her earpiece, but nothing happened. There was a brief crackle of static, but that was it. "You try. My batteries must be low or something."

Avery tapped her earpiece and shook her head. "All I have is constant low static. That's it."

Quinn checked her belt pack. When she pressed the button once, the tiny LED lit up green. "It's not my battery. Maybe something around here is interfering with transmissions. We should move back until we can reconnect."

Quinn turned to move away from the corner behind which they hid. She stopped as four figures stepped out of the shadows behind them, blocking the way.

"Going somewhere, Huntress?" The brunette demon-kinder leading the group asked. She pulled a curved dagger from her boot.

Avery spun. "Quinn, there are people coming this way from the print shop. We're trapped." She brought her arm around, her sword appearing in her hand.

Quinn didn't wait for the others to act. She charged, drawing her Bowie. She and Avery had to break through fast and get away from whatever had jammed their comms.

Using her forward momentum, Quinn dropped to the ground, sliding in the loose gravel as she ducked beneath the swipe of the curved dagger.

Overextended, the brunette tried to twist to the side to avoid Quinn's blade. She was unnaturally fast, like all the Hunter demon-kinder were, but not fast enough.

The blessed silver alloy hissed as it sliced deep into the woman's side. Tendrils of smoke escaped the wound, followed by dripping black ichor.

The demon-kinder gasped and went to one knee. She

was down, but probably not out of the fight. Quinn had to keep going and hope it would take the woman time to recover. Blade clashed on blade as more attacks swept in at her.

Luckily, she wasn't on her own. She parried a heavy saber stroke aimed at her neck. It left her exposed so she couldn't get around in time to stop in the incoming tanto blade aimed at her back.

Avery's sword drove in just in time to bat the blade away, and her follow-up stroke took off the demon-kinder's arm midway between wrist and elbow. The woman howled in pain. She groped on the ground for the dropped weapon with her other hand.

Quinn's broad blade came down at the back of her neck, severing the spine, and the woman dropped to the pavement, unmoving.

"Keep going," Quinn called. "We've got to break contact before the others come around the corner to help them."

Avery took down one of the remaining two but caught a narrow slash across her back in the process.

Quinn's roundhouse kick dropped the final demon-kinder. Lifting Avery upright, Quinn supported her as the pair raced across the street before turning the corner of another building.

Shouts behind them announced reinforcements had arrived. Quinn didn't think anyone had spotted them turning the corner, but they'd search this way eventually.

She stopped and grabbed the knob on the nearest building. "It's locked. Come on."

Avery said, "Wait." She reached out with one hand and spread her fingers wide, rotating her wrist.

Quinn picked up on a slight glow of magic. Then the knob turned, and the door popped open.

"Quick, get inside." Quinn shoved Avery in ahead of her and checked the street behind them before slipping inside and closing the door. "I heard voices, so they're close, but no one saw us."

She checked the door from the inside as shouts on the other side grew louder. Spotting what she'd been looking for, Quinn reached up to a sliding metal bolt at the top of the door and pushed it into place.

The voices ran past their hiding place and faded.

Quinn stepped back, looking around.

Avery leaned against the wall, her breathing heavy as she grimaced.

"Here, let me look at that," Quinn said.

"It'll be fine, I just need to tamp the pain down."

"Nonsense, turn around. We have a break now. We might not get one later. Until we can get to someplace where Taylor can pick up our signals, we're stuck here."

Avery turned so she leaned against the wall with one shoulder. The blade had sliced away the bottom half of her shirt and left a gash running from her right shoulder blade diagonally down to her lower ribs. Blood ran down her back, smeared with dirt from the metal wall.

"We need to clean this up, then I can heal it." She spotted an old porcelain washtub against the wall nearby. The rusty faucet above it looked older than she was, but maybe it still worked.

Quinn tore the rest of the bottom half of Avery's shirt away. "Stay here and try not to move."

Walking to the sink, Quinn tried the faucet. The lever

seemed rusted shut, and for a moment, she was sure she'd break it off. It finally twisted, and water flowed. It was brown and rusty at first, but then it ran clear.

Soaking the scrap of Avery's shirt, Quinn returned and cleaned the wound and the area around it. The bleeding had slowed to a steady ooze, which helped.

Having done the best she could, Quinn laid both hands flat on Avery's back. "I'll use my reserves to close up the wound. That's the best I can do for now. I'm afraid to access nearby ley lines directly. That kind of magical draw might point Gemma and her allies to our location."

"Don't drain yourself too much. I'm quite all right, really."

"Hold still and be quiet. I'll be careful, but we'll be better off if you're able to move well."

Quinn drew on her mana store, supplementing it with her stamina, and focused her energy on the open wound beneath her palms.

A warm, faint golden glow showed around the outline of her hand. Avery sucked in a sharp breath as the healing flow took effect.

Quinn took her hands away. The angry red scar left behind still looked painful, but at least the edges of the skin had closed. It would heal on its own in time, especially with her Hunter background.

"How's that feel?"

"Better. You did too much."

"Shut up. I did what I had to. We're not out of this yet, and if you think I'm doing all the fighting from here on out, you are mistaken."

Avery smiled. "Fair enough. Now what?"

Quinn checked the comm again. Still nothing. She and Avery couldn't even hear each other transmitting on the circuit. "Whatever's dampening our system is still there. The last time we called was all the way back at the Fae bar. That's blocks from here. Who knows how wide the area of effect is?"

"How did they know to use it? Did they expect us?"

Quinn shook her head. "I don't know how. Gemma and the Fae know some of our tech capabilities, though. That has to figure into their planning. Maybe stopping our communications is part of a bigger issue. Maybe it's hampering their ability to recall us via the VR rigs."

"So we're stuck here. Great."

"It's not so bad," Quinn said. "As long as they think we got away, we can hide here. Once things calm down, we'll slip out and make our way out of the no-fly zone."

Avery smiled. "You're always such an optimist. How do you do that?"

"I have too much to look forward to. I only just got you back. Come with me. I saw what looked like a break room. We can sit down and rest for a bit. Once some time passes, I'll look around the building to make sure no one's outside. Then we can escape."

Avery and Quinn walked to the door near the sink. There were a few tables and folding chairs inside. They weren't all that comfortable, but they were better than nothing. The pair of them settled down to wait it out.

CHAPTER TWENTY-FIVE

Taylor cringed as Clark shouted again.

"Well, where are they?"

"I told you. I don't know. It's like they disappeared off the map."

Naomi leaned over to look over Taylor's shoulder. "You mean like they're dead?"

"No, nothing like that. Unless someone dropped a bomb on them, they wouldn't wink out simultaneously like that." Taylor pointed as she played back their tracking data. "Look. They're moving across the neighborhood toward this industrial park here. Just before they cross this street, poof, they're gone."

Clark growled, "I don't like poof. That means they could be anywhere."

Miranda came to Taylor's aid. "Use whatever word you want then, Clark. They reached that location, and then we lost tracking. That could mean anything."

"Can't you increase the power or something?" Naomi asked.

"It's not that easy," Miranda interjected.

"Besides, I tried that already," Taylor said. "Something pushed back when I increased the magical energy flowing into the interface."

"Pushed back, how?" Clark asked.

"It was like I was trying to force my way into a rubber ball from the outside. The harder I pushed, the more resistance I met."

Naomi said, "That sounds like protection magic. Could it be a counterspell?"

"Maybe, but it's not just my magic. We can't reach them on the comm system. It worked fine just days ago in North Carolina."

"A magic and electronic counterspell?" Naomi asked.

Clark took a deep breath and scratched his chin. "Just because we haven't seen it before, it doesn't mean it doesn't exist. Look at all we've been able to do with this VR stuff."

He stared at the screens for a few seconds, then started for the door.

Taylor asked. "Where are you going?"

"It's still a few hours until dawn. Naomi and I are going down there to test our theory. You keep track of us, and we'll do the same. If we lose signal, we'll backtrack until we get you back again. Between the two of us, we should be able to sense any magic."

"Be careful," Miranda cautioned.

Naomi nodded. "We will. You two stay here and keep trying to locate them."

Taylor smiled. "I won't give up on this end. Besides, they could show up at any moment. I'm holding out for simple comm failure."

"Both of them?" Clark asked.

"It's not probable, but it is possible."

Clark looked at Naomi. "Coming?"

"Right behind you."

The two left Taylor and Miranda alone in the workshop. Taylor sat back down and started tapping on her keyboard, trying to find a way past whatever had swallowed their VR signal. The more she worked, the angrier she got until she couldn't hold back, and her werewolf's claws emerged from her nail beds.

The clack, clack, clack of the sharp claws on the keyboard didn't faze Taylor. She planned on doing whatever she had to do if it led to finding Quinn again. She kept coding until Miranda floated between her and the screens, partially blocking her view with her translucent face.

"Taylor, stop right now. I mean it. You need to get yourself under control."

The tech witch looked up from the keyboard, trying to understand what Miranda was saying to her. The words made little sense.

"It's too close to the full moon for you to let stress get to you like this. Refocus your attention on me. Listen to my voice. Come on, you can do it."

As Miranda continued to soothe her with gentle requests, Taylor's mind cleared, and she realized how close to fully shifting she was. Coarse hair had sprouted along her arms, her claws had grown in, and she ran her tongue over her elongated canines.

Taking a deep breath, she closed her eyes and settled down with calming exercises she'd learned from the local pack leader since she'd first shifted. When she opened her eyes, her arms and hands looked human again.

She glanced at Miranda, still hovering in between her and the three monitors. "Sorry. I guess I lost control a little."

"I'd say. You haven't slipped like that in a while. Come away from the keyboard for a minute or two. Let Clark and Naomi take the lead on this. They'll contact us when they get close. With fresh eyes on the ground, maybe we'll get a better handle on what we're looking at."

"Sounds like a plan," Taylor said. She picked up the comm headset and walked out from behind the monitors. "Let's go. I need to get something to eat and drink while I wait. That partial shift used up a lot of my reserves."

CHAPTER TWENTY-SIX

C lark made a left turn and pulled over on the street a block away from where Quinn and Avery had dropped out of VR. Naomi alternated between watching the street and staring at the comm unit's tiny gray and black signal indicator.

Clark glanced at her. "What's it say now?"

"Still three out of four bars. But we knew that. They called us from this location after they arrived."

"Let me pull up the map on my phone and look at it. I need to pinpoint the location where Taylor said they disappeared."

He scrolled the map until he found the right area and zoomed in on the street on which they'd parked. He leaned over so Naomi could see.

"This is where we are." He slid his finger across the screen to show the area around them. "It's mostly residential and pretty run down, at least to outward appearances. The Fae like it that way. The few places I've visited look rough on the outside and pretty swanky on the inside."

Naomi pointed to an area to the south. "This is where Taylor said they disappeared."

Clark scrolled down and zoomed in again as far as he could. "Looks like a manufacturing or industrial zone. Those buildings are too large to be homes, and the extra parking areas are probably for contractor vehicles."

Naomi leaned back, staring out the windshield at the dilapidated row homes around them. "So, all these homes are really occupied by the local Fae community?"

"Most of them, yes. Why?"

"If Gemma came to town with a sizeable group of demon-possessed human Hunters, would the local Fae hide them and keep them a secret?"

"A few might. The ones that are in on Filippa's and Aurora's evil plot would for sure, but I can't believe that is more than a few of the locals. The others have businesses and family roots here. They wouldn't do anything to create chaos in their own community."

"That's what I'm thinking, too. They're probably all staying together with whichever dark Fae they've contacted locally."

Clark looked at the map again. "Let's head that way and see what happens to the signal. If you're right, it'll drop out before we get there."

Naomi nodded and held up the comm so they could both watch the signal. He pulled away from the curb and turned right, heading south toward the business park. They'd gone three blocks and were nearing the edge of the residential neighborhood when Naomi held up her hand.

"Stop. The signal is gone. One second I had three bars, then nothing." She showed him the comm pack.

Clark did a U-turn and drove back a half block. Naomi nodded. The signal had returned.

Naomi tapped her earpiece. "We found the dampening area. It's south of their original location, right where you said it was."

"Any sign of them?" Taylor asked.

"No, but now we know where to look," Clark said. "Any change on your end?"

"We just got back into the workshop. I had to get some food and stretch. Let me look."

Clark sat waiting until Taylor's voice returned a few seconds later.

"Nope, things are the same as when you left. I can see you both via GPS, but they're not on the map."

"Okay," Naomi said. "I'm going to walk that way again. I'll leave my comm unit on just in case the field dissipates."

"I'm not staying here while you search for them," Clark grumbled. "We'll cover more ground with two of us."

"What if one of you gets into trouble?" Taylor asked.

"We'll remain in sight of each other," Naomi suggested. "That way, we can lend aid if needed."

"That'll work," Clark said. "Let's go."

Taylor said, "I'll keep trying to break through on this end. I'll let you know if I hear from them. This spell has been in place for at least an hour now. It can't last forever."

Taylor cut the connection, and Clark and Naomi got out.

Naomi pointed at the opposite side of the street. "I'll go that way, and you stay on this side. We'll check the buildings as we go. I think I can smell Quinn if I'm close enough to somewhere she's been recently."

Clark nodded. "Sounds like a plan." He could use targeting and tracking magic on his end, too. It might help him see where they'd gone.

Naomi got the first hit on the missing Huntresses. She caught his attention and waved him over. He crossed the broad street, racing to catch up with her.

"What is it?" he asked as he reached her side.

"Blood, and it's fresh. Someone tried to wash it away with a hose or a couple buckets of water, but they didn't do a very good job."

Clark studied the asphalt pavement where she pointed. He could still make out stains where someone or several someones lost a significant amount of blood.

"Any of it belong to our ladies?"

Naomi crouched and leaned forward, then moved to another spot and repeated the move. She stood and nodded. "At least some of this blood was Avery's, but the rest isn't blood at all, at least not anymore. It's corrupted somehow."

"Demon-kinder, then," Clark said. "That means it has to be Gemma and her crew." He scanned the nearby buildings. "There," he said, pointing at the metal siding on the nearest building. "That looks like a smear of blood."

Naomi followed him over. He could make out the slight crimson tint even at night under the streetlights. "They fought a group of demon-kinder back there and then got away or ran away. That's why it's been cleaned up. Gemma doesn't want to leave a mess out in the open for everyone to see."

Naomi stared down, beckoning Clark to follow her. She peered at the pavement as she moved along until she stopped at the corner. "There are a few tiny drops of blood on the sidewalk. It's just a drop here and there, but I can sense it if I concentrate." She scanned the sidewalk in both directions and then pointed left. "They turned here and went that way."

Clark looked back. "If they were trying to evade pursuit, that makes sense. This corner would break the line of sight. Keep going."

Naomi moved on and stopped by a steel door in the building's side. "They stopped here. Try the door."

Clark checked the handle. "It's locked. Did they keep going?"

Naomi continued down to the end of the building with Clark right behind her. She stopped.

"There's nothing after they stopped at that door."

"Then that's where they are. They must have gotten inside and locked it from there."

Returning to the door, Naomi shrugged. "What do we do, knock?"

"I wouldn't answer. Would you?"

"No, I guess not." Naomi looked at the two-story structure. "There must be another way in. Let's see what we can find."

"Let's circle the building in different directions. We'll meet up on the far side."

The two split up. Clark headed to the right and Naomi to the left. He moved faster since they'd already covered the first two sides. He turned up the street one block over. There was a fenced-in parking lot, empty except for an old trailer. The sign on the side showed a print shop had used it.

Naomi came from the other way. She picked up speed when she saw him. He pointed at a door with a sign reading Office over it. It was made of heavy steel with a large window in the top half. There were also two sliding overhead garage doors along the parking area.

"Jump the fence?" Naomi asked.

"I'll just pick the lock." Clark held the padlock holding the gate closed in one hand and passed his hand over it twice. On the second pass, the hasp popped open. He unwrapped the chain holding the gate closed, then he and Naomi walked across the lot to the office door.

"My turn," Naomi said. She turned and leaned against the door. After scanning the street for anyone out at this hour, she slammed her elbow backward into the window. Her heavy leather jacket kept her from getting cut. She cracked the sturdy security glass on the first strike and broke all the way through on the second.

She reached inside and unlocked the door, letting them in.

"That was subtle," Clark said as he passed her.

"I'm getting impatient. Avery's injured. Quinn might be, too."

"Don't borrow trouble. Let's find them first."

It didn't take long to search the small office area. They weren't there. A door led to the printer's warehouse. Old printing equipment lined the shop floor, with pallets of paper stacked near the garage doors.

They split up again until Naomi got his attention with a low whistle. He joined her by an old work sink.

"What did you find?"

"More blood smell here. I think they used the sink to clean up or maybe wash out Avery's wound."

"Good, so we were right. They came in here. That door is bolted from the inside. So, where are they?"

Naomi pointed to the door in the wall by the office. The word Crew was stenciled on the door.

Clark nodded.

He walked over and reached for the handle. As he started to open it, the door slammed outward, pushing him backward. He fell to the floor and reached for his sword.

"Quinn, stop, it's us," Naomi shouted.

Clark let go of his sword and stared up at the dark, partially hidden figure above him. The shadow glamor faded, revealing Quinn.

She reached down and offered him a hand up. "I'm glad to see you two."

"We're glad to see you as well," Naomi said. "Is Avery all right? I sensed her blood outside."

"I am, or I will be soon enough."

Quinn asked, "What about the demon-kinder? Did you see any outside?"

"Just traces of their foul blood," Clark said. "How long ago did you last hear or see them?"

"It's been at least an hour," Avery said. "Right?"

Quinn nodded. "We decided to lay low until they'd given up the chase. I guess they gave up sooner than we thought."

"There's no sign of them," Naomi confirmed.

Quinn pointed toward the printer's offices. "They came from a building a block farther down the street out front.

If they were there or still watching, I'd imagine they would have come after you too, if they were still around."

"But where did they go?" Avery asked.

"I guess we need to find out," Naomi said. "Avery, should we leave you here? We can come back after we check to see where they are."

"Not a chance. I'm well enough to lend a hand if needed."

Clark sighed. "Then let's go see where they are."

The four of them walked back through the office and out the gate to the sidewalk. Quinn pointed down the street. "They were in that second building there, the painter's shop."

"The lights are out," Naomi said.

Avery shook her head. "They were on before."

The four approached the building, taking their time. Clark tried to watch every direction at once, fearing a trick or trap. Nothing happened, though. They reached the building, and all was quiet. Quinn glanced through the office window.

"Anything?" Clark asked.

"No sign of them."

"I know what I saw," Avery insisted.

"We believe you," Naomi said. "But now we have a problem. Where did they go?"

Clark shook his head. It made little sense that they'd bug out if this was their local staging area. "I think we have to assume they've pushed up their plans after your scuffle with them on the street. That's what I'd do if I thought they had discovered me."

"Okay, but where will they put their plan into effect?" Avery asked.

"It has to be the Crystal Well," Quinn said. "That's been Gemma's and Filippa's focus since the beginning. Ever since we uncovered their plot, we keep going back there."

"It's close," Naomi said. "Only five minutes from here."

Clark glanced at Avery as they walked. She definitely favored her back. If they ran into trouble, she'd have to hold back.

"We have to follow them, Clark," Quinn said. "That's the only place they could have gone."

"I don't disagree, but you and Avery are still in VR. Can you stay in this long?"

"We can ask Taylor once we clear this dead zone," Quinn said. "I feel fine, and when we get there, I can recharge via the ley lines running beneath the Well."

Clark grimaced. He hated it when she did that. It made all kinds of noise for those who could sense such things. Still, they'd need Quinn at full strength if it came to a fight. Avery, too.

"Let's go. My car's this way. If we hurry, we might catch them before they begin whatever ritual they have planned."

CHAPTER TWENTY-SEVEN

Taylor saw Quinn's and Avery's comms come back online and keyed her mic seconds later. "Hey, you guys all right?"

Quinn answered, "We're good. We ran into trouble but got away clean. The problem is, so did they."

"Who, Gemma and her demon-kinder?"

"Yes. We think they got spooked when we found their hideout. Clark and Mom are here with us. We all agree they've pushed up their schedule. I'm pretty sure they're on the way to the Crystal Well to open the portal to the netherworld."

"That's not good," Taylor said. "How did you discover that was where they were going?"

"Just guessing," Quinn replied. "I mean, where else could it be?"

"I bet you're right. What do you want us to do?"

"You all hold down the fort there. Avery and I are remaining in the VR system for a little longer. At least in here, I can spot them on my map when we get close enough. That'll give us an advantage."

Miranda leaned close to the mic. "Be careful. It takes powerful magic to open a gate like that, especially with all the magical wards between the planes. It'll have side effects if it shuts down prematurely."

"We'll watch out. I'll check in again when we get closer before we go underground and lose the signal."

Quinn cut the connection, and Taylor leaned back. "At least Quinn and Avery are okay."

"Yeah," Miranda said, "but if they really *have* pushed up the timetable for releasing their spell, there could be powerful repercussions all over the city."

"You're right. I'd better go wake up Paddy. He might want to spread the word through his network so the city's supernatural leaders know to expect trouble." Taylor stood, holding out her arm for Sylvie to climb up to her shoulder. The dragon was curled up on the table where Quinn would reappear when she returned. "Come on, squirt. I'll see if we can get a treat for you from the kitchen."

"Eeeep."

Miranda laughed. "While you two do that, I'll look in on Tadpole and the girls. They should've all been tucked in their beds hours ago. I'm sure they're asleep, but it doesn't hurt to double-check."

Miranda turned left down the long tunnel leading to the Hunter chambers and Taylor turned right, passing through the hall and storerooms behind O'Malley's pub. She'd check his office and then the pub. Paddy might still be up. He liked to hang at the bar and watch late-night infomercials. He'd once told Taylor he was convinced his next pot o' gold would come from making one of his own.

Taylor almost reached the door leading to the pub when she heard the crash of breaking furniture and glass from the other side. Yanking the door open, she spotted shadowy figures racing through the darkened pub. Two of them wrestled with Paddy near the bar.

The shift to werewolf form started at the first sign of a threat. It brought her wolf's night vision online.

Two women held Paddy down atop the bar while a third pummeled the small man's face. There were at least a dozen others in the bar, and more coming in from the alley entrance. Taylor didn't know who to attack first.

Gemma entered and called orders to the invading forces. She pointed right at the storeroom door.

Taylor pulled the door closed and said, "Sylvie, go tell Miranda to hide the girls. Go *now!*"

The dragon pushed off Taylor's shoulder and flew back down the long hallway. The tech witch's talons sprouted from her fingers, and her canines emerged and grew. As she readied for the coming fight, something bothered her. Why were they here? They were supposed to be at the Crystal Well.

She cracked the door enough to see inside the pub and got her answer. Behind Gemma and the leading demon-kinder walked Filippa and Aurora with a group of black-clad Fae enforcers.

That was all the information Taylor needed. Quinn had been wrong about the location of their planned gateway. It wasn't the Crystal Well. It was all happening here in the Hunter center of power.

Twisting in place, Taylor bolted back toward her workshop. She only had a few seconds before they found her. If she hurried, maybe she'd have enough time to start the recall sequence before anyone caught up to her.

Behind Taylor, Gemma shouted, "After her!"

Taylor ran as fast as her partially shifted form would allow her to, not just for her life, but to save everyone she knew and loved.

Racing into the workroom, she slammed the door and pressed her fingers wide against the stout wooden door. Summoning a surge of her magical energy, Taylor muttered "warp" while she drew in power.

Beneath her hands, the wood fibers roiled and expanded. The stout boards making up the newly replaced door and frame bent. The timbers creaked as they pressed outward and wedged the door closed.

Taylor smiled. It was the best she could do, and it might slow them down a little.

Pounding fists more powerful than a normal human's beat on the door from the other side. The frustrated shouts told her they'd be awhile getting through.

Taylor sat down behind her triple monitors and started typing, prepping the system to bring Quinn and Avery home as quickly as possible. She usually had this part of the system constantly cycling so she could bring them home in an instant, but when she'd gotten up to go to the pub, she'd let it wind down. Now she needed two minutes for the magic/technology interface to spin up and bring her friends back home.

The timer on the screen started counting down just as the door burst inward in a shower of splinters. Gemma stood outside, one hand splayed out wide as she directed her powerful magic against the door. The remaining planks on either side of the door tumbled to the floor.

Snarling, Taylor let the rest of the shift to werewolf come over her, shredding her clothes in the process. Leaping from behind the monitors, she charged the evil sorceress.

If it had been just the two of them, Taylor might have had a chance.

Two demon-kinder women stepped in Taylor's way. Though she clawed and bit both of them, ripping out the throat of one of them, others came in and wrestled her to the ground.

Taylor was mostly lost in her change. She couldn't speak the words she wanted to say. Instead, she snarled and bit at the four women holding her down.

Gemma stared down at her. "Bind her with silver. Tightly. She will be part of our sacrifice."

The sorceress turned and bowed to the two princesses standing behind her. "We will capture and bind them all, Your Highnesses. Then you will have all the revenge you need. I promise."

Filippa glared down at Taylor, a savage grin baring her perfect white teeth. "See that you do, Gemma. These upstarts have been too much trouble. It's time you made up for all your missteps in stopping them."

Gemma gave a slight bow. She waited until the two Fae princesses and their entourage started down the long corridor, then followed. She left Taylor thrashing to break free from the quartet of powerful demon-possessed women holding her down.

She let out a long, pained howl when the first of the silver restraints touched her arms. The agony got worse until it nearly blinded her while they wrapped her wrists and ankles in silver cables. Eventually, it was too much. The pain drew a veil of darkness over her and she lost consciousness.

CHAPTER TWENTY-EIGHT

Quinn tried the comm unit again from the basement in Federal Hill that led down to the old silica mines and the Crystal Well.

"Still no response?" Clark asked.

"No. I don't understand. You can hear me, right?"

The others nodded.

"We've had comm issues all night," Avery suggested. "It's probably more of the same. It could even have to do with them starting the ritual below."

Quinn nodded. "We'll try again after we stop Gemma and the others. Come on."

She pulled open the secret door and entered the old mine tunnels. As soon as she did, the comm signal dropped to zero. Taylor would have to wait for them to come back up if she wanted to know what they were doing.

Quinn, Avery, Clark, and Naomi walked down through the tunnels carved from the old silica mines that laced this part of the city. The two werebadger caretakers who lived in the home above the entrance had told Quinn and the others that no one had come or entered the mines in quite some time.

As Quinn neared the oldest part, she expected to feel some response from her amulet. The Hunter charm usually warned her when dangerous magic was nearby.

There was nothing, no chill or tingling or anything. She checked her HUD. Nothing there either.

"Something's wrong."

"Why do you say that?" Avery asked.

"You've got your amulet. Are you getting any warning about what's up ahead? Anything telling you of evil magic at work?"

The other Huntress shook her head.

"Exactly. Neither am I."

Clark reached up to touch his amulet. "I'm not either. I'm not as attuned to it as you are, Quinn, but I should feel something from magic as powerful as what they're planning."

Naomi said, "Maybe they're masking the power somehow. They masked the magic and tech in the VR comm system."

"Maybe," Quinn replied. It was possible, but she wasn't convinced. "Come on, the Crystal Well is just around the corner."

Quinn drew her Bowie. The others armed themselves as well. They picked up speed and raced around the bend, entering the open circular chamber that was the Crystal Well.

Their pounding footsteps echoed off the glass dome overhead as they entered the empty circular chamber.

Quinn stopped and stared, searching the brightly lit

room. "Where is everyone? They should be here. They *have* to be here."

Naomi placed her hand on Quinn's shoulder. "It could be that you two showing up when you did earlier caused them to rethink their plan and bug out."

"She's right, Quinn," Avery said. "If they're not here, where else could they be?"

"This is happening tonight. I can feel it."

Naomi shook her head. "Quinn, it's okay to be wrong, especially about this. It'll give us more time to prepare."

Clark walked to the center of the room and looked up at the gold chain dangling from the ceiling. "Quinn's right. If I've learned nothing else since we got together, it's to trust her instincts."

Quinn shot him a look of gratitude. He nodded in reply.

"Okay," Avery said. "If it's not happening here, where is it?"

Quinn stared at the ceiling. The glittering cut glass lining the dome above her shot refracted rainbows from the electric bulbs strung along the walls. There was something about this place that could help them. Something someone had said when she first came here.

"Upwood, the original caretaker of this room, told me this place could be used to pinpoint weak spots where demon incursions could happen around the world."

"I don't suppose he told you how?" Clark asked.

"No, but I wonder..." Quinn's voice trailed off. She stared at the long gold chain just above her head. She could feel the inherent power behind the walls. It lay dormant, waiting to awaken.

"The people who built this place were ancient. They

worshiped old gods and nature. Their magic would have been old too."

Naomi stepped up beside Quinn and nodded. "Of course, wild magic."

Quinn lifted her blade and placed the razor-sharp edge on the palm of her other hand, then drew it through her clenched fingers, hissing at the fiery pain from the shallow cut she'd just made.

"I don't know if this will work or what it will do, but be ready for anything."

Reaching up, Quinn wrapped her bleeding palm around the gold chain, gripping it tightly, then closed her eyes and opened her HUD. The gold wild magic icon glowed brighter than ever before at the top. Depressing the icon, Quinn gasped as a flare of energy coursed through her.

In an instant, her consciousness filled the entire room, her mind and awareness connected with the glittering dome. Each twinkling facet represented a distinct place of magical power across the world. She could sense and feel the power coursing through each of them.

The sensation overpowered her. Her mind was filled with so much input, it threatened to burn her out in a flash of magical feedback.

Focus, Huntress. Use what you have learned to let the power pass through you. Give in and let it use you as it will, not as you would will it.

The old woman's voice rang through her head, relaxing her. This was wild magic. By its very nature, it couldn't be controlled.

Quinn did the impossible. As every muscle in her body

tried to tense and spasm, she relaxed. She gave in fully as the surge of magic coursed through her.

She'd feared it would snuff out her life. Instead, the life of the world filled her. In a single instant, she saw all the wild magic nexus points in the world.

She sensed the power of the deep blue lake in the mountains of western Maryland. She soared over the peak of the mountain beside the lake. She dove deep beneath the bay and circled the dragon's den.

In that split second, Quinn visited thousands of wild magic loci around the world. Also in that split second, Quinn knew exactly where Gemma had gone. The nexus of wild magic beneath the Hunter clan chambers had gone dark. That could only mean one thing.

"Oh, my goddess."

"Quinn," Avery asked. "What is it?"

"It's not here. It was never here."

"Where is it, then?" Clark asked.

"Home." Quinn's eyes opened. She looked at her companions. "It's our home."

Realization bloomed in three pairs of eyes at once.

Quinn released the gold chain and ran for the chamber's exit. "We have to hurry. There might still be time." Her heart sank, realizing what Gemma might do to Taylor and the girls. Without Quinn there to protect them, Gemma would take every ounce of her revenge out on them.

The thought spurred her to run faster. The others strained to keep up. As she neared the surface, Quinn started keying her comm unit, trying to reach Taylor, praying she was wrong.

There was no answer.

Quinn stopped as she skidded out of the tunnel into the old basement. "Clark, we'll need help."

"Who?"

"Everyone. Anyone."

"They'll be watching the entrance to the pub," Clark said. "We'll have to fight our way in. You and Avery can go back directly and bypass any wards. Naomi and I can't."

"Call Ariel," Quinn said. "She mentioned an old water entrance used to smuggle people and items into the Hunter stronghold. She can take you there."

Clark nodded. "How are you going to get back if Taylor isn't answering?"

Quinn didn't answer, then she felt the familiar tug at the back of her mind. Taylor was calling them back via the VR.

"Oh, dear," Avery said. "I feel strange."

"Go with it. It's the recall sequence. Taylor is bringing us back, even if she can't answer us."

Quinn laughed and held her Bowie in front of her, ready to fight as soon as she woke up in the workshop. "Mom, Clark, see you back home. Don't be late and miss all the fun."

Before either could answer, she closed her eyes, and the familiar welcome darkness washed over her.

CHAPTER TWENTY-NINE

Miranda had almost made it to the tunnels connecting the upper passage to the Hunter chambers when Sylvie caught up to her.

"Eeeep, eeeep, *eeeeeeeeeeep*!"

The dragon's keening cry would've sent chills down Miranda's spine if she'd had one.

"Slow down, Sylvie. What are you trying to say?" Reaching out with her ghost consciousness, Miranda tried to build a mind to mind connection. She wasn't sure it would work, then a flood of images surged into her mind all at once.

Black figures beating Paddy on the bar. Angry women charging Taylor. None of it made any sense, then the blur over one face cleared enough for Miranda to make it out.

"Gemma. Oh, no, they're here. Quick, Sylvie, we have to wake up the girls and Tadpole. We have to hide everyone."

"Eeeep."

Sylvie took off down the passage before Miranda could

begin moving. She was a ghost, however, capable of moving at the speed of thought. She raced after the speeding dragon, passing it with ease as she wove through the passages. She zoomed into the hallway where the girls were staying.

Miranda stopped outside the first of the rooms. Sylvie zoomed down the hallway behind her.

"Eeeep?"

"You go wake up Tadpole."

The dragon headed for his room while Miranda passed through the closed door and into the first of the girls' rooms. This was where Brea and Kami stayed. Both were sound asleep. She didn't think they would be happy to awaken to a ghost hovering over their beds. There was no choice, however.

"Brea, wake up. Quickly. There's trouble coming."

The girl's eyes fluttered open. "Wha…"

"Wake up. Wake the others. Gemma, the demon-kinder, and the dark Fae are coming for us."

Brea sat up, her eyes wide. It wasn't fear, though. She had a look of grim determination as she turned and stared at Kami for a few seconds. The youngest of the group also sat up, suddenly wide awake.

She looked at Brea. "I heard. We must prepare."

It was a strange thing to say, but Miranda was just happy they were both up. Before she could tell them what to do, the two ran into the hallway in their pajamas.

Miranda floated after them. She turned to wake up the next set of girls, but there was no need. The other four already stood in the hallway, eyes turned to Brea.

Suko said, "They are close. I can sense them. We must not let them use us to open the portal."

The other five nodded in reply.

"Wait, 'use you?'" Miranda asked. "How would they use you?"

The six girls didn't respond. They all ran toward the training room at the end of the hall. Miranda followed, still trying to understand what was happening.

When they reached the training room, Tadpole stumbled out of his room at that end of the hall. Sylvie perched on his shoulder. Her head bobbed toward Miranda and the girls. "Eeeep."

"What's going on, Miranda? Why did Sylvie wake me up?"

"Trouble, I'm afraid. We have to hide the girls. Gemma and the two princesses are here. They plan to use the power inherent in this place to open the portal to the netherworld."

The orc warrior's eyes narrowed. "They want to hurt the girls?"

"Yes, Tadpole, and hurt you. We must hide until Quinn and the others get back."

Shouting echoed up the passage behind Miranda. "Oh, no, it's too late. They're here. We've got to hide the girls."

Kami said, "Hide and seek. I remember the best hiding place. Don't you, Tadpole?"

All six girls nodded and turned to the big orc. He grinned and pointed at the armory.

"Go. You know how to open the wall. Go inside and wait. I will stay and protect you."

The girls ran into the armory.

Tadpole grabbed the gold spear from the rack by the room's entrance. "Go with them, Miranda. I'll slow them down."

"Tadpole, they are too powerful. You cannot defeat them. Come, hide with us."

"No, Quinn would want me to fight."

Miranda tried pleading with him again, but it was already too late. Four demon-kinder Hunter women charged into the practice chamber.

Tadpole bellowed a challenge and brandished his spear. Arcs of gold lightning ran up the shaft to crackle from the spearhead. He charged the women on the other side of the room.

The lightning shot from the end of the spear, striking the lead demon-kinder. The blast lifted her from her feet and slammed her into the wall.

Tadpole bellowed a challenge at the remaining three, slashing and stabbing at them to keep them at bay.

They spread out to divide his attention, but he was too quick for them. In a blur of motion, Tadpole slammed the butt of the spear into the gut of the attacker behind him.

The woman doubled over, dropping her sword as she vomited black ichor from her crushed internal organs.

Tadpole reversed his move, skewering another demon-kinder on the leaf-shaped gold spear blade. Magical energy arced from her open mouth and eyes as the orc warrior pulled the blade free, leaving a smoking husk of a person behind.

The final demon-kinder backed toward the exit.

Tadpole shifted his grip and threw the spear, pinning the woman to the stone wall with the force of his blow.

Dead, her body sagged on the shaft pinning her in place.

"Miranda, go with the girls. I'll take the fight to the enemy." Tadpole yanked the magic spear free, dropping the woman from the wall.

"You can't win, Tadpole. Come with me. Hide."

"No, Quinn needs time to come back. I must fight to give her that time. Go to the girls. They are preparing themselves for what they must do."

"What are you talking about?"

"Go and see," he replied, giving her a fierce grin that showed all his teeth.

More shouts came down the hallway. Tadpole ran toward them in surprising silence for his size.

Miranda floated into the armory. A section of the wall had opened, revealing a hidden room beyond with more weapons and armor. The girls were inside. Brea stood by the open panel, waiting.

Miranda appeared again. "Go inside. Close the wall. I'm right behind you."

"What about Tadpole?"

"He fights to give you time to hide. Don't waste it. Close the panel."

Tears streamed down the oldest girl's face, but she pulled the panel shut until it clicked closed. A single overhead bulb lit the hidden room. Sylvie flitted around and settled on a rack by the panel. All six girls pulled on the armor Tadpole had found for them.

"What are you doing?"

Brea wiped her tears away. "They will find us, Miranda. Gemma will not give up now that she's here. We have to fight her. We can't let them take us and use our power for their ritual."

"But you're just little girls. You'll die if you fight them."

Suko said, "They plan to kill us in the ritual anyway. They can't afford to let us die before then. They will strive to take us alive, and we will make them pay."

The clash of steel reached them, though it was muffled. They could also hear Tadpole's defiant roars and screams from dying demon-kinder and Fae. Then a flurry of gunshots was followed by two explosions. The blasts shook the room in which they hid.

The fighting outside stopped. Tears flowed anew as realization dawned on the young ones what had happened outside.

Gemma's voice just outside their hiding place said, "There's no sign of the girls. Search the tunnels. They're here somewhere. Bring the injured orc. We'll use him to boost our sacrificial rites."

The voices trailed off and disappeared, leaving them in silence.

Sylvie let out a low, sorrowful "Eeeep?"

"Yes, Sylvie. I fear you are right. At least the girls are safe for now. That is something."

Miranda stared at the closed secret panel. She feared Brea was right. They would eventually find the group in the hidden room. She wondered how long it would take Quinn to arrive with the others and rescue them.

The crying stopped, replaced by quiet discussion.

Miranda looked around to see the three oldest girls huddled together, talking about something.

"What are you up to?"

Brea lifted her head. "We must prepare to fight."

"What? No, stay here and hide. Quinn and the others will be back soon. They'll come and take care of the intruders."

All six girls shook their heads in unison as Brea said, "They won't come in time to help Tadpole. If he is to be saved, it must be us."

"Girls, I know you want to help, but this is not what Tadpole would want you to do. I know him."

"We know how to fight. He selected the best weapons for each of us, and armor, too. Why do that unless he expected us to fight for him and ourselves?"

"Look, I know how you feel," Miranda began.

Ola said, "No, you don't. You're already dead. We have to help ourselves. If they come for us, you cannot do anything."

Miranda started to speak but stopped. The six children checked the fit of their armor, tightening straps and buckles. A minute later, they all stood in front of her, armed to the teeth. Each girl wore tight-fitting leather armor covered with small rectangular metal plates. The fierce expressions on their faces would have been inspiring if they weren't so young.

Brea said, "Miranda, we will be more likely to succeed if you help us. We will leave and attack either way, but we would rather have your help."

Miranda's thoughts swirled. She couldn't stop them from leaving if they wanted to. They'd made up their minds, and she could not change their decision.

"What do you want me to do?"

"It's simple," Brea said. She outlined the plan for the ghost, giving her a simple task: Distract and delay.

CHAPTER THIRTY

Miranda floated down the corridor, remaining invisible for the moment. Chanting voices ahead alerted her that the ritual had started. She had to hurry. If she could distract the casters and guards, it might be enough to force them to start over from the beginning. That would buy them time.

She lifted her shoulders and held her head high as she flew through the entry to the ceremonial chamber to the center of the room.

Twenty women lined the walls. The negative energy emanating from them was easy for her ghostly self to read. They were demon-kinder, the last of the women Gemma had trained for tonight's attack and ritual. The center of the room held five Fae, three women and two men. All knelt, rocking back and forth in a circle facing each other. Their chanting filled the room with eerie voices.

She could hear other voices murmuring in side corridors. A glance down one showed a four-person Fae assault team in black body armor, armed with swords and pistols. There were likely others around.

She turned her attention back to the five Fae spellcasters at the center of the room. Miranda didn't speak Old Fae, but she recognized enough to realize that was the language they spoke.

To the side stood Gemma, Princess Filippa, and Princess Aurora. All three stared at the spell circle with intense fascination. At their feet lay Taylor and Tadpole. They were bound with thick ropes even though they both were injured and unconscious.

Miranda flew to the center of the circle and revealed herself, floating above the spellcasters. The evil magic emanating from their chants gave even her insubstantial body a chill.

"Stop!" She drew upon her limited spiritual energy, glowing with a white nimbus so she was no longer transparent.

The chanting faltered and then stopped as the Fae casters looked up at the woman in their midst.

"Ignore her," Filippa shouted. "She's a spirit, already dead. Continue the spell before the energy dissipates."

The chanting began again, but it lacked the intensity it had before. Miranda smiled. "I warn you, this is a holy place. Not only will your spell fail, but the Hunter protections here will curse you and your eternal souls."

The chanting faltered again. Several glanced over their shoulders at the princesses.

Filippa snarled, "Get back to it, you fools."

Miranda continued, "You will all die. Nothing will save you from what is coming."

The chanting continued this time.

Gemma asked. "What is coming, ghost witch? We know your vaunted Huntress is elsewhere. It will take her far too long to return."

Miranda smiled. They didn't know she could return via the VR system. Besides, the immediate threat to them came from the six tiny armored figures sneaking down the corridor behind them.

Spreading her arms wide, Miranda spent the rest of her energy to let loose a burst of blinding white light that filled the room. Everyone blinked and shielded their eyes from the glare.

The chanting stopped again. Several of the Fae mages rubbed at their eyes after staring straight at Miranda when she flashed.

The witch's form faded to nothing. She couldn't even speak aloud anymore. She could do nothing more but watch, listen, and pray.

The flash of ghost light was the signal. The girls rushed into the room. Brea and Ola came first, followed by the twins and then Suko and Kami. They spread out, working in teams of two, each pair taking on a different demon-kinder.

Miranda watched, fascinated by the coordination of the girls' attacks. Two of the guards died, and they incapacitated a third before any could react to the sudden savage assault.

The paired girls moved on to fresh targets. This time, however, they had less success. The remaining seventeen demon-kinder rushed in and grappled with the armored attackers.

Two more died under the little girls' blades, then the attacking women wrestled them to the ground, stripping the girls of their weapons and holding them in place.

The youngest, Kami, got a hand free and pulled a small knife from within her armor. She slashed up, cutting the throat of the woman holding her down.

Another of the Hunter-trained demon-kinder was dead.

Three demon-kinder kicked and beat the girl while Miranda silently wailed at them to stop.

Gemma stalked over to where the girls struggled. "Stop beating her. She's learned her lesson, and we need her alive. We must have all six for the final spell."

Gemma stood over them. "Hello, Brea. How nice of you and your sisters to come to us. I was just about to send a party out to search for you."

"You cannot use us, Miss Gemma. We will not let you."

"*You* will not let *me*?" Gemma threw her head back and laughed. "You've been hanging around those Huntresses too long. You forget what I'm capable of."

Gemma glanced at the other five and said, "Bind and gag all of them. I don't want to hear any more of their insolence."

"Gemma," Aurora said. "they have broken the spell. We must begin anew."

"Very well. Let's use the innocents' blood to fuel our magic. We will now be able to open an even wider gateway."

"Just get on with it," Filippa snarled. "This has already taken too long."

Gemma nodded a bow to the princesses and pointed at the center of the spell circle. "Drag them over there once you've secured them. Tie the knots tight. I don't want them wriggling loose."

She waited as the women dragged the six girls to the room's center, next to Taylor and Tadpole. Gemma drew a small curved blade from her robes and followed the women who pulled the struggling girls to the room's center. The demon-kinder used another length of rope to tie them back to back, facing outward.

Holding her dagger at her side, Gemma circled the six captive girls. "I had so many wonderful plans for you until Avery corrupted you with her enlightened ideals. Now you will serve an even darker purpose."

She stopped in front of Brea, and before the girl could react, slashed down with the curved dagger, cutting a deep gash into her forearm. Blood dripped to the floor in a steady flow. Each drop caused a ruby flash when it hit the stone.

Gemma moved around the circle, repeating her move with each of the girls. None of them cried out, though Miranda saw a steady stream of tears running down young Kami's face.

Miranda let out a scream of rage only she could hear as she watched the lifeblood leak from the six brave children. It formed a small pool around each of them and released pent-up energy into the room. The witch sensed that whatever made the girls so special was now feeding the magic's intensity as the five Fae spell casters began their rocking chants again.

Unable to do anything but watch in silence, Miranda wept as everything they'd worked so hard to stop moved closer to happening. They were running out of time, and Quinn was nowhere in sight.

Miranda hoped Sylvie had understood her instructions. It was up to the little dragon to bring help.

CHAPTER THIRTY-ONE

Quinn's eyes opened, and she sat up. A glance at the monitors told her Taylor wasn't here waiting for her, which was odd.

"Avery, you awake?"

"Does your head hurt like this every time you return, too?" She lay staring at the ceiling, rubbing her temples with both hands.

"You get used to it. Come on. Taylor's not here, and she should be. We need to find her and the others."

Quinn hopped off the worktable and saw the door, or what was left of it. The splinters and wooden scraps that had been the door covered the floor by the entrance.

"Damn, I was right. They're here."

"I'm sorry, Quinn. That means they have Taylor, and probably the others."

"We need help. I was counting on having a little time to mount a defense. Clark and Mom won't be here for ten or fifteen minutes."

"Where are we going to get help?"

Quinn walked to the door and turned toward the pub. Down the hall, the door to O'Malley's was wide open. Inside, she could see a few of the patrons and servers cleaning up a mess. Tables had been overturned and chairs thrown around.

She ducked back into the workshop when a figure dressed in black body armor walked past the opening to the pub.

"They left guards in there. It looks like there was a fight when they arrived."

Avery asked, "What's the plan?"

"I'd say leave them for now, but I think we'll need help to get down to the tunnels. Let's dip into the shadows and sneak up on whoever they left to guard the entrance."

Avery nodded, and the pair both engaged their shadow-hiding abilities. Quinn stepped into the lead. Avery still moved with the stiffness of someone recovering from an injury.

Glancing into the pub from the doorway, Quinn saw only two guards pacing past where she and Avery hid. She pointed at the closest one and then at Avery. Her partner nodded and brought up her katana.

Quinn waited until the two Fae enforcers passed each other again, then darted forward. She stabbed up under the body armor with her Bowie while she cupped her hand over the man's mouth. His muffled scream died as she stabbed again, then she lowered his limp body to the floor.

Behind her, the nearly decapitated body of the other enforcer lay next to Avery. Quinn double-checked to make sure there were no other guards and then ran to the bar.

Juni tended to Paddy there. He sat on the floor with his

back to the bar while his daughter dabbed his bruised and battered face with a cloth.

"Was it Gemma and the Fae?" Quinn asked from the doorway.

"It was," Paddy said. "They killed the cook when he tried to help me and told me they'd be coming back to finish the job on me."

"They've gone down to the Hunter tunnels to open a portal to the netherworld. If they come back, everyone dies. We need help until Clark and Naomi get back."

Paddy gestured at the small group of waitresses and the remaining patrons who'd stayed to help. "You're welcome to ask them, but don't be surprised if no one takes you up on the offer. You're the fighters here."

Quinn raised her voice. "I need everyone's attention. Is there anyone here willing to join me in taking the fight to the ones who did this? There's just two of us for now, and we could use some help."

The few of the patrons and one of the regular waitresses glanced her way for a second but turned aside as soon as her eyes met theirs. Quinn knew she shouldn't have expected them to step up. They were ordinary folks who didn't have any training. Still, she had hoped one or two would volunteer. All were nonviolent shifter types, not werewolves or vampires, the most powerful of the supernaturals. Quinn shook her head.

Avery tugged at her arm. "Come on. We can't wait any longer. We have to get down there. There's no telling how close they are to opening the gateway."

Quinn nodded and turned away from the bar.

Juni called, "I'll come."

"Juni girl, no," Paddy said. "We're leprechauns, not fighters."

"We have magic, Da. I might not be much of a fighter, but I can help them. I *have to* help them."

Paddy held his daughter's gaze and then nodded.

Juni smiled, joining Quinn by the door.

"I'll get you a weapon," Quinn said. "What would you prefer?"

"Oh, I'm good." She snapped her fingers, and a gnarled, polished length of wood appeared in her hand. The stout stick ended in a rounded knob. "I've got a shillelagh."

"You know how to use that thing?" Avery asked.

"It's a club. Ya hit 'em with the big end, don't ya?"

Quinn nodded. "That's about it. Stay behind us, and try to keep anyone from sneaking up on us."

"I'm hoping I can lend a hand with some trickery. That's what my kind are best at."

"Do what you can, then. Anything that keeps them from overwhelming Avery and me. We have no idea how many there are."

"Over twenty, based on what my da said."

Avery shook her head. "This will be tough."

"I've taken on similar odds down there before. Plus, if we can stall and keep them from overwhelming us all at once, I'm hoping we'll get more help."

"What kind of help? You just said we can't wait for your mom and Clark."

Quinn shrugged. "I'm not sure. I get the feeling we're not alone in this fight. I can't say how, but there has to be some help, or we've already lost."

Avery said, "Let's see where the help we know about is,

at least." She tapped her earpiece. "Clark, Naomi, can you hear me?"

The comm circuit opened. A motor buzzed in the background. Naomi answered. "Avery, did you get back? Where's Quinn?"

"I'm here. Where are you?"

"We just met Ariel. We're in her boat heading across the harbor."

"How much longer 'til you arrive?"

Clark jumped in. "If she's going where I think she is, we will be there in about five minutes. This boat is fast."

Quinn thought about how much time they had. It would be close, especially if they had the numbers Paddy said they did. "Head straight in when you get here. You should hear fighting. We will try to stop their ritual, then work to delay them as long as we can. Hopefully, you two can hit them from the rear."

"You can't wait for us to get there?" Naomi asked.

"No time, Mom. We've no idea how close they are to opening the portal or what they've done to our friends. Just get here as fast as you can."

"We will," Naomi replied. "Be careful, Quinn."

"I'll do the best I can, but I can't let them get that gateway to the netherworld open."

Quinn cut the comm signal and checked the time. Five minutes was forever in a fight like the one to come. A glance at Avery told Quinn she was thinking the same thing.

"You ready?"

Avery nodded. "Let's get down there."

"Juni, what can you do? I'm not familiar with leprechaun magic."

"It sounds like you need a distraction. We're not great in a standup fight when we defend our gold. Instead, we distract and disorient. I can probably get a few of the guards to chase me if that'll help."

Quinn nodded. "That would be good. What will you do if they catch up with you?"

"They won't catch me. I might be able to take a few from behind while they're lookin', though." She patted the bulbous end of her shillelagh.

"Okay, do that. I'll go first so I can sneak up on anyone they might have left guarding the tunnels. Once we get closer, I'll give you targets for your tricks."

Juni smiled and nodded, and the three of them started down the stairs. Quinn and Avery dipped into the shadows again. Juni snapped her fingers, and her outline blurred as she too disappeared.

They'd almost reached the bottom of the stairs when Sylvie flew out of the darkness and swirled in a circle around Quinn's head. The dragon always seemed to be able to see Quinn, even when she was hidden in the shadows.

"Eeeep, eeeep, eeeep, *eeeep!*"

A flurry of images flashed through Quinn's mind. They went by too fast for her to register, though.

"Sylvie, slow down. Show me what you're saying one thing at a time."

Sylvie stopped circling and hovered in front of Quinn's face. Her emerald eyes bored into Quinn's.

The first thing Quinn saw was Taylor in shreds of

clothing, bound and unconscious on the floor. Beside her lay a similarly bound and bloody Tadpole.

Quinn's lips pressed together in a grim line as she looked at the scene. "What else?"

A motion sequence played this time, showing the six girls attacking. Then it shifted to them sitting bound in a circle as Gemma slashed them one by one and left them bleeding on the floor.

Avery gasped. "I'll tear that woman's evil heart out."

"You getting this too?" Quinn asked.

Avery nodded. She'd gone white with rage. "She'll kill them. That bleeding will drain them if it's not stopped."

"We don't know that they'll die," Quinn countered. "That's why we have to hurry."

She turned to leave but stopped when Juni grabbed her arm.

"I have another quick trick that might give you an advantage when you get there. It'll make it look like there are eight of ya instead of just two."

"How's it work?"

"I'll snap my fingers before you show yourselves to them, and you'll appear from different directions at once. Your voice'll come from the projections, too. They won't know which are real." She shrugged. "It might make them split up at first. As long as I can see them, I can make them run away, Maybe some will give chase."

Quinn nodded. "It's worth giving it a shot. Okay, one last thing. Sylvie, I need you to find the place where Clark and Naomi are landing. It has to be down in the maze of tunnels. Go find them and bring them as fast as you can, okay?"

"Eeeep!"

The dragon flew into the darkness, and Quinn turned to Juni. "Stay behind us and do whatever else you can to start, then lead those who follow our doubles as far as you can. And be careful. This is going to get ugly."

CHAPTER THIRTY-TWO

The trio started down the tunnel toward the central chamber. Chanting drifted up the corridor.

As Quinn walked closer to the Hunter ceremonial room, her amulet grew ice-cold. She held up a hand, stopping the others. They crouched in the shadows by the entrance.

Quinn could just make out Juni's blurred outline. "You're up."

Juni's broad grin appeared in the middle of the blur, and fingers snapped. "You girls are ready. Good luck."

Quinn and Avery walked the last steps to the bend in the tunnel. They were just a few feet from the chamber's entrance. A squad of Fae enforcers stood with their backs to her, watching the ritual in the center of the room.

She craned her neck and stared at the entrance opposite hers. Her face stared back at her. Avery stood beside the replica Quinn.

She couldn't make out the other exit, the one leading to

the training room and armory, but she assumed there were duplicates there.

Quinn sucked in a deep breath and bellowed, "Stop!"

Gemma threw her hands in the air as the spellcasters in the center of the room fell silent and looked around for who had called out.

"What now?" Gemma groaned. She twisted her head until she spotted the duplicates of Quinn and Avery directly across from their true hiding place. "Oh, it's you two. Just in time to provide more blood for the rites."

"The only additional blood spilled today will be yours and your followers'."

Avery nodded. "We'll add a splash of Fae blood, too. It'll brighten things up a bit." She brandished her sword.

Gemma twisted her head around as Quinn's voice came from all three entrances at once.

"Get them, you idiots," Filippa yelled. "They can't all be projections."

The four Fae enforcers in the group just ahead of them turned around, realizing the voices were right behind them. Quinn and Avery killed the first two before they reacted.

The remaining two brought up their swords and charged, trying to take advantage of the tight quarters in the tunnel entrance.

Quinn ducked aside and under an incoming sword, then lunged forward to sink her Bowie into the enforcer's throat.

Beside her, Avery finished the last guard. Juni laughed and ran past them, blurring into invisibility again. Across the chamber, the two nearest duplicates ran down the far passage. At least four of the closest demon-kinder raced after them.

The remaining demon-kinder around the chamber's perimeter jumped into action. Two came up the tunnel toward Quinn and Avery.

Quinn raised her Bowie and parried the incoming blow with a clash of steel on steel. Beside her, Avery lunged. The woman she targeted bounced backward, avoiding the attack with ease.

She dodged away from Avery's katana, but that put her in range of Quinn's follow-through. A quick strike buried the Bowie in the demon-kinder's side, and the Huntress twisted the knife as she yanked it free. Thick black ichor flowed from the wide-open wound.

Avery's long blade flashed past Quinn's face, parrying the incoming sword strike from Quinn's original foe just in time to keep it from decapitating her.

Quinn reversed her grip on the Bowie and slashed backward, drawing the blade across the sword wielder's throat with enough force to cut three-quarters of the way through her neck.

Gemma's head turned when she heard the sound of blade on blade. She shouted, "This way, you fools. The others are fakes. The real intruders are back there." Her arm extended, pointing out the real Quinn and Avery.

Quinn shrugged as she stepped over the two twitching bodies on the floor. "Juni bought us a little time to narrow the odds."

"What say we divide and conquer? First one to Gemma or the princesses gets extra points."

"Deal," Quinn shouted. She darted forward to take on the rush of demon-kinder coming from the left.

Avery turned to take on those coming around the room on the right.

To call the fighting desperate didn't come close to describing the struggle over the next minute and a half. Initially, Quinn and Avery carried their surprise forward, downing several more scattered attackers each.

Then the resistance coalesced into a solid mass of the demon-possessed women facing them.

They forced Quinn to back up so quickly, she almost tripped backward over the body of a woman she'd killed a few seconds before. Now she backpedaled while parrying a dizzying array of bladed weapons that sought to take her.

Avery cried out behind her, but Quinn couldn't spare any attention for her girlfriend. It was all she could do to bat away the flurry of incoming attacks. Quinn searched for some way to break away and regain the initiative.

Quinn dialed down her remaining stamina, putting most of it toward a speed boost to match the unnatural quickness of the Hunter-trained demon-kinder. With the last of her reserves gone, Quinn wondered how much longer she could hold out.

An opening appeared in the attacks, and she executed a desperate lunge at the exposed torso of a tall raven-haired woman. The Bowie sank to the hilt in the woman's gut, causing what should have been a fatal wound.

As Quinn tried to yank her blade free, the woman's hands came down, gripping Quinn's wrist and keeping the blade in place, Quinn with it.

Her moment of hesitation exposed her for a tad too

long. Other attackers' blades came down at her from different directions.

Quinn twisted aside and avoided the first incoming swipe at her midsection. That opened her up to the other two attackers, and she let out a surprised grunt as the first sword slid past her ribs and into her chest.

The second blade pierced her shoulder and pinned her to the stone floor.

The woman Quinn had struck fell back, and the Bowie slid free to clatter on the floor.

Quinn tried to reach for it with her working right hand. A swift kick from one of the three remaining demon-kinder sent the blade spinning across the stone floor.

Quinn lay back and stared upward, awaiting her fate.

Two sword blades went up, ready to deliver their killing strikes. Quinn winced, waiting for them to fall.

"Stop!" Filippa yelled. "Bring them both here while they still live. Their blood is more valuable for our rite."

Rough hands pulled Quinn to her feet, twisting her exhausted arms behind her back and marching her stumbling body over to where Gemma and the two princesses stood.

Two demon-kinder held a struggling Juni in the second corridor. Four others dragged Avery over and dropped her on the floor beside Quinn.

At first, Quinn thought Avery was dead. She let out a small sigh of relief as the other Huntress groaned when she hit the stone floor. Avery had blood all over one side of her face from a horrible gash to her forehead. Other wounds seeped blood into her shirt and pants.

"I told you they'd come," Gemma said to Filippa and

Aurora. "They'd have to come back and defend their home."

Quinn sneered. "What, does that make you a genius, to predict I'd come home? Wow, your self-esteem bar is seriously low."

"Quiet, girl. I didn't get to kill either of you before, but I will finish the job this time."

Quinn smiled. "I'd give up and run now if I were you all. We've killed half your demon-possessed guards and most of the Dark Fae goons you brought along. When the rest of the clan arrives, they'll make short work of you."

Aurora tilted her head back and laughed. "Girl, you still believe you've assembled something special here. Our presence in this place of power tells us all otherwise. There is no clan. Your collection of misfits failed to stop us, and we've started the rites. They'll be even easier to perform, thanks to the extra power of your blood to fuel them."

Filippa nodded. "We tricked you into holding the six girls for us here where we needed them. Once we've drained the blood from those six future Huntresses, we'll move on to the two of you." Filippa glanced at the bound girls in the center of the chamber. "I find it strangely appropriate we got to use them for this purpose. They would have been the ones to rebuild the old Hunter clans if Gemma hadn't gotten to them first."

"You're lying," Quinn snapped. "Avery rescued them."

Gemma nodded. "An unfortunate setback in the short term. However, I found them first. If Avery hadn't intervened, I would have possessed their souls too." Gemma glanced at Filippa. "I thought I'd lost them and their unique hold on power until Her Highness reminded me where

Avery would take them for safe-keeping. It made us move up our plans a little, but nothing we couldn't account for."

Quinn stared at the six listless girls, still bleeding out their lives in the center of the room. They were the future Huntresses? She realized they were all orphans, just like she had been for so long. The symmetry of it struck a chord inside her like a bell ringing. Now they were here in this sacred place with her. Was this foreordained, and did it offer a slight glimmer of hope?

She searched the room, looking for a tiny sign that might show this was a plan of the light. Her eyes scanned the stones marking the tombs of the past clan chiefs. They'd helped before, but not this time, it seemed.

There was nothing.

Wait.

A tiny flash of crimson light on the floor beside Brea.

Quinn stared at the center of the room until she spotted what had caught her eye. Next to each of the girls were the almost imperceptible flashes of ruby brilliance from the dripping blood. It flashed each time a droplet of the girls' blood struck the chamber's floor.

Was there still power there, something she could use? She had to get over there.

Quinn sagged in the arms of those who held her. It was only partly an act. The gash in her chest still bled, and she was having trouble breathing. She'd probably die from her wounds without medical attention or healing.

"I'm done, Filippa. I've tried to fight you, and you keep coming back stronger than before. Just get it over with."

Gemma laughed. "See, ladies? I told you she'd submit to us eventually. She grew up alone and on the streets. How could she possibly have the strength or wherewithal to face us?"

Aurora sounded almost disinterested as she said, "I had expected more from the girl. I suppose you were right after all. We should get this over with. I for one would like to receive all that is due me at the end of these rites. I tire of waiting for our brethren from below to return and the reward that comes with it."

"Agreed, cousin," Filippa said. "Take them to the center with the others. Let's not waste any more of their precious Huntress blood."

The demon-kinder dragged Quinn and Avery to the room's center and dropped them to the stones beside the six girls. Quinn hoped she was right and hadn't been hallucinating. If she was, they'd just brought eight Huntresses together in the center of a Hunter ceremonial chamber. That had to be significant.

Quinn hit the floor, her face landing in the expanding circle of blood. A flash of ruby light blinded her for a moment as her blood mingled with Brea's. She waited, hoping for something—anything—to tell her she was right.

Nothing changed.

Quinn's ability to hold onto consciousness slipped away with her will to keep fighting. Gemma shouted at the Fae spellcasters, "Start again. Nothing will stop you this time."

With a small sigh, Quinn let go and drifted into darkness.

CHAPTER THIRTY-THREE

"*What are you doing here, my daughter?*"

The voice whispered into her head, not her ears. Quinn's eyes fluttered open. A rose-colored haze hung in the air, partially obscuring everything—not that there was anything to see. Nothingness stretched in every direction.

I'm dead.

What makes you think that?

I lost, and they won. I must be dead.

The voice in her head turned disapproving.

You surrender so easily? I'm not sure what I saw in you if that's the case.

Quinn twisted her consciousness and searched for the voice's origin.

She saw no one.

I didn't go easily. They overpowered Avery and me. We failed to push them from the chamber.

Was that your only plan? To push them away?

The voice was right. There had been something else.

Quinn shook her head. *I'm tired. You're the goddess. You tell me what's next. I'm all alone right now, so I don't have any options.*

Another wave of disappointment swept over Quinn. The goddess' emotion sapped her stubborn resolve to give up.

Daughter, you are never alone. You are the Huntress. The one who connects all who came before you in the old clans and all who would come after you in what is to be. That is far from being alone.

Did she mean the little girls? They weren't able to fight anymore. They struggled to hold on to life, just like Quinn did. Her only connection to the old clans was her mother and Clark. They would not make it back in time to stop this. The mental gymnastics annoyed Quinn.

I know what you're trying to do. You're trying to get me to fight back, even when there is nothing left to carry on the battle.

How is there nothing if you and I talk, daughter? If all was lost as you believe, your soul would be damned and your body possessed.

Damn it, I don't know what you're talking about. Quinn's anger exploded at last. *Avery's dead or will be soon. The children were taken and will die. I tried to build a home and family here. Once again, someone came and took it all away from me.*

The image of her foster father sneaking up behind her played in Quinn's mind. She had beaten that man senseless before running away to live on the streets.

You didn't let that one take your belief in family away from you. Good came even from that bleak moment in your life.

I found Taylor because of him. Without that, I wouldn't have a sister.

You've lost nothing but your way, child. Your clan, your family is still with you. Yes, your enemies have sorely injured you, but they haven't told you the complete truth. They made one fatal error, one I foresaw long ago on the day of your birth.

You're speaking in riddles again, Quinn said. *I can't think. Tell me what I need to do. Please.*

If I do that, I take away the power of the Huntress. You must draw upon the power of the clans past, present, and future. Only then will you expose their error and take back what is rightfully yours.

Damned riddles again. Tell me in plain language.

There was no answer.

Quinn didn't bother asking again. She knew the goddess was no longer in this place, midway between life and death.

What did she mean about drawing on the power? Quinn had no power left. The six girls were dying, their blood leaking to join hers on the chamber's floor. Clark and Naomi, her connection to the past, were still too far away. The other Hunter clans were dead and gone.

She stopped herself.

"No, they're not," Quinn whispered, as if afraid to let anyone else hear the secret she'd just learned.

A smile crossed Quinn's lips. She knew what to do.

CHAPTER THIRTY-FOUR

The droning of the Fae casters' magical chanting filled Quinn's ears as she opened her eyes just enough to look around. Her face was pressed into the sticky blood pooled on the floor.

Through slitted eyes, she watched the two Fae spellcasters sitting closest to her. They rocked back and forth, eyes rolled back in their heads, chanting with increasing intensity. Even though she wasn't a spellcaster, the energy around her vibrated a black place within her. Quinn knew they were close to opening the portal.

Quinn closed her eyes again and opened her HUD, studying it and taking stock. She had barely any mana left. The blue bar continued draining as her blood dripped away.

She struggled to hold onto consciousness despite the thick fog filling her mind. There was something important she had to do, something only she could accomplish. Every time she got close to remembering what the goddess had told her, the haze rolled in, obscuring the answer.

Angry, Quinn exerted her will, forcing the clouds and fog out of the way so she could see again. Her mana drained even lower. How was she supposed to use her power as it literally leaked from her body?

The five Fae still recited their droning chant, louder than ever. Quinn tried to lift her head from the sticky puddle, which caused another of those strange ruby sparks to appear between her face and floor. She jerked at the sudden static shock.

Gemma and the others watching those dying in the center of the room laughed at her involuntary spasm.

Angry at their laughter, Quinn lifted her head again. She worked up the strength to tell them what they could do with their humor. This time, she wouldn't jerk for their amusement.

Quinn anticipated the spark, gathering her will to control her body.

She lifted her head a little, and the spark appeared. To her amazement, the flash didn't just spark; a red arc of energy ran from the puddle to her temple. It only lasted for a second. That was enough, though. She saw her blue mana bar increase a little.

Quinn's lips curled ever so slightly into a grin. Bless the goddess, the mother had told her everything she needed to know. She only had to believe.

She let out an involuntary chuckle.

"Look, the spell makes her delirious," Aurora said. "She has lost her mind. She is smiling at us like an idiot."

"Well, we'll see about that," Gemma said. She barked an order. "Ellis, go over there and put another hole in the Huntress with your sword. She's not dying fast enough."

One of the women lining the wall grinned from ear to ear. "Yes, mistress. I would be happy to hasten her trip to the netherworld. She will be fine stock to fuel our waiting army."

The demon-kinder wove her way around Taylor and Tadpole, stepped between two of the Fae spellcasters, and stood over Quinn. Drawing her curved sword, she pressed the tip against Quinn's side.

"Push it in slowly," Filippa called. "I want to hear her scream one last time."

Quinn shifted her eyes to stare up at the woman standing over her and lifted her head once again. The demon-kinder's body would block what she was about to do from Gemma and the others.

Once again, the red energy arc connected to Quinn's blood-smeared temple. This time Quinn drew upon it, and the flow thickened as it drew power from the pooled blood.

The energy flowing into her reached a tipping point in just a few seconds. It had filled almost half of Quinn's stamina bar. That was enough.

The sparking energy arc changed color to pale blue, like the hottest part of a gas flame. Quinn's eyes flew open as she pulled in the flow even faster. Both her mana and stamina bars were filled to bursting.

The energy didn't stop. It continued to course into her.

The blood energy touched the three crossed ley lines running beneath the chamber. Triple arcs of gold energy, pure wild magic, flowed into Quinn.

She trembled as it filled her.

"Mistress Gemma," Ellis said. "Something isn't right."

"Just finish her. You don't have to give me every little update."

The demon-kinder nodded and shoved the sword at Quinn's side.

What happened next occurred in the space of a split second. Despite the unnatural speed of the demon-kinder, Quinn had grown both faster and stronger.

Her hand snapped out and halted the descending arm. Quinn twisted her grip, shifting the curved blade so it missed her body, the tip skittering across the stone floor.

Ellis's eyes widened, and she tried to pull back. Tried in vain to break free.

It was no use.

Quinn's other hand snatched the sword away and spun it to reverse the grip. She lunged upward, the long blade's tip passing up through Ellis's throat and into her possessed brain.

It was over before anyone in the chamber had a chance to react.

Quinn leaped to her feet. Her eyes glowed with pure golden wild magic, drawn directly from the ley lines.

Her awareness expanded outward. She could see everything.

Clark and Naomi stood just outside the chamber, readying what they thought would be a final useless assault.

Sylvie, who'd been perched on Naomi's shoulder, went rigid as Quinn's mindvoice spoke in her head.

Come.

Sylvie launched like a rocket and flew straight to Quinn, who was standing inside a column of golden light.

The Huntress didn't hold onto the energy filling her. She waited for her dragon and redirected it with a single word of power.

"Sylvie!"

White-hot magical energy exploded from her open mouth and splashed toward the ceiling. The tiny dragon darted up and intercepted the bolt of power.

Sylvie hovered, wings spread wide, as she directed individual energy streams into seven of the still forms slumped on the floor below.

All that happened in the space of two seconds.

The others in the room finally reacted, but it was too late.

The five Fae spellcasters were the first to die.

Quinn released the last of the excess power into the dragon. In the blink of an eye, she raced around the circle of casters, swinging the sword in a broad arc. By the time she'd completed the circle, the first two of the five Fae heads rolled free to tumble on the floor.

Behind Quinn, Avery and all six of the young Huntresses stood. Golden light glowed from all their eyes as well.

The six younger Huntresses spoke as one. They sounded almost sad as they asked, "Must the chamber be cleansed?"

Quinn nodded. "The goddess orders it."

Avery answered, "Her will be done."

The hands of eight Huntresses came up as one, summoning their individual weapons.

The remaining demon-kinder and Fae enforcers

charged to the room's center from their places along the walls.

The summoned blades arrived a split second before the first of the attackers.

That was plenty of time.

Quinn, along with Avery and the children, struck out as parts of one whirling silver circle of death.

Only a few of the intruders escaped the carnage. Clark and Naomi rushed in and finished those who staggered away.

The Huntresses—Quinn, Avery, and all six girls— fought with one mind. Quinn saw herself everywhere at once, seven other awarenesses reacting with her as their bodies fought with a coordination a single person couldn't achieve.

Gemma snarled a magical command. The rune she sketched in the air blasted toward Quinn's back as a lance of midnight-black magic.

It didn't matter that Quinn had her back turned and couldn't see it coming. The communal mind did. Without raising her head from the fight with a demon-kinder, Quinn reached out with the palm of her free hand. The black energy splashed into her hand, and she redirected it harmlessly into the endless well of wild magic coursing below the chamber.

The collective consciousness saw the two Fae princesses racing toward the tunnel that led to the surface. There was no one close enough to intercept them. A minor flash of annoyance passed through the joint mind. They wouldn't get far. Others were coming from above to help.

Gemma saw them leaving too. She moved to the wall

and chased the retreating Fae, but the communal mind sent Avery after her.

She caught up with Gemma at the doorway to the surface, cutting the sorceress down from behind.

As Gemma fell, the other seven parts of the Huntress stood still, scattered around the chamber's blood-stained floor. All turned and faced inward as Avery returned. The only living beings remaining inside the circle were Tadpole and Taylor. They still lay injured and bound.

Quinn asserted her individual self long enough to say, "They must be healed."

"Agreed," echoed the others.

The eight approached to stand around the pair on the floor. They reached out, resting their hands on them. Golden magic flared around the bodies.

The bindings fell away, and the two clan members stirred.

The eight stepped away until they stood with their backs evenly spaced around the circular chamber.

Taylor and Tadpole sat up.

Taylor asked, "Quinn, what happened here?"

"Leave us," the eight said as one.

"But—" Tadpole began, confusion twisting his wild green brows.

"I think we should go," Taylor said.

Clark and Naomi rushed over and helped the two of them limp from the chamber.

Tadpole hesitated, staring at the bodies strewn about the floor. He searched for something unseen. Taylor tugged at his arm, but he resisted. Bending down, he moved one of the demon-kinder bodies aside, uncovering Juni. He scooped the unconscious leprechaun into his arms and followed Taylor into the tunnels with Clark and Naomi.

"The way is clear," Quinn stated.

The six girls said, "The chamber must be cleansed."

"Her will be done," Avery responded.

All raised their hands, palms facing the center of the ceiling. Sylvie still hovered there. The tiny head nodded.

"Eeeep."

As one, all eight released the remaining power they held, focused on one point.

Sylvie let out a screeching cry and once again drew in the golden energy beams, this time coalescing the streams into a single column of power that returned to the floor.

Slowly at first, the column of magic turned until it had completed a single rotation. It twisted faster and faster until a cyclone of magic spun in the chamber's center.

The swirling cone expanded across the floor. As it widened, it scoured the stones of all that didn't belong.

It continued to expand out from the center until it had burned away all the bodies, blood, and debris. The magical energy dissipated, returning to the triple ley lines beneath the floor, leaving eight figures along the chamber's walls. A youngling dragon hovered at the room's center.

The vanishing energy flows pulled the group consciousness with them, at least from Quinn's mind.

Quinn shot a glance at Avery, checking on the most important person in her life. Avery gave her half a smile, deep fatigue showing in her eyes.

The exhaustion struck them all a second later. Two women, six girls, and a tiny green dragon slumped to the stone floor, leaving the chamber in peace at last.

CHAPTER THIRTY-FIVE

The Fae court entered the Crystal Chamber and once again took seats arrayed against one of the glittering walls. The five magistrates sat.

Quinn smiled. Finally, they'd get justice.

The woman who was the chief magistrate nodded at Clark. "You have asked the court to assemble here again, and we have granted your request. Present your case."

"Magistrates, I bring you a request for justice." He gestured at two hooded figures dressed in black who were bound with silver chains, shackles, and manacles.

He continued. "These two attempted to use murder, blood magic, and a link to Hunter magic to dispel the barrier between this world and the netherworld."

"That is a bold accusation. You have witnesses, I assume."

"We do, magistrate."

"Reveal the prisoners for the assembled guests of the court and us. Remove the hoods."

Quinn and Avery, standing behind the accused, pulled

the hoods away. The two Fae women lifted their heads and directed defiant glares around the room.

Clark said, "I present their royal highnesses Princess Filippa and Princess Aurora."

Filippa laughed. "Release us, magistrate. These humans have no right to hold us prisoner like this. It's an affront to—"

"Silence!" the lead magistrate shouted. "In this setting, only we five may say who has what rights."

The initial shocked expression on Filippa's face relaxed into her usual haughty one after a second, but Quinn had seen it. The princess had not expected to be corrected. Clark had refused to allow Quinn and Avery to kill them outright after the pub staff apprehended them trying to leave through O'Malley's.

The magistrate gestured at Clark. "You may present your case and the evidence against the accused."

Clark nodded and laid out their evidence. He addressed each charge with relevant quoted testimony. As he listed the witnesses, Naomi brought forward scrolls with wax seals, the witnesses' affidavits.

Quinn had wanted to testify in person, but Clark had told her it wasn't the way of the Fae court. Only the advocate bringing charges could speak. He explained it was their way of avoiding unnecessary drama in court.

It took over an hour to lay out the multiple charges and present the relevant affidavits.

An impressive pile of scrolls sat on the silver tray mounted on a stand in front of the magistrates.

"Does anyone here have anything else to add to the

charges?" The magistrate waited for a few seconds, then asked, "Who would defend those charged here?"

To Quinn's surprise, no one came forward or spoke up. Judging from the looks on the five magistrates' faces, it surprised them too.

The woman at the group's center spoke to the two accused. "Since no one here will speak on your behalf, one of you may speak. Given the gravity of the charges, it *will* be brief."

The two princesses must have arranged this ahead of time. Aurora spoke immediately. "Magistrate, these humans have no jurisdiction to hold or charge us with anything. We've violated no human law in this jurisdiction. They hold no sway over our use of magic. We request the court throw out all charges and release us at once."

Quinn could take no more. Despite Clark's warning to remain silent, she couldn't hold her words any longer. "No human laws? You nearly killed both of us and several other members of my clan. We nearly bled to death while you tried to harness our power for your plan to rule the world."

"Enough," the magistrate said. "Since you have chosen to add your voice, you must answer for what you have said. Step forward."

Clark glowered at her but said nothing. Quinn was pleased. He'd been wrong when he'd said they wouldn't hear her out. She stepped forward and waited for the magistrate's questions.

"Since you spoke out of turn, Huntress, it falls to me to assess the validity of your claims."

Quinn nodded. This would be easy. This woman was on their side. All she had to do was tell them what had happened. Then Filippa and Aurora would get to follow Gemma into the grave.

"You claim to have been sorely injured, yet I see no injuries on you. If there are injuries I cannot see, you may disrobe to display them to me."

"I'm no longer injured. Our Huntress powers healed us."

"So you've been made whole, then?"

Quinn nodded. "Yes?"

Before Quinn could ask what was happening, the magistrate continued, "Please tell me which of the accused assaulted you directly or killed a member of your clan."

"What? Neither of them. Like they would get their pretty hands dirty."

"Where are the bodies of the dead or the injured persons so we can view them?"

"I told you, we healed their wounds with our Huntress magic."

"So, once again I ask, have you been made whole?"

Quinn glanced over her shoulder at Clark. She didn't understand. "Uh, yes, we healed them."

"Very well, we have examined you. Return to your place."

"But—"

"I said, return to your place, Huntress."

"Quinn," Clark said, "get back over there."

She shot him an angry glare but returned to her place beside Avery and behind the two princesses.

Aurora smiled and said, "Considering the newest testimony presented to the court, I believe there is only one ruling you can return."

All five magistrates fixed Quinn with their aged Fae eyes. After a second, they turned and talked among themselves. Once again, they somehow cloaked their voices so no one could overhear their discussion. Whatever was said, a few of the magistrates became quite animated.

After about five minutes of the silent discussion, the chief magistrate waved her hand, dispelling the silence.

"Though the evidence of injury is scant, the weight of the affidavits now on record is paramount."

"What?" Filippa said. "You have the girl's own testimony that she and the others have been made whole. There's no crime here. You must free us. I insist upon it."

Quinn tensed, afraid that was just what the magistrate intended.

Instead, the old woman fixed Filippa with a baleful look. "Princess, I have been privy to your machinations for many centuries. Each time you have come before this court for wrong-doing, you have skated away with nothing more than a slap on the wrist."

Filippa grinned and held out her hand. "Would you like to slap it now, or is there some wrist-slapping ordinance that must be followed?"

"Your flippancy betrays your true intent and contempt for this court and its purpose. Long have you twisted the law to your own ends. This time, however, you have gone too far."

"What's that supposed to mean?" Aurora asked.

"Don't worry, cousin. She probably means we have to pay a fine or something."

"Or something," the magistrate repeated. "An appropriate use of words for what will befall the two of you.

Since you have tried so hard to reunite with those lost Fae brethren bound to the netherworld, it is the sentence of this court that you join them."

Quinn's jaw dropped.

Filippa shrieked. "You cannot. I will appeal. There is no way you will get away with this."

"The court has spoken its sentence. Appeal is denied. The sentence will be carried out forthwith."

The chief magistrate raised both hands and sketched glowing black runes in the air before her.

A black and purple glowing oval appeared in the air beside the princesses. Both tried to run for the exit, but their silver manacles yanked them back around to face the widening portal.

A tall Fae stepped through the gateway. His skin was so pale it almost seemed translucent. He wore red plate armor, spikes jutting from the shoulders and elbows. He sneered at the onlookers as he glanced around.

His eyes fell upon the seated magistrates, and he inclined his head in a brief bow. "I see you have need of my services. What miscreants are you entrusting to my care?"

"The two women to your right have defied the law dividing us. It is our judgment that they be sent to join those they wish so dearly to rejoin. Take them away."

The netherworld Fae removed his gauntlet and chewed his thumbnail while he considered the two princesses. "What if I decide I want to stay? You opened the gateway freely. What's keeping me from returning after I take them to the place of their sentence?"

The magistrate didn't answer. Instead, her eyes darted to Quinn, concern wrinkling her brow.

Quinn took the hint. "Then I'd have to kill you. Take your pick. You can have the princesses and stay on your side of the barrier or die. I care not. I'm sure we can find another demon to take them off our hands."

Out of the corner of her eye, Quinn saw the chief magistrate nod in approval.

The netherworlder eyed Quinn, appraising her abilities, or trying to. When he didn't discover what he wanted on his own, he asked, "And who are you?"

"I'm the Huntress. We have restarted the clans. There will be no more incursions into this world by your kind unless you're summoned. We will meet any violations with lethal force. We won't send you home. We won't imprison you here on Earth. We'll just kill you and burn the body." Quinn settled her hands on her hips and squared up to the demon. "What's it going to be? I have somewhere to be, and I tire of this conversation."

When the demon paused a bit too long, Quinn dropped her hand to the Bowie sheathed at her waist. She traced the hilt with her forefinger as she stared him down.

The netherworld Fae cleared his throat, "Yes, well, there's no need for that. If you want me to take these ladies off your hands, I'm happy to do it."

He clapped his hands, and the silver manacles yanked the women toward the portal. Filippa and Aurora wailed and tried to pull away, but the force dragging them was too strong. With a last cry, both disappeared into the swirling black and purple oval.

The netherworld Fae bowed to the magistrates and nodded at Quinn, then stepped back through the gateway. As soon as he passed through, it snapped shut.

Silence hung over the Crystal Well for several seconds. Then the five elderly Fae magistrates stood, and without a word, processed in a line out of the room. The other onlookers, most of them Fae, muttered to each other as they followed the judges out.

That left Quinn, Avery, Naomi, and Clark in the room. Since it was the full moon again, Taylor had opted to remain at O'Malley's and help Miranda and Tadpole watch the newest members of their clan. The abilities of the six newest Huntresses weren't fully mapped yet, and everyone was still adjusting to them being around.

Quinn smiled. "At least we don't have to deal with the two of them again."

"There'll always be something that needs doing," Clark grumbled.

Avery nodded. "There will, but Quinn's right. We can at least take some time to enjoy our growing clan. Who knows, it might be downright peaceful."

Quinn took Avery's hand as they walked toward the Crystal Well's exit.

She looked over her shoulder once at the glittering chamber behind her. A single point of light flashed in the ceiling, a little brighter than the others.

Well done again, my Huntress, my Defender. You've earned a time of peace with your new family. Enjoy your life in a world made safer for all.

THE END

Extreme Medical Services: Medical Care On The Fringes Of Humanity

Monsters, Paramedics, and Street Medicine

New paramedic Dean Flynn is fresh out of the academy.

Then he learns his patients aren't your normal 911 callers.

With patients that are vampires, werewolves, fairies and more, will Dean survive his first days on the new job?

Will his patients?

Come along now with Extreme Medical Services, a supernatural medical thrill-ride with the paramedics of Elk City by best-selling author and real-life paramedic Jamie Davis.

Jump on the ambulance with Dean, Brynne and the rest of the team.

Get the first book in this best-selling service at Amazon.com.

JAMIE'S AUTHOR NOTES
AUGUST 13, 2020

As I look forward to the end of the year ahead, I realize how much I miss seeing and meeting readers at local events. In the past, I always tried to attend at least one regional sci-fi or fantasy con. I looked forward to signing paperbacks and meeting existing reader fans and those who are new to my books. I hope 2021 brings us the opportunity to return to at least some in-person events.

I'm a rare breed among authors. I'm an extrovert, meaning I thrive, and actually need, people around me. Writing is a solitary task and as a full-time author, I spend lots of time alone with my thoughts. To most authors, who are usually introverts, this is how they thrive. Not me. I need crowds. I need to meet new and interesting people (I find I can discover something interesting about every person I meet).

The thing I've had to adapt to is finding ways to safely be around people. My wife has helped me out with opportunities to gather outdoors with family so we can mask up, stay six feet apart, and still have time together. I also meet regularly with a choice group of authors and entrepreneurs to share some time talking and sharing ideas. These things have served to help fulfill my extrovert needs.

The long and the short of it is, I had to change and adjust to find new ways to interact with people. I urge you to do the same. It's going to be a little while until things return to some sort of normal. Maybe the eventual new normal will be very different from the old. That change is inevitable and the road to successful adaptation is acceptance of what you can't control while controlling the things you can.

So, I end this little note with this mantra. Hopefully, it will resonate with some of you.

Adapt, Accept, and Overcome.

Until next time, thanks for reading my books. Peace.

Check out more than forty other fantasy books by Jamie Davis at https://jamiedavisbooks.com.

ABOUT JAMI DAVIS

Jamie Davis is a nurse, retired paramedic, author, and nationally recognized medical educator who began teaching new emergency responders as a training officer for his local EMS program. He loves everything fantasy and sci-fi and especially the places where stories intersect with his love of medicine or gaming.

Jamie lives in a home in the woods in Maryland with his wife, three children, and dog. He is an avid gamer, preferring historical and fantasy miniature gaming, as well as tabletop games. He writes urban and contemporary paranormal fantasy stories, and LitRPG/GameLit, among other things.

He loves hearing from readers and going to cons and events where he meets up with fans. Reach out and say "hi." Visit JamieDavisBooks.com for more books, free offers and more!

Author site is: https://jamiedavisbooks.com

Facebook group is: https://facebook.com/groups/funfantasyreaders

Twitter — https://twitter.com/podmedic

Instagram — https://instagram.com/podmedic